BEYOND RELIGION

BEYOND RELIGION

Robert Wagner

To order additional copies of this book, contact:
Xlibris Corporation
1-888-795-4274
www.Xlibris.com
Orders@Xlibris.com
28373

Dedication

Thanks to Cathie McEwen for making faces at the first draft. Also, thanks to Maureen Medved for her patience through numerous workshops. I appreciate Pat Anderson's hard work for fine-tooth combing the manuscript. Finally, thanks to Claire, my patient wife, who had the good sense to remain neutral.

Dear Jean.
I hope you enjoy the novel. If not, pass it on or burn it.
Best Wishes
Bob

16-16   he said   should be   he says

~~~~~~ wincinger

96-28 slices
        into my
        mud   — Slided

87— how difficult
      is for a priest   (for a priest to
      adopt to ..   adopt to

I-SINNER

92 — occupy   occupy
      my seat   his seat

CHAPTER 1

M y dream recurs. A breaking sun shoots sparkles through the skiff of fog that layers the lake. Father and I are fishing, trolling in his aluminum boat. The *putt, putt, putt* of the outboard, like the rhythm of a soft rock band, is easy listening music. I'm not quite awake. The sweater Mother knit for me is warm and only a bit itchy. Soon it will be too warm and too itchy. I tried to tell her we were fishing from a boat and there was no need for knee-high rubber boots.

Father wears a red plaid lumberjack shirt with the top two buttons undone. His fishing hat is emblazoned with a green-eyed hawk on a blue background. Across it are the words "Seattle Seahawks."

I lean back in the clip-on chair and tug at my line to see if I caught a fish.

Father's cap is low over his eyes. Tufts of red hair flutter in the breeze below the cap. His sleeves are rolled up now, and his freckled arms warm in the morning sun. His wide back is to me.

He is ambidextrous and holds his rod with one hand while the other grips a can of Coors.

I scan the water for ripples or the splash of a trout as it jumps for breakfast. "Patience," Father says, "you need lots of patience. Fish only bite when you think they won't."

I close my eyes only to be jolted by his yell. "They're jumping dead ahead."

The boat lurches forward, and I'm dumped into the lake in a torrent of bubbles and water. My heart races, and I kick my way to the surface. He can't hear my screams. My boots fill with water and again I sink.

I wake up gasping. My head is beneath my pillow and covers lie on the floor. I am cold. My sweat congeals. A film of ice envelops me.

Mother is beside me. She must have heard my screams and surrounds me with warm blankets, but I dare not close my eyes.

"Not the same dream?" she says. "Funny, you've never been fishing."

She presses a hot water bottle on my chest. Soon, my shaking hands are quiet enough to hold the hot chocolate that she made. "I don't want to go to school today, Mom."

"It's better that you go. Have a hot shower. You'll feel better."

I leave but not before I reluctantly eat a bowl of hot cereal. "Don't dawdle after class. Father's coming home from camp."

Rock, rock, rock. Swivel, rock, rock. I enjoy the motion as I lounge in Father's chair and wait. Soon he'll burst home for a weekend of R&R.

Our driveway abuts against an aging verandah. I feel safe here in the den behind the old porch that's a dry moat surrounding the house. And before Father can cross it to reclaim his den, I will find safe haven.

A low rumble, like gathering thunder, warns me of his arrival. His black mud-spattered truck with its ram emblem grinds into the driveway, brakes locked and spewing gravel. A terminal revving of the engine precedes its shut down. I relinquish the TV, Prime Star remote, and one hundred sports channels. Where would I rather be on a Friday night? Elsewhere, of course, elsewhere, with my friends, hanging out, driving around, and doing whatever.

I remain hidden under the shadows of the eaves as Father jumps out of his truck, lands like a paratrooper with both knees flexed, and slams the truck door with a backward kick of his right foot. A chirp of the remote irritates my ears as the truck locks down. In three strides, he is at the front door reaching for the handle. He pulls his cap from oily matted hair and slaps it across his knee to expel a week of accumulated sweat and sawdust. My sister and mother are on the porch waiting to greet him. Soon, they'll be surrounded by the smells that accompany him.

He insists that we spend our Friday nights at home.

"I work all week. What's the point in coming home if no one's here? We need family time."

The tightness in Mother's face reflects constant pain. Every Friday afternoon, she takes pills to ease her backache, removes the pillow from behind her knees, and twists herself out of bed to stand under a hot shower until it's no longer hot. She emerges with her hair neatly combed and a freshly made up face. Then, she waits like a sentry for her husband and smiles when his footstep shakes the porch.

"Welcome home, Bruce," she says, hands folded in front of her. He reaches for her, but she retreats and winces as a sagging floorboard jars her back. "Do you think you'd have time to fix that board, Bruce? It's in an awkward place, and I'm forever catching my heel on it."

"Guess I better. I told Tom to fix it. You'd think somebody in grade 12 could remove one board and replace it. I'll try to get around to it. Tom would only bugger it up anyhow. By the way, where is he?"

"He's around somewhere, but he never learned how to fix loose boards nobody taught him."

She squeezes the small of her back and sighs. "Why don't you take off your coveralls, dear?"

She flicks a few bits of sawdust off his shirt. "You have clean clothes in the bathroom and a cold beer in the cooler. I know how thirsty you get in a hot bath."

Bruce Spanner only grins when Mother insists that he remove his boots before entering the house.

"Thomas, where are you?"

"Right here, Mom."

"Well, don't just stand there. Get his bag out of the truck and take it to the laundry room."

"You OK, Mom? You don't look so good."

"Of course I don't. My back's killing me. I never should have let them talk me into a second operation. I've got screws and rods in my back. I'm so stiff I can't bend over to tie my laces. I can't get a decent back rub anywhere. All the doctors say is, 'It would really help if you'd lose weight.'"

Julie busies herself in the kitchen. She is cook by default. Mother can't stand long enough to cook. I'm unfamiliar with the culinary arts and therefore useless. Besides, she's my older sister; it seems a natural function. A pot of water simmers on the stove. Beads of sweat dot Julie's forehead, while her cheeks are pink in the kitchen's heat. A neat orange apron covers the yellow dress that she wore to work.

"Hi, Thomas. What're you up to?"

"Just hangin', sis. Waiting to have dinner with Father. Can't go out till later when he's watching some game on the tube."

"Don't be so selfish. He works all week. Why shouldn't he insist on dinner with all of us?"

"I guess."

Her slender hand automatically locates spices and utensils. Essential materials are at waist level. Mother insisted on this so there'd be no need to bend, even though she rarely cooks anymore.

"I suppose you're bored," Julie says. "How about setting the table so we don't have to eat with our hands?" Did it really matter if the fork was on the left or right? We could still reach the spoon even if the handle was up or down.

"Practice, Tom. You can't get married until you get it right."

Julie's hazel eyes crinkle at the corners and for a moment, I want to do it right.

"I don't want to get married," I reply. "Why should I get someone who'll boss me around?"

"You could take turns you know."

"Naw, I'm not a fighter. How about you? You ever want to get married?"

"Look around. Do you think it's fulfilling to cook a man's meals, do his laundry, and have him come to bed smelling of beer, hands all over you, and then snore half the night?"

"They've got separate beds. Besides, it doesn't have to be like that."

"Awesome, Tom. You get extra spaghetti tonight, but no beer."

"Come on, sis, I bet there are a lot of guys who really like you. Why don't you give one a chance?"

"Because nobody treats me like an equal. Most want only one thing. To the others, it's always the little woman or she's the best thing I've ever seen. It's like the church. Women aren't good enough to be priests and speak for their god, only good enough to serve. I wouldn't mind being a nun, but not the old kind, suppressed, inferior, and subservient. I do have some pride."

"It's cool the way you've got it figured. So chill. I was just asking."

"Oh, sorry, Tom, I got carried away. I'm frustrated having to look after Mom. Who else would? Everything hurts when she moves. I know she's seen every doctor, quack, and healer here in Bellingham. Even Seattle's specialists can't help her. All the chronic pain joints, MMPI surveys, electrical stimulations, antidepressants, physiatrists, and psychiatrists can't help her. Do I dump her? I can't, Tommy. I just can't."

"Holy shit, Julie. I hardly know what you're on about. It's different for you. You've got a job. You could split. And maybe, just maybe, Mom could start to do stuff and get it together. Then maybe she could get home care or something."

Mother shuffles into the kitchen. Her eyelids droop, and her voice sounds far away. "How are you managing? What can I do to help?"

"We're just about there," Julie says. "We only need to boil the spaghetti and make the sauce."

"That's great, sweetheart, I really don't know what I'd do without you."

Julie's smile verges on a grimace. "You would, Mom. You'd make do."

"Maybe, but you're a big help."

CHAPTER 2

F ather slouches at the kitchen table, fork in one hand and beer in the other. His hair, a curly mop, no longer matted, adds an inch to his height. Muscular forearms protrude beneath rolled-up sleeves. His hands are rough and scarred while fingernails are burdened with the perpetual grime of his job. Physically, we are opposites, he the bulldog and I the greyhound—a greyhound that can't even run. I'm two inches taller than Father, and his chest circumference seems twice that of mine.

A clean shirt, open two buttons at the neck, betrays the first signs of age. Some of his chest hairs have transformed to a subtle shade of gray.

"Hey," he says. "Where is everybody?"

"We're coming, dear," Mother calls from the kitchen, and we proceeded like three wise men bearing gifts. Mother carries spaghetti, Julie brings sauce, and I trail with miscellaneous.

"Looks great," he says. "Sure is nice to come home to a real meal. Not like camp where the cook doesn't give a shit."

Mother frowns and dabs at her lips with a napkin. "It's so nice to see you. How was your week?"

"It was a sonofabitch. I was setting up the trim saw and getting the angle just right. Ninety degrees up and ninety degrees lateral. I ran a test board when the blade exploded. Some goddamn tree hugger hammered a nail into a tree. Lucky thing, I wore a face shield—not a mark on me. The FN bastard could have killed me."

Mother savors a minor victory, Bruce Spanner no longer says "fucking" at the dinner table. He abbreviates it to FN.

"So what's up with you, guys?" Father asks between sips of beer. "What's new, Julie?"

"Oh, nothing much. I've reorganized the optometrists to actually spend time in shopping malls. Then people can get their eye exams and glasses with a minimum of inconvenience. It's turned out to be a real moneymaker. I got a raise."

"Smart girl. That's real good. I'm happy for you."

"And I'm going to be a nun."

"What?"

"I think I'm going to be a nun."

Father nearly swallows his beer can. His eyes bulge, and his neck veins stand out like breakfast sausage. "A nun? Like in penguin? What the hell for?"

"Well, Daddy, because I want to help people."

"Shit. So you're going to help a bunch of drunks and wimps that won't help themselves. And where's that going to get you?"

"I'll have a good feeling."

Bruce Spanner fixes his bright blue eyes on his daughter. "You're young, smart, and pretty. You've got a real good future. What pervert have you been talking to?"

Father glares at Mother. "Do you know anything about this crap?"

"Oh no, sweetheart. This is the first I've heard of it. But we did raise her Catholic, and she still goes to church on Sundays."

"I don't give a shit if she goes to a mosque on Saturdays. It's the stupidest goddamn idea I've ever heard. You better get it out of her pea-brained mind."

Mother smiles.

"It's OK," Julie says. "I haven't decided for sure. I need to give it more thought and prayer. Perhaps counseling too."

Father upends his beer and squashes the helpless aluminum can. Then he turns his sights toward me, swiveling slowly like a tank turret. "What have you been doing?"

"Nuthin'."

"What do you mean, nuthin'?"

"Just going to school and stuff."

"What kind of stuff?"

"Oh, you know, the usual. English, math, socials—stuff like that."

"You still working at McDonald's?"

"Yup."

"Well, ain't that something. Working and going to school."

He opens another Coors. "Where have we gone wrong, Judith? One wants to be a nun, and the other goes to school and does nuthin'."

"Oh relax, Bruce. He'll get it all together. It's just that he's a slow starter."

"Well, it's un-American. But then what can you expect. He was born premature when we were on holiday in Canada."

Julie rolls her eyes. "Just how slow are you, Thomas?"

"Just what I need," I say, "two of you on my case."

"You know," Father says, "when I was your age, I was in the army and—"

"We know," Julie says and rolls her eyes once more.

"Never mind. How are you coming along, Judith?" he says turning to Mom.

"Slowly. When I move the wrong way, pain goes down both my legs; and when I cough or sneeze, it just kills me. Sometimes I'm so numb that I don't know where my legs are. Dr. Johnston says it's my proprioception that's impaired, and that's why I don't have a position sense. He doesn't think the surgeon did anything wrong, but I was a lot worse after the operation. As a matter of fact, I got worse right after the myelogram. I've heard they didn't have to stick a needle in my spine and put x-ray dye in. A CAT scan or MRI would have told them all they needed to know. Look at Elsie Waterton. She's in a wheelchair from a myelogram. Maybe I should see a lawyer. These doctors always stick up for each other. What do you think, Bruce?"

"What?"

"I said—oh, never mind. You weren't even listening. You don't even care enough to pay attention. Go. Take your beer to the den. Watch your sports on TV. It's my body. My problem."

"Sorry. I didn't mean nuthin'. My mind wandered for a minute."

Mom gets up slowly, with both hands braced on the table, her suffering etched on the crease lines of her face. "Julie, help me to bed. There's no reason to stay up. Do the dishes, Thomas. Your sister's done enough. Besides, she's going out."

"Julie, can I get a ride to Bill's house? He's got a big collection of videos, and we were just going to hang out."

Father's face reddens. "That's bloody great. I work all week, look forward to seeing all of you, and what happens? Everybody disappears. What am I, a bloody mule?"

I cringe. Soon he will yell.

Julie steps toward him and puts an arm around his shoulders. "Oh, what big muscles you have, Papa, but I work too. After I finish my job, I come home to cook and look after the house. And Tommy works too. He vacuums, dusts, waters the plants, takes out the garbage, cuts the grass, and does what he can to keep this place going. It may seem like mostly women's work to you, but it all helps. Besides," she says, pushing her lips into a pout. "I know you're going to put your feet up and watch TV. So I'll go out tonight and socialize. All work and no play, you know. If I don't have a social life, I might just become a nun."

I leave with Julie, amazed at how she softened Father.

"I have a pain, Julie. Will you teach me how to do that?"

She grins. "I can't teach you. It's an inborn thing."

Bill's house overlooks Bellingham Harbor. A wrought iron fence guards the manicured lawn and sculpted plants. Interlocked bricks pave the driveway that leads to high double oak doors. Recessed to the left of the house, a three-car garage blends with the shrubbery.

Bill's new in school. He wanted to be friends so he threw a party at his house. We're curious about Bill and his 911 Porsche.

He's standing at the open door. Baggy pants drag on the hardwood. A T-shirt with a nude picture of Marylyn Manson hangs over his belt. A plain gold chain encircles his neck. Hidden by his shirt is a muscular body. A Seattle Mariners baseball cap sits backward on his spiked hair. From time to time, a casual hand checks the diamond in his ear lobe.

"Enter," he bows. "We got popcorn, 'n' beer, 'n' pizza. Glad you made it. There are a lot of people here already."

He hands me an imported beer in green glass bottle. I knew there was beer other than Coors in a can. He says, "The women are waiting. What kept you?"

"The old man came home. He only let me go after he had enough beer."

Nearly the whole class is here. Most just stand around with drinks and talk. Some sit on sofas, smoking grass, and nodding to the music. No other cigarette has that smell.

She must have come up from an angle at my blind side. I feel the softness of her breast against my side and enjoy her arm around my waist. Moira squeezes close and says with a laugh, "I didn't know you were a party animal, Tom. Are you having a good time?"

"Oh, yeah sure."

"Sure you are," she says and giggles as she leaves.

For a while, I stand in a corner and drink my beer. I try unsuccessfully to look cool. My fingers keep time with INXS, Sting, and Backstreet Boys. A few couples, glued to each other, sway under the subdued light in imitation of a dance.

I nod to people and some even talk to me. It's not necessary. I only need to be here. After a few more beer, I loosen up and mellow as the hours pass. In the morning, I have a job. Reluctantly, I decide to go home. I try to find Bill to say good night. He's wrapped around a girl and can't see me. I decide not to bother him.

When I leave after midnight, no one offers a lift, so I walk. Dew slicks the grass. I discover this when I accidentally walk off the sidewalk and fall on my bum. Soon I need to stop and pee into a hedge. More than dew moistens my shoes.

I near my house and see the light is on; I decide to sneak in the back. It's no use; all the doors are locked. I use my key and tiptoe past Father's den. He's still watching TV.

CHAPTER 3

Saturday morning and nothing is stirring except a thump as Father's feet hit the floor. Vibrations initiate a pain in my head. I scramble into my clothes, eat two peppermints, and ignore my headache. Father sometimes yanks off my covers and pulls me out of bed by one leg.

"C'mon, sleeping beauty," he'd shout. His lips twisted somewhere between a sneer and a smile. "Or is it sleeping ugly?"

Bacon smells waft through the house. Father, dressed in jeans and sweatshirt, scowls over the frying pan. "Good afternoon," he growls. "About time you got up. Are you rested from a tough night?"

"Guess so."

He shakes his head, cracks four eggs into the pan, swirls the mixture until it congeals, and plops it onto a plate. Then he sluices down the whole mess with two pieces of toast and two beer.

"Frying pan's still hot. Help yourself. Ya gotta have a good breakfast if you're gonna amount to anything."

He inspects me as if he were still in the army. I wear the Puerto Vallarta T-shirt that Julie gave me. It hangs loosely over my baggy jeans. "No shoes," he says, "You'll catch cold for sure. Wouldn't hurt to exercise. Maybe your clothes wouldn't flap in the breeze."

Then he sniffs, twice in rapid succession. His nose crinkles like a rat after cheese. "Have you been smoking?"

"Who me? No."

"Yeah, you. Is there anybody else here?"

"I was at Bill's. He smokes."

He rinses his dishes and drops them in the sink. "I'm going to town in a bit. I need some tools and parts for the mill after those tree huggers fucked it up. And I'm going to pick up a plank for the porch, so your mother won't kill herself. You can come along."

"I can't. Julie's going to give me a driving lesson, and I have to go to work later."

Father stomps out of the house. His boots, still on the porch, detain him for only a few moments. From the kitchen, I hear the rumble of his truck spurting gravel as he leaves. A soft hand covers my eyes. Over an enticing perfume, a warm breath whispers, "Guess who?" Julie grins as if she'd won a prize from a popcorn box. A pink striped blouse accentuates the flush of her cheeks.

"You're mixed up, Cinderella. This is Saturday morning. Not the night of the ball."

"Yes," she says, "but I still have the same dull sibling."

"Oh, oh, you met a prince. What happens to the frogs now?"

"Don't worry. I still love you."

She whirls a banana into her diet milkshake. "Get your shoes and wallet. Last lesson before the driving test."

She tosses her keys at me. The metal tab announces, "Expensive but worth it." Her red Miata convertible gleams in the garage beside Father's pride, a '49 Buick Roadmaster. "Give me a hand," Father said to me a few weeks ago. "Let's move some of this crap. So your sister can park her toy car inside. Those rag tops rot in the rain."

The Miata looks like a midget beside a giant.

"Careful when you open the door," Julie says, "one scratch on the Buick and you're dog meat."

As instructed, I allow the car to idle for a few minutes and ease it out of the garage. By now, I am programmed: four way stops, parking, parking on the left, stop on hills, go on hills, playgrounds, school zones (I remember not to slow down on Saturday), passing, pedestrian rights, gear up, gear down, seat belt on. After the lesson, Julie sits, hands folded on her lap. Then her suppressed smile escapes. "Excellent, dude. You'll ace the test."

Flashbacks to lessons past flicker through my mind: Julie wincing as I ground the gears.

"Keep your hand on the shift, gentle pressure. She'll shift herself." At times, a whack on my thigh, hand on her forehead. "Gear down. I can smell my brakes." Frowns, eyes rolled, hands braced on the dash, hands over her face. At the end of each lesson, there are two lists: skills learned and skills to learn.

Father comes home as I'm leaving for McDonald's. He had a lot of supplies to get and, as usual, he had a few beers with the boys. When I get home from work at midnight, I trip over a piece of lumber at the weak spot of the porch. Father must have put it there so he won't forget to fix it before he leaves. At times, Mother complains that his forgetting is becoming a habit.

On Sundays, Father sleeps until 9:55 AM At ten, the TV blares, "Seattle Seahawks versus Oakland Raiders." Beer smells, and curses explode from the den. "Kill the sonofabitch. Break his fuckin' back. Nail the cocksucker. This is real football. Not some limey pansy game. Oh Jesus, you pussy."

Mother leaves for church before the game. Father's truck step is out of reach for her, and Julie's car too low. Every Sunday, at 9:45, the Wilsons collect her in their van, loaded with kids. Mr. Wilson, a graying gaunt man in his late fifties, hunches over the wheel while one of his adopted, challenged sons scampers out to help me get Mom into the van. "There are so many kids," Mom observes. "There's always somebody on someone's lap. Eleven of them and half are adopted." Mrs. Wilson always smiles and folds her hands when questioned about her brood.

"Life is precious," she announces, in her verbal neon fashion, and then bestows her benevolent smile. "What you do for the least of these, you do also for me."

When Mother asks, "How do you provide?" the answer begins with an expression to envy the *Mona Lisa*, "Behold the lilies in the field . . ."

Mother's back is really sore today. Sometime, I go to church with her. Today, I ignore the hint and cringe at Mother's tentative steps that jar her back. Mr. Wilson looks at me in that serious, holy way of his. "Come with us, Thomas. Your mother needs more help than my son can give and you look in need of uplifting. We'll wait five minutes. That's all a young fellow like you needs to get ready."

What do I hate most about church? Not the service, not the sermon. No, it's the old chronic attendees who turn to me and say, "Welcome" or "Bless you" or "We hope to see you more often." As if I need to come, as if it would make any difference I've seen and heard it all before. Father Delorme recites Mass and recycles a sermon—blessed are the meek, blessed are those who suffer, blessed are those who mourn. Ask and you shall receive."

Do pain and suffering create blessing? I'm inclined toward Bill's heathen saying, "I'd rather be rich and happy than poor and miserable." Mother suffers. It seems there is nothing else she can do. Turning water into wine or calming a storm is more important than relieving her pain.

Sometime after Mother's return from church, Father stumbles out of the den. He rubs his eyes and squints like a gopher caught in a flashlight. "Goddamn stupid buggers blew it. They could have run out the clock; but no, they pass and that skinny nigger drops the ball."

"Oh, that's too bad, dear," Mother says, "I've made some sandwiches for you before you go."

"Thanks, Judith. I sure hope you have a better week. I gotta run and get the mill going for Monday. Damn tree huggers ought to be paying for it."

He turns to me. "I bought you a board so you can fix the porch. There's nails and tools in the garage. Have it done before I come back."

I open my mouth in protest but think better of it. Boards come from trees, and there my knowledge ends.

Mother smiles and waves good-bye. She continues waving while saying, "Don't worry. He's always like this after a few drinks and when his team loses. By Friday, it's always easier. Good thing it's a dry camp."

At mid afternoon, Julie unravels herself from her bed. Even in jeans and a sweater, she looks fresh. "Sit down, Mom," she says, "Put your feet up. I'll cook dinner."

"You shouldn't, dear," Mom replies, "I'll manage."

"No hay problema, mi madre," she says with a Spanish lisp. "It's done. The roast and potatoes are in the oven. Veggies in a pot, gravy from a package, and Mario Andretti here has volunteered to set the table and do the dishes."

"You should be in management, sweetheart." Mother smiles and pats Julie's hand.

"I already am—Julie B. Spanner, executive secretary of the Bellingham Optometrists Association."

On Wednesday morning, Julie wipes the milk moustache left by her diet drink. "Come home right after school, Tom. I have a surprise for you."

"What?"

"If I tell you, it won't be a surprise."

After school an old Chev truck coasts into the driveway. A tall man in his late twenties unwinds himself from behind the steering wheel. Even in September, his skin has a tanned outdoor appearance. He wears blue jeans and a red plaid shirt. Julie holds his hand and tilts her head to look in his face.

"This is John. He's going to save your butt."

John raises an eyebrow. "I hear the verandah needs attention?"

"Yeah, I guess."

"Let's have a look. It's unusual for only one board to rot."

He squints at the floor, taps it with a broomstick, and at times, stabs it with a screwdriver. "Needs a whole new deck pretty soon. That two by six won't help much."

He squats, like a man careful about his back, and marks a red X on four planks. Then he says to me, "How'd you like to come along to the lumberyard and get some boards? We can patch it, paint to match, thinner, and a brush. Needs two coats and some spiral galvanized nails so the boards won't lift."

He puts on work gloves and selects four boards from a pile of planks. "We might as well get preserved lumber. You never know how long it stays on."

On our return, Julie meets us on the front steps. "Did you get everything?" she asks and squeezes John's arm.

"Sure did," he nods. Then turning to me, he adds, "If it's OK with you, I can give you a hand fixing the deck."

"I don't know how to fix decks."

"You will. I can show you."

It isn't hard. Remove the rotten and replace with the new. I think I am of some help. I excel at cutting up old planks and taking them to the garbage.

"Looks good," John says. "You got potential."

Julie voices her agreement, hands each of us Coors, and salutes, "To a job well done."

I hesitate until Julie gives my shoulder a friendly punch. "Bottoms up, Tom. I know you drink it, and I know you like it."

She slides an arm around John's waist. "It looks really good. Thanks a lot."

Mother steps on the verandah. "I think I'll have a sip too. Thanks Tom. And my back thanks you too."

CHAPTER 4

Another Friday. Father removes his boots, grunts at me, kisses Mom on the cheek, and proceeds to his bath with two cold beer.

He is just out of the tub when Julie announces that dinner is ready. She looks out the window and forgets her usual offer of second helpings. Dessert is a cake with one candle on it and an icing sugar picture of a car. The flowery writing says, "Congratulations, Thomas."

"What's the occasion?" Father asks.

"Tom got his driver's license today. Isn't that neat?"

"Well, it's about time. I was driving for four years when I was his age."

"Can't be," Julie says pouting her lips and blowing a kiss. "There weren't any cars when you were that age, and there weren't any roads either."

"Oh yeah, what's that Buick in the garage?"

John's old truck rumbles up the driveway. Before he can get out of the cab Julie sprints from the house.

"What's going on?" Father asks, looking first at Mother then at me.

"I'm sure I have no idea," Mother answers.

"How about you, Thomas, have you got any idea?"

"Julie's got a date. His name's John."

"Oh, OK. Is she ashamed to bring him in or what?"

Over the next week, Julie talks more quickly, smiles more often, and walks faster. She comes home later most nights and doesn't always cook dinner. "Thomas," she says, "I've been thinking. What's the use in having a license if you don't drive? If you can get your buns out of bed on Thursdays and get me to work by eight, you can have my car. It'll cost you, though. You'll have to cook. I'm sure Mom can teach you. John's picking me up after work."

Awesome. I have a car one day a week. I park at school when Bill slides in beside me with his black Porsche. His hair is freshly spiked, and he flexes his biceps until it stretches the barbwire tattoo.

"Jeez," he drawls, "ya got a car."

"It's my sister's. She let's me drive it every Thursday."

"It's kind of cute and little, but that doesn't matter. When you got wheels, you get pussy."

School becomes bearable even though math is boring; chemistry, dry; and biology, no use. I am now motivated to maintain my 55 percent average. Biology has a bright spot: Moira. *Anaphase* and *metaphase* are mere words. My focus is on wavy hair that reaches her shoulders. Brown eyes, full lips, melodic voice, and swaying hips mesmerize me when she walks. I am concentrating on her dimples when Mr. Sinclair interrupts. "What would you surmise, Mr. Spanner, is the function of the metaphase?"

"Would you repeat the question?"

"It's a straightforward question. I'm sure your mind was elsewhere—metaphase."

"Something to do with cell division stuff."

"You're in the ball-park and be thankful this isn't an English class. What kind of stuff may I ask?"

"Ah, I'm not sure."

Snickers in the background increase my discomfort.

Sinclair continues. "Ah, I sense a learning opportunity. For tomorrow, Mr. Spanner, please prepare a three-minute presentation on this topic so that you will be as enlightened as everyone else."

My face reddens. Moira peeks at me over her shoulder and sticks out her tongue.

On sports day, I volunteer to help with the refreshment stand. Moira's name is listed just ahead of mine.

"Let's move this table," she says. "The tablecloth is on the counter. If we put the pop cans here, they'll be out of reach of the customers."

"Looks good. We should make a bundle."

Moira finds an empty jar and with a red marking pen writes *tips (or else)*.

The hot, the smelly, and the watchers all buy from our stand. We are a monopoly. "It's location, Tom, and prompt service. Don't forget to smile at the customers." She laughs at her enterprise, and I laugh with her. "More hotdogs," she orders.

"Right away." Moira could have all the hotdogs from an overcrowded dog pound. She only needs to ask. During a pause, she wipes my face with a cool cloth. "Let's cool you down. You're getting hotter than the dogs you're boiling."

"That's great. One more time."

She complies and gives me a small hug.

A sweater with big block letters wants two beer and a bloody Mary. He thinks he's funny and then asks Moira, "Who's your chef? Can he cook anything else?"

"Oh no. He has only one specialty."

Is there a track meet in that world beside our stand? There must be.

After the meet, Moira empties the tip jar and divides the money into three piles. "One third for the school. They didn't expect it. It's a bonus—one third for you and one third for me. Why should we work for nothing? Why should anyone?"

"You capitalist."

"Yup," she says, "watch my smoke." Then kisses me lightly on my cheek.

"Damn, Tom. I have to run. I've got to baby-sit my stepbrother. These blended families can be a real pain."

"I can give you a lift."

"I didn't know you had a car."

"It's my sister's. I get it every Thursday so I don't forget how to drive."

"Well, in that case, I'll help you clean up."

It's late November, and Father arrives home unexpectedly on a Wednesday. Julie's still at work, and I'm lodged in front of the TV.

"Bunch of chicken shits," he grumbles. "Couple feet of snow and a little cold, these guys run home to Mama. We're shut down till Monday."

"Well, what a pleasant surprise," Mother says. "Get cleaned up. I'll put on some spaghetti. We can have a nice family dinner when Julie gets home."

Mother is happy tonight. She actually hums as her face reddens over boiling spaghetti. At dinner, she squares her shoulders. "I have an announcement," she says. "I've decided to hire a lawyer. He thinks I have a legitimate case, and it won't cost me anything."

"Who'd you get?" Father asks, "not that weasel Braxton? Better read the fine print."

Julie breezes in, hums her way through the house, and washes up in a few minutes. Even after a long day, she looks radiant. I assume what's-his-name is still in the picture. Toward the end of the meal, when everyone is too full to argue, I break the silence. "Hey, sis, can I borrow your car? I've got stuff to do."

Julie stares at me while half-rolled spaghetti droops in white strands from the fork. Her forehead gathers a quizzical frown as she stares at me with her hazel eyes. "What kind of stuff?" she says.

"My god," she sighs, shaking her head. "You're in grade 12, and you still can't speak English. Yes, you can borrow my car and, no, you may not."

"Oh, sorry, Julie. What I meant was that I'd really like to borrow your car for a few hours. Pete and I want to study for the geography test, and we don't have a computer at our house."

"I don't believe any of it," she says. "Are you going to study before or after you take my car to the lookout? You know it still bugs me that you spilled ketchup on both sides of the driver's door."

"I really tried hard to get the ketchup off, but it stuck and dissolved some of the paint."

"I might lend it to you. What will you do for me if I lend it to you?"

"What will I do? I'll promise anything. I'll learn to cook."

"Wonderful," she says. "I'll enjoy teaching you."

Father snorts. "Bull, it ain't going to happen."

I can tell Mother disapproves. She tightens her lips until they disappear. Then she twirls her narrow wedding band around her puffy finger, a sign that she is gathering her thoughts.

"I think it's just an excuse," she says. "You're too young to be driving at night and going out on dates."

"Aw, c'mon, Mom. Can't I have any fun? All work and no play. I could turn out even duller than I am now."

She sighs, dabs at the sweat on her forehead, and wipes her palms on her apron. Hot food adds discomfort to her overweight frame.

Father is still eating. He grasps his fork as a man would grasp an oar, shovels food into his mouth, and leans over his plate to bite off the excess. Then he repeats the process with shorter lengths of spaghetti.

"Jesus Christ," he says between mouthfuls, "when I was his age, I had two jobs, a truck and knew how to drive. In my day, a real man wouldn't ask a woman for her car."

Julie puts her arm around his shoulders. "Modern times, Daddy. They don't make men like they used to. It's that darn women's lib stuff that preaches kind, caring, and considerate. No wonder they're wimps."

She pats the back of his hand. A slender white clean hand rests on his sledgehammer fist. Each imbued with its own power and control. For a moment, Bruce Spanner studies his hand: its grime and cracks and scars. His massive hand circles the beer can until a grimy thumbnail nearly opposes dirt engraved fingernails.

I look at my hands: white, uncalloused, unused to work.

Julie winks and tosses the keys at my nose. "Here are the keys. No chores for me for a year," she says pointing her index finger at me. "Just be sure that my car's home unscratched. Since I taught you to drive, I guess I need to let you practice. By the way, don't forget to put gas in. The tank's low."

I jump from my seat and bolt for the door. "Who's going to pick up your dishes?" Father bellows.

Like a well-trained dog responding to command, I scramble back, pick up my plate, and try another exit.

"And who's going to wash your dishes?"

"I will," Julie says. "Let's go, Tommy, I'll show you where the gears are."

Father's voice follows me. "There he goes and without his books."

"Jeez, Julie, I didn't want to say anything in front of Father. You know how he rides me. But I've got a date with Moira."

She grins and nods. "Well, have a good time."

CHAPTER 5

Pete and geography evaporate from my mind. Moira lives in the Uplands Subdivision. I coast into a circular driveway to park beside her father's Oldsmobile. She's waiting. Before I turn the engine off, she's in the car.

"Hi, Thomas, you look frazzled. Have you been studying?"

Then, without waiting for a reply, she says, "Let's get out of here before my parents want to meet you. I'm on curfew tonight. So let's boogie."

I laugh. "I'm always on curfew, even when Father's out of town."

She tousles my hair. "Good boy, Tom. You can figure a way around. Let's skip the burgers and just go to the lookout."

Only a few cars dot the lookout, but it's still early. The party crowd will arrive after movies and more after parties. Later on policemen with Breathalyzers and ID checks will disturb the heat behind fogged windows. It's still daylight but half-moon hangs low on the horizon waiting to displace the sun.

My main preoccupation is to dislodge a smiling Moira from the passenger door. I'm disappointed. She wants to talk. She licks her lips, dry in the autumn air. I misinterpret the gesture and reach toward her. She puts one arm over the seat and another on the dash. "It sure is hard to get away from anybody in this car."

"I don't know," I say, "you don't seem to have any trouble."

"Oh, Thomas, you guys are all alike. You think if a girl doesn't climb all over you, she doesn't like you."

"That's not true. I like you. But if you were over here, I might like you even more. But if you'd rather be there, it's OK."

"Sure?"

"Of course."

"Have you ever wondered why I go out with you, Tom?"

"I try not to."

"You're so funny. I go out with you because I like you. You don't try to prove stuff to me, and you don't brag. There's a freedom with you, Tom. What I want matters."

She takes a deep breath, looks at the moon and the river. "How do you like school, Tom? What are you going to do after grade 12?"

"Oh, I dunno, get a job I guess, make some money. What about you, Moira?"

"I haven't decided. Guess I'll go to college, take courses, join a sorority, and party. Could be fun."

Moira wipes the fog off the window and looks over the river.

"I just don't want to do like everybody else. Get a boyfriend, get pregnant, get married, have kids. I don't think I even like kids. My stepsister takes up enough of my time. I don't want kids that will grow to have kids that are just like me. I want to do something meaningful, something relevant. Not just a rerun."

"Well, I couldn't do what my father does. It takes a lot of strength. Course he's built like a horse, and it's easy for him. I have to do something with my brain. And that's the other problem. My best mark so far is a C-."

She comes closer, touches my face. "Oh, Tom, there must be something you can do that doesn't require brains or brawn."

She giggles at her observation, but the beginnings of tears are in her eyes. Then, for no reason at all, she kisses me on my mouth, on my neck, on my ear.

"Oh, Tom, I could just hug you. You're so needy. I like to hang with you. Sometimes I think you could be my crush."

It all feels so good, living above the clouds for a moment. She likes me, likes to touch me, and I like to touch her. Then she takes my hand and slides it under her sweater. "Oh, Tommy, you have really soft warm hands."

I reach with my other hand, and she pulls away to plaster herself against the door.

"That was nice," she says, "but let's save some for another day. I'm not ready for more tonight."

My beginning arousal subsides. I'm not ready either.

I drive in silence to the circular driveway. She kisses my cheek and ear. "Don't get out of the car, Tom. Let's go out again, and if you're good," she says, "I'll let you touch the other one."

I float home unaware that time actually passes. The garage door thuds to a close. I remember. *Get gas.* The gauge reads one-eighth full—more than enough for Julie to get to work.

Lying naked on the covers, I postpone sleep. Moira fills my mind—smiling lips, fingers brushing mine, hands tousling my hair. Memories transform to dreams while she laughs and frolics in the joy of my restless night. I sleep in.

From the edge of my contentment, I feel a sudden coldness or thunder that precedes a storm. Cold puckers my skin, and I wrap myself tightly in the covers. Without a knock and with a painful roar, my door shatters. Light, intense, a bright arc weld blinds my sleeping eyes. Father's face, a purple rage, lips compressed to a thin pale line fills my world like a close up horror movie. Stale beer and staler breath push me to the edge of vomit. I pass out.

Fists, like pile drivers, wait in ambush while the cold water he doused on me mingles with my colder sweat.

"Get up," he rasps. "Julie's dead. Car accident. Killed in a head-on with a semi."

Mother screams, hands over her ears to stop the noise. "Julie's dead," she shrieks and then falls to her knees. "The trucker tried to miss her," Father says. "He rolled his rig. He thought she just froze or ran out of gas."

Tears stream and form a drop at the tip of Mother's chin. She doubles over as if kicked by a giant boot. Great wrenching sobs wrack her, and she grimaces as each sob jars her painful back.

Julie never froze.

Father stares at nothing, his face contorted. His favorite child lies chilling in the morgue. Her brother, the ugly duck, moves its bill and cannot even quack. He faces me with knotted fists, waist high, like a confident boxer whose only need is offense. Then he shoves his contorted face inches from mine. "Did you put gas in the car?"

"Yup."

"How much?"

"Three bucks."

"When?"

"About nine thirty."

"Where?"

"At—"

"Stop, Bruce!" Mother screams. "Stop! One loss is too much. What's the matter with you? Do you want to alienate your son too?"

She crumples into a whimpering heap. "Stop it. Stop it."

Neighbors and friends arrive to mill about. Mrs. Wilson hugs Mom and then passes tea and cookies. Her husband stands silently, hands in pockets. Our next-door neighbor so stooped that she can only see the floor shakes her head and says, "It's so sad, dear. I know only too well."

Others hug Mother in silence and mingle their tears with hers. Some shake Father's hand and mumble at the floor. The few who came soon leave.

Mother rocks in Father's chair. He kneels beside her, holds her hand, and strokes her arm. For once, he has no can of Coors. She screams and pulls at her hair. I see her clutch a knife and feel its sharpened edge.

Doc Murphy visits. He no longer works at the hospital but looks after patients in his office and in their homes. He frowns and touches Mother's forehead. After a few words, too quiet for me to hear, he rummages through his black bag and injects Mom with a yellow fluid. Eventually, she sleeps.

Sometime after midnight, I climb the fence to the impound and find Julie's crumpled car. The dent of her head, outlined with bits of blood and strands of hair, is stamped against the shattered windshield. Where her lap would have been, the engine rests bleeding oil. I pour a gallon of gas into the tank. In the cracked mirror, I see my twisted face—*killer, liar, cheat*. From somewhere inside my head, I hear a whisper—*guilty, guilty, guilty.*

I will be punished according to my own patent. Father has not earned the right. My mind conjures whips, chains, hair shirts, bamboo splints, gasoline, and matches.

Between midnight and morning, I wander. No searching police encounter me. No worried Father tries to find me. I sleep on the floor beside my bed and wake to the stench of burnt coffee. Father gives Mother more pills. Then he glares at me through the slits of his puffy eyes. "Did you sleep?"

I hang my head and blink away my tears.

"Let's go," he snarls, "the impound opens at eight. We'll see if you put gas in the car."

We arrive early at the closed impound. Five minutes later, Hunchback Hal exits his shack and opens the gate.

"Where's the Miata?" Father asks.

At the crumpled car, he snakes a short garden hose into the tank and pulls it back. The tip is moist. Once again, he scowls, reinserts the hose, sucks on the end. "Shit!" He spits when he inhales only fumes. He slides under the car, squirming like an overgrown snake, and unscrews the gas drain. Fuel gurgles from the tank. He stares at me in disbelief. I raise my eyes and glare into his for only an instant. Then he turns and drives home without me.

CHAPTER 6

What perversity decrees an open coffin? Does death require the dead displayed? What gain comes from torture that disrupts the unhealed wound of grief?

I sit in a pew one space from my parents. Julie lies among white silk decorated with lily of the valley. From her hand, a bouquet of roses sends out its perfume. At rest, her face is calm. No impish grin, no playful teasing, no touch tells me that I'm still worthwhile.

Painful words assail my ears. In life, there is death; and in death there is life everlasting. Numb and silent, I have no prayer. What life is there in death that a mortal man can know? In life, there is life; and in that life, there is joy; in death, only memories and nothing.

Father allows me to ride in the back of his prized Buick. It is a new honor for me. I have never been inside his car. And now, at the end of Julie's life, I sit in his Buick, in the backseat, hunched against the door. Father's eyes flash in the mirror. Perhaps I could oblige and fall under the wheels.

We trudge to the grave. My legs move as if in a muddy ooze.

Mother, her expression dull, pill suppressed, mouths futile prayers. Dust to dust with a spatter of life between. A handful of dirt drums on the coffin of her child.

Father's arm holds Mother. Otherwise, he stands at parade attention, eyes fixed on the horizon. I dare a glance at him. Two vertical streams, irregular, streak his face. He refuses to blink or swallow. Jaw muscles jump in series, knotted in their anger. Holy water rains on the coffin and muddies the dust. In the end, no words remain. Father Delorme, his knobby arthritic hand on Mother's elbow, leads her from the grave. Father follows.

Numbed, I remain rooted. Father finds no resolve to show a gentle touch. He makes no effort to retrieve me from the grave. He shoots a glance, like a man about to vomit, and drives away.

By the grave, alone with my sister, I weep and shovel dirt on the coffin until my hands are raw. Pain and tears cannot repay my debt. *How can I go home and live with my guilt? Where will I live? How will I eat?* A shadow casts over me. I shiver. From behind me, a policeman pats my shoulder. "It's time to go," he says, "your mother wants you home."

I look up. He is neither angry nor friendly. "She's really worried about you."

"I'm not going."

"That's up to you really, your choice. But it doesn't make much sense to bite a helping hand."

He shrugs and walks away. "I'll tell your mother where you are."

I keep shoveling but soon become dizzy. Maybe I dozed off or got hypoglycemic. I wake up surrounded by pale yellow hospital curtains. Mother kneels over me, clasping her trembling hands. "Tommy, oh, Tommy, I was so worried about you." She touches my face, strokes my hair, and kisses me.

"Please come home. Let me take care of you."

Mr. Wilson is beside her. He extends a hand. "Let me help you up, Thomas. Your father's back at camp, so your mother asked me to help. We've been praying for you."

Mother anchors herself to me in Wilson's van as if afraid I might escape.

"You're cold, Tom. Your lips are blue, and you're shaking. Here, I brought some hot chocolate."

I let Wilson help me into the house. "You need a hot bath and hot soup, young man."

He leaves with a litany—Samaritan, lost sheep, helping hand, forgiveness, faith.

After my hot bath and soup, I watch TV. *How could I be so crude? Accepting kindness after what I'd done.* Mom tries to talk.

"It's so hard. We'll always miss her. She was so close to you, to all of us. It was a gift, the way Julie could bond and relate. Don't you think so?"

I nod with an inarticulate reply.

"Let's try to get some sleep."

"I can't, Mom, I'm too wired."

"I've got some sleeping pills. Take one."

Next morning, groggy, after a fractured sleep, I lie inert to ease the pounding of my brain. Mom has pain pills that reduce my headache to a dull throb. Soon I need three pills to help me sleep. When I ask for three, Mom frowns. "I think you better stop the pills. They're habit-forming."

"Oh, but they really help. I'd be a case without them. Can't you get some more?"

"I talked to Doc Murphy. You can't have any more. If you need more, you have to see him."

I wait an hour on a wooden chair. Dressed in his doctor coat, he frames the doorway and peers down at me over half glasses. "What's a young fellow like you need pills for?" he grumps.

"Can't sleep since my sister died."

"Have you talked to anybody about her, about how you feel?"

"Not really."

"Well, do it," he scowls. "It's more important than any pills I give you. You've had all the pills you need."

"Asshole," I mutter after he leaves. "One hour waiting, two minutes listening to his preaching. No pills. Waste my time."

Sketches scrawled in shades of gray torment my nights. Julie's face appears, recessed in a black cowl. Her skeleton hand draws shadows across her battered face. An accusing arm extends to me and then she gestures, "Come." I scream in the night. Mom is beside me. "Hush, Tommy, hush." She rocks me until my sobs subside.

"It's OK," she says. "Try to get some sleep. Let me get some sherry. I'll slip in a couple of Gravol. It's a trick I learned from Doc Murphy."

After another bad night, I visit Bill. His spiked hair pokes upward from his open doorway. He stares. "What's goin' down, man? You look like boiled shit."

"My sister died in a car accident."

"Tough. I heard she bought it. So what are you going to do? Fall apart and go to rat shit? Life goes on. Don't be an idiot. There's nothing you can do to bring her back."

"You got any tokes?"

After a smoke and a beer, I feel better. "Thanks, Bill. What is this stuff? Grass?"

"Not grass," he sneers. "Grass is for wimps. This stuff's traditional. The Chinese used to smoke it."

Bill and I are buds. His Oriental grass brings serenity. But it's only temporary. Soon, I become irritable and short tempered. Once again, I can't sleep. I complain to Bill. "This stuff's not doing it for me anymore."

"It can be like that," Bill nods with understanding. "The strength varies. Everybody's different. You get used to it. Tell you what. Try a couple more, have a beer. If it doesn't get you there, I got better shit."

Two more tokes and two more beer (not Coors, thank Christ) don't get me there. I'm on edge, irritable, sweating. Anger, guilt, depression plague my tired mind.

"Roll up your sleeve," Bill says.

He has a syringe, the size of a pencil. *God what a rush! God what a calm!* "Thanks, Bill. That was awesome, rad."

For a few days Bill is my best friend. Then he disappears. He's not home or at school. Maybe he's on holidays or had a car accident. I can't find him.

Mother's pills—Serax, Ativan, Demerol, MSContin—fill my needs. At first, she seems puzzled then hides her pills. Beer, scotch, and sherry temporize. I see Julie in my nights. Her tears flow, and she shakes her head.

Bill, where is Bill? Finally, I sit on his steps and wait.

"Hey, Tom, bud. How you been? Long time."

"Trying to find you. I need more stuff."

"Bad timing. I got none. I need cash up front to get some."

Nausea hits me like a kick in the groin. "Don't you have a spare toke even?"

"Sorry, Tom. I got nuthin', and I'm broke. You can't get unless you give. Now bugger off. I got a date."

I no longer have my job at McDonald's. I lost it when I was unable to explain how my till was fifty dollars short.

Mother keeps money in her purse. She also keeps charge cards and pin numbers written in her address book.

Mom avoids me. She goes to evening service and is invited to the Wilsons'. I sleep during the day. She sleeps at night. I'm feeling better. Bill's medicine keeps me together. Mother won't miss a few Royal Doultons, and Father has more than one torque wrench.

One evening, Moira phones. Her voice is cheerful. "How are you, Tommy?"

"I'm OK, I guess."

"C'mon back to school. We miss you."

I can't get up in the morning, but I do make it to biology. It never occurs to me that I am offensive. No shave, no hair combed, teeth not brushed. *When did I last change my clothes, have a bath?* Mr. Sinclair takes my arm and directs me to the nursing office.

A few weeks later, I'm sitting in a psychiatrist's waiting room. The school insists. Father even takes a day off. *A psychiatrist? What can a neatly dressed man with a pipe and sports coat do? Will he ask about my childhood? Bedwetting? Nail biting? Ask about my dreams and nightmares. Will he ask if I sleep well?*

I am greeted by two hundred and forty pounds of unexercised flesh. "You don't mind if I smoke," he says. It is a statement, not a question. He stands to let his belly fall over his jeans. "I'm Dr. Simpson," he says, "I'm a psychiatrist."

It's awkward. This stranger extracts words from me like a verbal dentist.

"Mmm," he says, "I see, go on. Is that so?" Then, "Do you ever feel rested? How much alcohol do you drink? Pills? Injectables? Have

you ever thought of injuring yourself? Tried? Thought of suicide?
Tried?"

My fumbled replies are noncommittal grunts. Finally, he blows
smoke at the ceiling and tries to read my downcast eyes. "You know,
Tom, you've been had. You're a sucker, and your father's whipping
post. It goes with being a good lad and believing your elders.

"Nothing in this world is perfect. Accidents happen. Intent to
injure is evil. Injury as the consequence of intent is a crime. Your
sister had an accident." My eyes remain downcast, yet I cling to
his words. Words that carry the first hint of absolution. *You're
human. Your pecker ran away with your memory. It happens all
the time. You grieve. You must. Would your sister approve of how
you're living now?*

"Go to confession. Exorcise your Catholic demons. Get on
with your life. Find your old friends. Make new ones. Now let's
talk to your parents. They need to get off your case."

I think I feel better. I'm not sure, yet I'm hopeful. But when
we return home, Father sits in his chair and pronounces, "Bullshit.
Don't change nuthin', just words farted by a fat old man. And I
wasted a day's work."

Mother only sighs and shakes her head. The glimmer of my
fledgling hopes is extinguished by Father's edict.

"Shit," Father says. "I can't piss around here all day." He tosses
his bag into the truck and leaves with a growl of gravel and squeal
of tires on the pavement.

Mother puts an arm around me. "It's not all his fault. I couldn't
be a wife to him after I had you."

*Confession, the fat man said. Exorcise your demons. Forgiveness. What
can that senile Father Delorme do? Bring Julie back? Bless me, Father,
for I have sinned. I stole my father's beer and killed my sister.*

I'm losing weight. Mother insists that I have a physical. "Well,
if you won't see Doc Murphy," she says, "I'll take you to one of
those walk in clinics."

The doctor looks about my age and still has peach fuzz, but a
label with his picture on it says "John Mills, MD"

"We should do some blood work," he says.

He phones in a few days. "We should get more blood work. We have to rule out diabetes."

On the morning of the lab test, I eat doughnuts and drink Coke with plenty of sugar. There is no doubt. I am diabetic. I get pamphlets, a glucometer, insulin, and syringes. Two clean syringes per day, I reuse some and sell the rest.

Mother is happy. I have a disease, and it causes everything I have wrong with me.

Bill's heroin calms my nerves; and for weeks, I am calm like a meditating monk. Then, after a joyous hit, I wake up attached to an IV. "I found you unconscious," Mother explains.

Standing beside her is a short woman dressed in hospital greens with a name tag around her neck. "It's not diabetes," she says. "We gave him a glucose bolus, and nothing happened. He was breathing one per minute, and his pupils were pinpoint. And there are these," she says, pointing to my needle marks.

Mother seems confused.

The short medic purses her lips. "We gave him a narcotic antagonist. He woke right up. He's a junkie."

"Fuck you," I tell her. "Give me my clothes and take out this IV. I'm leaving."

"You haven't been discharged," short ass says. "You'll need to sign the release form."

"I'm leaving. I got my rights."

A hollow expression falls on my mother's face. A tear shatters on the floor. She shakes her head and whispers to me, "Can you think of no one but yourself?"

On weekends, I move out of the house. Father is still furious that I signed his name to a check I made out to me. When he's home from the woods, I go to the woods. There, among defunct logging roads and game trails, I feel safe. Solitude is bearable. On the edges of canyons, my irritability and moroseness offend no one. By Sunday evening, my legs ache and I sweat. Cravings overpower me. I need a fix, nothing else matters. I am in pain, therefore alive. Even my bowels begin to move. Constipation is the price of tranquility.

I wait and listen for the rumble of Father's truck as he leaves for camp. I sneak into my bedroom and avoid Mother. But she knows and brings a sandwich or bowl of soup. She has no words anymore, and I cannot meet her eyes. She now wears earplugs at night to suppress my screams. When I'm awake, a constant flipping of the TV is muted from her mind.

My sense of time is day and night. One day is like any other. Late one afternoon, I am still in bed. I don't know it's Friday. Father barges into my room. Most of his tools are missing, and all the beer has vanished.

His bear-paw hand encircles my neck. Squeezes it like a cold can of Coors. His normally reddish face is purple. Neck veins throb. At the corners of his mouth, two mounds of spittle protrude. Bulging eyes and pointing fingers make words superfluous. He opens the door with one hand and tosses me with the other. "Get out. Stay out. If I ever see you, you stinky weasel, I'll kill you with my bare hands."

Mother appears with my runners and throws them at me one by one.

CHAPTER 7

I need drugs. My hands shake; and I'm nauseated, but more than that, I'm cold and need a place to stay—*Moira's?* "You have to be nuts, Tom, my parents would freak. Besides, you're over the edge. Try an alley or under a bridge."

"Pete, old pal, can I stay in your basement tonight? My old man kicked me out."

"Bill, old pal, buddy. Can I stay in your house tonight? There's no room in my house anymore."

"Who are you?" Bill says. "I don't know you."

On Sunday evening, the Bellingham Sally Anne has room for one more. "I'd like a private suite with bath," I say to the attendant.

"Wouldn't we all," he says. "The best we can do is a public shower and community bedroom. We've washed the rubber sheet and boiled the bedding. Will that be adequate, sir?"

Sally Anne keeps me for the night. I'm warm and dry among a row of army cots. A smelly old bum tries to crawl into bed with me. Another keeps singing "The Old Rugged Cross."

Just before daylight, a bearded wino with a pickled brain mistakes my cot for a urinal. I leave. The bleary-eyed attendant stops me. "Have some porridge," he says, "and remember, Jesus loves you."

Would he blow a trumpet? "Here," he says, "take this jacket. It's cold out."

My hands shake so much that I can barely mop my forehead. My guts twist into knots. Porridge backs up and spews a gray pattern on a grayer sidewalk. I slither into one of those methadone clinics. An arrow on a beige wall points up a flight of stairs where an opaque plastic window allows light from the inside. Under the window is a sign, Dr. Emile Dickson, MD.

He doesn't stand as I enter. He's leaning back on a wooden chair and has his hands clasped behind his head. A brown plywood desk provides a place for cowboy boots. Faded blue jeans and checkered shirt complete his doctor outfit. I see no white coat or name tag. He squints at me through rimless glasses, sniffs and furrows his brow.

"You the doctor?"

He moves some papers on his desk and points to his name. His lips separate to expose yellow teeth, but the corners of his mouth don't move up. His eyes squeeze shut, and he frowns like a man with a headache.

"Why are you here?" he asks.

"I need some methadone."

"Wrong answer. Nobody needs methadone."

He scratches his nose. "Would you like to get off drugs, enter a rehab program, partake of counseling, cooperate with a methadone program, and submit periodic urine samples?"

"Yeah, that's it."

He writes on a prescription pad. "What's your name?"

Before long, I feel better, but there's no high, not that orgasmic rush of a heroin. It's only bread and water not a full course dinner.

Next morning, I sit with my back against a brick wall. People rush by on their way to work. No one donates to the upended baseball cap at my feet. After a while, I become aware that someone is beside me.

"Kicked you out, eh?" He smiles and passes a cigarette. "This one's on me. Hi, I'm Alex."

He looks fourteen, maybe fifteen—long lashes, innocent eyes, blond curly hair, baby face, voice not yet entirely broken.

"What are you doing here?" I say. "Shouldn't you be in school?"

He laughs. "This is school. What am I doing here? Surviving, same as you. You need a friend when you're here, somebody to watch your back and show you the ropes."

"You been here for a while?"

"Oh yeah, man, a whole lifetime. Just remember, when you live here, nobody gives a shit if you live or die."

I watch Alex's back as he stands on the sidewalk in the glow of a neon night. His white muscle shirt outlines his body, and his faded jeans are too tight at the hips. He only accepts rides in Porsches, BMWs, Mercedes, and occasionally a Cadillac. He spurns the pickup truck driven by a longhaired man with a tattoo on his shoulder.

I write down license plates and carry a beeper.

"If it goes off," Alex says, "phone this number and leave the license on the answering machine. Don't phone anybody unless it beeps. I can be gone a long time. That's the nature of my business. I got to look after myself."

I have two columns: time and number.

Some evenings he's bruised around his arms and neck. He doesn't seem to mind.

"We should trade one night," he says. "Let me write the numbers down."

I shake my head. I couldn't.

One evening, Alex and I are sitting near a theatre entrance. "Look pathetic, keep your eyes down. If you look up, they think you're challenging or threatening."

He holds up his cardboard sign: Hungry and Homeless. I hold mine: Homeless and Hungry. Black platform shoes impinge on my vision; above them are Calvin Klein Jeans and a name brand sweater. A face from the past, still much alive in my memory, wears her clothes like a skinny runway model. Moira smiles at the creep in Hilfiger's that walks beside her. He laughs, squeezes her hand, and tries to kiss her. He looks like some arrogant rich kid loser that she picked up from a college mixer, probably a frat rat. I raise my collar, pull down my cap, and fix my eyes on the sidewalk.

She brushes past me and never slows. I imagine the scent of her perfume. Flashes of what might have been flicker through my mind. I shovel away my feelings and regain that hollow state—the eggshell that remains after the core's sucked out. I'm desperate for another hit.

Alex straightens my collar and puts my cap on the ground. "We need it for them to put money in," he says. Then he puts an arm around me, gently like a young girl. "It's tough, man. Shit happens."

Alex has disappeared. After two weeks, he just shows up. He's tanned and a little fat. "You look great, Alex. What's up?"

He smiles, almost bashful, a little proud, but mostly defiant. "Sugar daddy," he says.

Alex only hangs with me a few days. We do some great hits. In the calm after a rush he says, "You should try my line of work, Tom. The money's good. Most of my clients are married men with money. I'm not cheap you know. Actually, I'm quite pretty. Don't you think so? What do you say, Tom, a real team?"

Pictures of naked fat old men, sweat, saliva, and semen jam up my brain. I gag and throw up a few ounces of bile.

Alex takes off again. It's getting to be a habit. I look for him on the street, in shelters, and even churches. I ask the street kids and the do-gooders who roam offering help if we want it. No Alex. After a few weeks, he's just there, in the condemned Avalon Hotel. I brush away spoons and needles, kick at used-up lighters and sit on the floor beside him.

"Bad trick," he hisses through wired jaws.

We go begging. "Could I please have some food for my friend, Alex? Could you put it in a blender? Do you have a straw? Look, Alex, I got us a treat, a vanilla shake." In a few weeks, his jaw is unwired, and he's back working the streets.

The next time I see him, he's sprawled limp in the dumpster behind the Kong Lum Restaurant. A purple Kaposi blemish on his chest announces he has AIDS.

Below his left nipple ring, the handle of a steak knife forms an indent on his skin. Purple and yellow bruises pattern his beautiful face. His eyes are partly open. I try to close them, but they won't stay shut.

I roll him over and look for his wallet.

I only want to see Moira one more time. Maybe even talk to her, try to explain. I dress up in a brown corduroy jacket with frayed cuffs, a gift from the Sally Anne. When Moira leaves her house, I follow far behind but never closing the gap. I nearly ring her doorbell but lose my nerve. I could phone, but I'm afraid she'll hang up.

Leaves and apples have long fallen from the tree in her backyard. In the darkness under its gnarled branches, I reminisce as Moira deftly works in her kitchen, cutting carrots, peeling potatoes. She lifts a lid and tastes her cooking. Her cheeks are flushed, and a wisp of stray hair sways over her forehead. I imagine she's humming.

Tightened handcuffs bite my wrists and two cops frog-march me to her door.

"We caught your stalker," the paunchy cop says.

Moira narrows her eyes. "Oh, God, Tommy. It's you."

"You know this creep?" the cop asks.

"No," she whispers. "I only know who he used to be."

CHAPTER 8

No Alex. No Moira. No Mother. No Julie. Those that matter are dead or distant. When I'm in the mood, stealing and begging help me survive. I've conned everyone I know. I still go to the methadone clinic when I'm near the edge.

Sometimes I bed down in the condemned Avalon Hotel. In my dreams Alex laughs. He clutches a roll of money and throws knives at me. I yell at him to stop. A kick in the ribs wakes me. "Shut the fuck up, shithead. This ain't no goddamn zoo."

In an alley, a stranger stares at me. Maybe he knows me. His left hand is in his pocket, perhaps clutching a knife. I've seen those bushy eyebrows and that short red beard. I try but can't connect them to a car or license. He follows me, but I elude him in the familiar geography of my lanes and alleys.

Midnight drizzle penetrates my donated clothes. They stick to me and chill my body. An old raincoat keeps moisture in. My crotch and armpits grow an itchy fungus. I walk miles, unable to sleep, safer awake. I stay at the outskirts of town. Sometimes I walk along railway tracks. I've mastered the technique, much like a blind man with a stick. *I think I'll lie down and catch a train. Don't be stupid. Only freight trains run at night.*

In that wedge of time between night and morning, before shadows appear and shapes are not yet substance, I walk alone beside a deserted highway. Moisture coats my new wool sweater. I traded the raincoat. After all, wool keeps sheep dry too. The B&E I just did was so easy. Signs on the windows warned—Nixon Alarm Co. A lot of people never activate alarms. If they do, I am long gone. Cops are fed up with false alarms.

I walk briskly on the left side of the road when bright lights blind me. I freeze, immobile like a forest deer. *Oh shit! Cops!* The bumper indents my pants but not my leg. From the dark beyond the headlights, I hear a whispered voice. Not cops—worse. A familiar voice, almost a hiss, assaults me from the darkness. "I told you I'd kill you if I ever saw you again. Now's a good time."

"What are you doing up this time of day, Pops? Insomnia or are you looking for some action?"

"No," he sneers, "I was just going to run over you. But then I figure you'd just mess up my truck. So, I'll just off you—slow and painful."

I pull a syringe out of my pocket. "Come and get me, Pops. I've got AIDS and a used syringe. Maybe I'll get lucky and stick your drinking hand. Maybe I'll just sneak into our house and do you when you're drunk and tired."

He jumps into his truck and squeals a U-turn. The smell of burning rubber hangs in the morning mist.

My nightmares begin to drive me crazy. I can't sleep and only doze. I'm losing weight; and even with my drugs, I'm always hungry. Julie haunts me. Alex laughs. I have to get away. The living want to kill me, and the dead do as well. I panic and am bound by a compulsion that demands. I leave. I must escape. I will flee to my mountains; never to return. There I will be safe. I will survive. Indians have for centuries.

My life as a junkie pays dividends. I steal a tent, sleeping bag, food, hunting rifle, ammunition, and alpine clothes.

Silver birches in their autumn glory line my path. I'm going home. Giant spruce saved by tree huggers block the sunlight. Game trails wind past distorted, stunted trees to reach the brown grass of an alpine autumn.

How long had I climbed? Two days? Three? Vomiting no longer plagues me. My cramping bowels ease, and my dripping nose no longer trickles on my shirt. Gone too is that persistent sniffing, annoying even to me.

Strange, the faster I climb, the better I feel. *I'm not paranoid about Father. He'll never find me here. Jubilation! A natural high!* I toss my Valium away. Drugs only impede my mission.

Raleigh's Canyon gapes below me. Its granite walls face each other like giant Siamese twins separated in their primordial past. A howling wind tinged with the perfume of winter funnels through the canyon walls. I struggle to peg my tent. Fingernails break backward as they dig into nylon. Another gust threatens to tear my shelter away. Finally, by bracing myself against an earthen bank, I anchor my tent. An accomplishment.

Morning shelters my tent in virgin snow under the clearest blue of a mountain sky. No wind stirs. Only silence pervades when a storm is spent. I have time for meditation, time to plan, to reflect. After five days, I'm bored. There's no TV, cards, or telephone. No company. No Moira, Julie, or Alex. No fix, no pills, no methadone.

Some nights, I look for stars I know. Tonight the Big Dipper is upside down and the little one too.

At first, it seems a whisper, then more like a hum that rises from the canyon. I go outside to be kissed by a warm breeze. I close my eyes and listen to the whispering mountain wind. Music like a symphony drifts to my ears.

"Hush, baby brother, don't you cry. You'll be better by and by." Julie, dressed in sandals and daisies in her hair, walks to me with arms held wide. She continues her rhyme. "You have yet to see the best. This chapter's just a test—and you flunked."

Her laughter echoes from the canyon. She holds her sides and laughs at her own poor joke. I run toward her, but a gentle hand detains me and leads me from the canyon's brim.

Julie lives! Her spirit rides the western wind. The hand of God has touched me.

I am sheltered from the brink. Warm rain falls upon me. Beneath it, I dance naked and wash my sins away.

Can I stay on this mountain forever? Already boredom and loneliness engulf me. Before a snowstorm can seal my exit, I load my pack and leave. Distance. I need distance from other junkies or I'll hang out with them again. Most of all, I need distance from the derelict self, that self that still stalks me. To get away, I hitchhike north to Canada, and then follow the railway tracks across the border. I thumb a ride in a dented brown Chevy with rusted fenders. Its driver, a man with a big pockmarked nose, reaches over and shoves open the passenger door. His gut indents the bottom of the steering wheel. On his right middle finger, he wears a chunky gray metal ring.

"Wanna lift, Sonny?" he says.

"Sure."

"Well, hop in. I'm going to Vancouver. Tell me when you want out."

He drives in silence, then somewhere between a strip mall and a river, he stops. "Get the fuck out, Sonny. You're skinny and smell funny."

This must be Vancouver. I recognize a bridge from a postcard I'd seen. Narrow houses on narrow lots line the side hill like rows of army barracks. Scattered playgrounds relieve the sameness. Several blocks from the muddy river, a church with its white steeple beckons me. On the uncut lawn is a sign. St. Mary's Catholic Church. Everyone Welcome. Father Alan Maguire, Pastor.

The rectory is tucked behind the church. I suck in my cheeks, hunch my shoulders, and try to look pathetic. From inside the house, I hear the echo of the doorbell, but no one answers. A man in rubber boots and work gloves rounds the corner of the house. "Hello there," he says, "looking for somebody?"

"I'm looking for Father Maguire."

"That's me."

"Oh, I thought you were the gardener."

"That's me too." He says with a smile. "And who are you?"

"I'm Tom. I've been traveling, and I'm starving. Could I trouble you for some food?"

"Well, Tom, this church has a policy. You don't get something for nothing. There's grass that needs cutting. Do that, and I'll get you some food."

My mouth falls open. Every other Christian is happy to give. It's his duty and makes him feel good to help those who are less fortunate. Maguire raises an eyebrow. "It's a fair deal, isn't it?"

Even in autumn, Vancouver is warm and grass is still lush. I push the manual lawnmower until sweat trickles from my face. Obviously, this is penance.

We sit across from each other at a scarred oak table. Dinner is a bowl of clam chowder, a slice of brown bread, and a glass of milk. I finish eating and am ready for a quick getaway before the inevitable preaching starts. Maguire drops his spoon into the empty bowl.

"It's my business to ask," he says, "and I don't like to do things for people that they can do for themselves. You're not going to find a job in those rags and no bath. You're welcome to use the shower. I've got some spare clean clothes that I'll trade for yours. We're about the same size. You can sleep in the basement until 6:00 AM. Then you have to go.

"I have a job for four hours every morning," he adds. "The immigrant workers of my parish can't support an able-bodied priest."

CHAPTER 9

"Make sure you wear gloves when you do dishes," Ronaldo says, "and put the leftover meat scraps in this little garbage can. I take them home to feed the dog."

His friends call him Rolly. He is perpetual motion. His hands mimic his speech and never linger on a topic. Often his head oscillates as if he trying to get a full view around his hooked nose. The dog is probably a Doberman and hyper too.

"Just remember," Rolly says, "we don't pay much, but we share the tips equal. If the dishes are dirty, the customer don't tip. If the food's crappy, he don't tip neither no matter how much the waitress smile or how big a tits she got."

I wash dishes, dry dishes, clean counters, take out garbage, and sweep floors.

"Don't mop the floor until everybody's gone. Somebody might fall on his ass, and I have to pay compo." Rolly smiles and adds, "You do good job."

Good job and no place to stay. I return after work to find Maguire napping. I give the hammock a strong push that startles him.

He barks at me. "Have you no sense of decency? I was having a wonderful dream."

"Oh, sorry, the devil made me do it."

"Well, now that I'm awake and you're employed, there are terms and conditions. You can stay in the basement. The rent is half of your tips to a maximum of five dollars a night. If you wake me again, it's seven dollars."

One month later, I say to Maguire, "I'm moving out. The rent's too high. I've got my own place, a furnished one-room suite."

He shakes my hand and says. "Congratulations. You've come a long way, baby. If you'll kneel, I'd like to bless you."

I decline the blessing and refuse to feel joy. Even Julie would have raised an eyebrow and said, "You've only done what's ordinary. And you're still just an almost graduate."

Even though I've moved, I still keep in touch. There are no appointments. I just show up and am always welcome. Al's not always home, but I wait. If he's gone too long, I go home. I don't live far.

One evening, I'm caught in a downpour and escape into Maguire's church. The sign reads, Welcome to St. Mary's. The Door Is Always Open.

Suckers. The loot from here could buy a lot of fixes. I take off my coat and slouch so that my head rests on the back of the pew. Like a hypnotist's watch, the altar light waves to me and does a dance in red behind the glass. Hands of flame in ceaseless motion capture my vision and enter my mind. The squeak of the confessional breaks my dream. Maguire emerges, squints, and stretches. He runs a hand over his balding youthful head. He yawns and stretches again. Then sees me in the periphery of his vision and smiles, "Hello, I thought I was through, but there's always time for one more confession."

"It's OK, Father. I'm just here for some peace and quiet. Besides, my sins would take all night to confess."

"You don't have to confess them all at once. It can be done by categories. We could set up a series of appointments and have you come back on a regular basis. Just like visits to the orthodontist."

I smile. Maguire is also amused. He treats sin as if it were a subject for banter.

"Seriously," he continues, "I have a proposition. There's a youth group in the church basement on Thursday's at 8:00 PM, nothing fancy, just a get-together. Talk. Kick around a few ideas. We've got a few projects. Why not stick your nose in. Have a sniff. If you don't like it, feel free to go. We don't take attendance."

"Maybe."

I don't go that Thursday, but I go to the next meeting. I'm a little late on purpose. I don't want some nosy do-gooder talking to me.

My well-worn jeans are comfortable, and I wear a clean shirt that I have actually paid for. Now I blend in. Maguire introduces us, first names only.

He interjects Bible quotes. "What you do for the least of these you do also for me." He's setting me up. "We are all made in God's image. Honor is due us as we also honor others."

Within a week, I am a passenger in Maguire's VW Beetle. He believes in 100 percent occupancy. His left foot occupies the clutch; right, the gas; right hand, the shift; and left, the steering wheel. There is no spare leg for brakes. He executes a sudden left swerve past a blurred sign that announces Welcome to St. Alphonse.

Ramps nestle against the brown sides of a U-shaped building. Wire grids cover the windows. "It's only minimum security," Maguire says, "to keep the inmates safe."

We wait at the Plexiglas entrance. A woman in jeans and pink sweatshirt waves at us.

"Father, I'm so happy to see you," she says. Then, turning to me, she added, "I'm Anna. You must be Tom. I've heard so little about you." She chuckles at her own little joke and extends her pink hand.

"Pleased to meet you," I reply and shake her hand.

I follow her into the labyrinth. I sniff urine. Not ordinary urine in a washroom or disguised with talcum powder in a kid's diapers. This was moldy, cloaked with Nilodor.

"This is Alice," Anna says, "Don't get too close. She's a biter. That's why she's got a red name tag."

A hunched old man shuffles toward us, both feet always in contact with the floor. His hands are in constant motion, like a bank teller counting dollar bills. When he gets past me, I notice his buttocks enjoying fresh air through his backward dressing gown.

Anna taps on a closed door and enters before it's answered. Inside is a silver-haired man rocking in his chair. "This is Sourdough," she says." His other name is Earl. He's a prospector."

"You mean was," I say.

"Was," she says, "and still is."

His bright blue eyes pierce into mine and squint as he tries to remember. Anticipation cheers his face. "Yes, yes," he says, "it's so good to see you." He pumps my hand in both of his and gives me a tattered book. He sits in his rocker. I read *The Cremation of Sam McGee*. Earl falls asleep.

I continue to read. Maybe he can still hear me. One part is underlined:

> How good is God to me.
> For I have not a mansion tall,
> With trees and lawns of velvet tread.
> With beauty is my life abrim.
> With tranquil hours and dreams apart;
> You wonder that I yield to Him
> That best of prayers, a grateful heart?

Anna appears and shakes his shoulder. "Did you like that, Earl?" He smiles and nods. Clear blue eyes again seek mine. "Thanks, Eddie," he says.

Anna gives me a cookie when I leave.

I walk beside the river and watch the log booms and barges aided by the current. My life is drifting on the tide. And in my heart, I know that I have yet to yield to him.

I skip the next two Thursday meetings and avoid church. When I return, Maguire seems neither surprised nor happy. After prayer and discussion, he has another do-gooder Catholic project waiting to be launched. It seems that some of his parishioners are from Mexico. Their town orphanage is in dire need of school supplies. Would we look around for items to make a package?

Against my natural instincts, I buy paper, pencils, and a pencil sharpener, the kind that screws into the desk and has a shaving catcher. I send a screwdriver, just in case. Maguire smiles, "Gracias, Señor."

Six weeks later, I receive a letter.

> *Esteemed Sr. Spanner,*
> *We, the Sisters of Orphanage Guadalupe, thank you for*
> *your gift to our children. We believe that education is the key*

*that unlocks a meaningful future. Your consideration helps to
ease the enslavement of poverty. God bless you.*

*Yours in Christ,
Sister Maria Gonsalves*

*PS: The pencil sharpener fascinates the children. I have instructed
them. Its main purpose is not to produce shavings.*

The lower half of the page has names in various crayon colors.
"Antonio, Roberto, Consuela, Eleanora, Sally . . ."

Next day I enroll in a course—finish high school in your spare
time.

Winter passes. Maguire insists I call him Al. I'm clean, negative
for hepatitis B and C, HIV, and STDs. I have a place to live. I still
wash dishes at Rolly's, pump gas, and work on my high school
diploma. In June, I pass.

One evening after track I say, "It's a good life, Al, but I'm going
nowhere."

He raises an eyebrow. "Where do you want to go?"

I shrug. "I dunno."

"Why don't you go on a retreat? Step back. Look at your life.
It's not all about religion."

I think about it and follow his suggestion. The retreat house,
nestled in the foothills, calms my apprehensions. People are
friendly and helpful. I hear a lot about love and the healing power
of forgiveness. Then there are themes about guilt, negativity, and
creativity.

In the quiet of night, free from traffic noise, junkies, and hookers,
I begin to find peace. Sometimes Julie enters my dreams. She
understands and forgives. It is something I cannot do.

The obvious reaffirms itself. There is life other than this one.
Spirituality is real. Al knows. Julie knows. And now I know it too.

On my return, I avoid Al and duck when I hear a Volkswagen.
Eventually, I return to youth group but decline to be helpful. Al

never asks. Never pushes. Early in September, after a meeting, Al says, "How would you like to tour the Pacific Coast?"

Al has a habit when he drives. He tilts his head to the left and combs his nonexistent hair. He aims the bug and ensures that only two wheels touch the pavement at any one time. I tighten my seat belt, brace my feet against the floor, and keep my hands on the dashboard. "Relax, it's perfectly safe. The Oregon Coast is made for this car. We can't go left. The mountain stops us. If we fall right, you'll be happy to know this car floats."

"Thanks a lot, Al. If you keep driving like that, I'll float too. You're supposed to be a Christian, not a Roman chariot racer."

I try to distract him. Perhaps he can't speed and talk at the same time. "So, Al, what's your idea of God?"

For a moment, his foot leaves the gas pedal. "What?"

"I said, what's—"

"I heard you. We're on holiday."

He frowns. "God is a concept, an ideal, an explanation for the incomprehensible. God has been maligned by people's efforts to define him. By all those who begin with, God is, God says, or God wants. Yes, I believe there is a god, not as defined in human terms, but as spiritual force that is part of our being, but it's more than our genes. We are human in the image of God, and at the very least, godlike. Some would say, in the biological sense, we are God."

"Jeez, Al, couldn't you get kicked out for thinking that?"

Al shakes his head. "No, not for thinking it, only for saying it."

He stops the car where, waves crash, recede, and once more, assault the rocky shore. Two girls stroll on the beach beneath us; their bodies neatly outlined under their shorts and halter tops.

"Al," I say, "do you like girls? Have you ever had a girlfriend?"

His laughter roars above the waves. "I'm not gay, Tom. If I were, you'd know by now. I don't have a girlfriend. It's against my religion. But I do like girls. Why do you think I work all day and run till I'm exhausted?"

"Sorry, Al. I know you're not gay. I just wondered how you do it. I had a girlfriend once, before I became junk, and she still bothers my mind."

"I've never had a serious girlfriend," Al says. "I wasn't brought up that way. My family is strict Catholic. There are quite a few relatives in the religious life. I was destined to become a priest. And I've never been sorry. It's been easy, Tom. Maybe too easy."

CHAPTER 10

On the anniversary of my last needle, I capture my anxieties, harness my apprehensions, and phone my parents. Mother answers with a tired, sleepy hello. Even at midmorning, her voice is mechanical, opaque.

"Who's this?" she says with just a hint of slur.

"It's Thomas."

"Thomas who?"

"Thomas, your son."

"No, it can't be. My son's dead. Is this some kind of bad joke?" Silence.

"Is it you, Thomas? Is it really you?"

"It's me, Mom. My life's better now. I'd really like to see you."

"It's been a long time, Thomas. How can you do this to me? Not even a postcard. What do you want?"

"Nothing, Mom. I just want to talk to you and see you again. I've been straight for a year. I don't want anything except to see you. That's all."

A long silence answers me. "Mom, are you still there?"

"Can you call me back Saturday when Bruce is home. I don't know what to think right now."

When I phone again, Mom is clear, precise. "You can't come over yet. Your father and I aren't used to the idea of you back in our lives. Write. Tell us how you are and what you've been doing. Make it straight. We won't be used or hurt again."

What could I tell her? "I've survived the streets and needles. Been high and bottomed low. My best friend Alex was a hooker. He was beautiful. He had AIDS. Then he got beat up and killed."

What could I say about my new life? "I saw Julie. She laughed and walked across the canyon. God touched me and baptized me with heavenly rain.

"My friend, Father Al, is a great friend. He isn't gay."

Dear Mother and Father,

 I'm sorry for all the grief I've caused. I am no longer an addict and haven't used any drugs for over a year. Between dishwashing and my gas station job, I get by. My high school is completed. Church attendance is irregular, but I do go. I've joined a youth group and the parish priest, Father Maguire, has been a guide and inspiration. Enclosed is a picture of me.

 I would like to see you again and make amends. I don't ask forgiveness, only a chance to balance my life.

Tom

I check my mail every day, sometimes twice. *Will they never want to see me?* Eventually, I get a reply.

Dear Thomas,

 I'm delighted that miracles still occur, and that you are alive. I am getting used to the idea. Father flip-flops. I'm not sure how he feels. We miss Julie, and Father cannot come to grips. The house is very lonely when he is at work. We will see you and try to curb our apprehension. I hope all continues to go well for you.

Mom

Is this really my house? Flakes of paint peel themselves from the wooden siding. The open front gate swings at an awkward angle. In contrast, tidy flowerbeds form a buffer between the fence and uncut lawn. A display of yellow dahlias hides a crooked leaning fence.

No echo sounds when I ring the doorbell. I knock and wait for permission to enter my house. Mother faces me across the threshold. She clasp and unclasps her hands. Then steps toward me and hugs me briefly. A small tear takes shape at the corner of her eye.

"You look good, Thomas. How do you like Vancouver?"

"It's fine. The weather's a lot like here."

"We've had a warm summer."

"Looks like it. Your flowers are really nice."

"I like flowers. They're a bright spot in my life."

"How are you, otherwise, Mom? How's your back?"

"I'm not well. My back is worse. The lawyers haven't settled yet. Everything gets me down. It's no fun." She winces to make her point.

"Have some tea, Thomas, and a cookie."

For a moment, she sits across from me, still working her hands. Dark circles rim her puffy eyes. Her face is fuller now. Even her wedding ring has buried itself deeper into the finger's flesh. She turns toward the kitchen. "Bruce, Thomas is here."

From my uncomfortable seat, I rise to stand almost at attention. Father, unshaven, barefoot, comes in carrying a coffee mug. His shoulders are hunched now. On the crown of his head, he's grown a bald spot. It isn't large. One of those Jewish beanies could cover it. He narrows his eyes and peers at me, then looks out the window. He leans toward me and nearly closes the gap between us. He lifts his hand from his pocket and begins to extend it toward me. Then, as if at an unseen barrier, the hand turns and strokes the stubble of his chin.

"Hello, Thomas. How are you doin'?"

"Fine."

"How are you, Dad?"

"How do I look? I'm still alive, aren't I?"

"How's the mill?"

"The mill's getting old, harder to repair, low on timber. Goddamn tree huggers all over the place. Some sonofabitch burned my truck. Now I'm driving a fucking Toyota."

I can only nod. Then he turns on a naked heel. "I gotta go. I've got a lot of things to do."

Mother's mouth drops open. "Bruce," she yells, "get back here. Don't run away. We've got business."

Then she grabs his collar. "Sit. You've complained a lot about Thomas. Now tell him to his face."

He sits, head bowed, shoulders hunched, like a beaten dog. He looks at me and says, "That night on the road, you told me you had AIDS."

"That must have been when you threatened to kill me. It was verbal self-defense. I figured you wouldn't splatter blood on yourself."

Mother steps beside him and yanks his ear. "What else, Bruce? What else is eating you?"

"Julie never froze. I still think she ran out of gas."

It was my turn. "And if she did? Would you call me a killer and seek the death penalty?"

His jaw clenches as he knots his fists. Mother squares her shoulders. "There's one more thing, Bruce. Spit it out."

"Who's going to pay for everything you stole?"

I hand him a check. "Here's four thousand dollars. It's all I have."

Mother snatches it from him and tears it up. "I'll have none of that, Bruce. There's a cost in raising children. He hasn't cost us for two years. Thank God he didn't go to Harvard. Do you know what the tuition is?"

She steps closer, engulfs me in her arms. "I'm so glad you're alive. Let's see each other more often."

Father stands in the doorway, hands in pockets.

Mother glares at him. "You've lost a daughter, Bruce. Make an effort, or you'll lose a son."

He remains immobile, hands cemented at his side.

"Al, I'm going to be a priest."

He looks up from his desk, raises an eyebrow, and combs both hands over his head. "I thought you might. Have you figured out how to go about it?"

"Don't you just apply?"

"Sorry, it's not that easy. Let me show you."

Al uses all the words—motivation, discernment, vocation, self-knowledge, commitment, and love of God, persistence, obedience, and celibacy. Then he added a few of his own—lonesome, horny.

"I'm going to be a priest, Al. God touched me. I belong to him. I'm going to be an inner city missionary."

"I'd be a little careful about that," Al says. "A week in a tent can do funny things to your mind. Some people hear things that aren't there, see things no one else can."

"I know what I saw, Al. And I know what I heard."

"I believe you," he says, "and I believe the people on LSD."

"What are you trying to do, Al?"

"You're still wet behind the ears, Thomas. There's more to this than a week on a mountain, or a year on the streets. People say a vocation is a call from God. Others aren't as kind. It's really your own psychology that matters."

My mouth falls open. "Is that really you, Al?"

He opens his hands and looks skyward. "Yes," he says, "it's really me and I'm doing you a favor."

"Gee, thanks."

"Just listen. You're a junkie who isn't using. You have a crappy job, no skills, and limited social ability. You break into a sweat when a girl puts her arm around you. You've a lot of work to do before you become an acceptable candidate."

"You're no help, Al. I'm going to be a priest. And you're starting to piss me off."

First he smiles, then laughs until his eyes water. I can't help it. My laughter joins his. What he says is true, but only for now.

"I don't mean to rain on your parade, Thomas, but it is immensely helpful if you do research first. Visit priests. They'll be happy to talk to you. Ask them how they sustain their faith, how satisfying is their life. Ask them what they say to allegations of alcoholism, child abuse, and the diminishing clergy.

"Perhaps some priests will let them accompany you in a job shadowing fashion. How do they deal with illness, death, Mass, tragedy? Ask about their vocations. Tactfully enquire about loneliness and celibacy. Then, Thomas, ask yourself if this is the life you want and why.

"Why do you want to be a priest, Tom?"

"I want to be a priest because God has chosen me. He touched me and converted me to himself."

Al becomes very quiet. He is motionless and breathes with his chest hardly moving. He stares into the distance at some point in the universe. I go to leave. Al makes no movement.

CHAPTER 11

To know others, I must first know myself. To love another, I must first love God.

Maguire plays the devil's advocate. At times he dissuades me more than he encourages. "How do you know God loves you?" he asks. "Look at the life you've had. Would he wish that on you if he loved you?"

"You know the answer, Al. God gave me a unique experience so that I can help others like myself. Besides, you can't second-guess God or see into the future."

I think I've shut him up until he says, "So God loves you because you think he does. Isn't faith wonderful?"

"I need faith, Al. It's what keeps me going. How do I know that I love God? How does anyone know?"

"Oh relax, Tom. I'm just asking you questions that you need to ask yourself, questions that everybody asks. It's crucial that you're sure. Is your vocation true? Everyone needs to pray for direction. Please don't forget the practical. You seem to like psychology. It could be a great academic degree for you."

Al encourages me to read. He says, "It's a great way to find out what others are thinking."

Of course, I've read and answered yes to most of what I read.

Would you like to make a difference in the world?

Do you like people?

Can you give to a cause greater than yourself?

Are you compassionate, flexible?

Do you have a developed personality?

Are you willing to learn from others?

I know I have shortcomings: flexibility, sociability, and personality issues. With prayer and effort, I will change.

I apply to become a priest. The easiest of my entrance tests is the physical. I manage to get three reference letters. One from Al, and one from Father Delorme. The third stumps me. I've run out of suitable people. Eventually, I decide on Rolly. He can certify that I work hard, am conscientious, and treat people with respect.

I have my interview in Seattle. No, I will not be accepted on face value. "Perhaps," says Bishop Rodriguez, "a trial period of two years will be appropriate."

If I am accepted, I will be a student at the university. I will follow the vows of the priesthood and regularly report to my mentor. Of course, I will attend daily Mass and partake in weekend retreats. I will also be subject to periodic interviews and psychological tests.

"Naturally," says Rodriguez, "You are free to leave at any time, with or without notice. Incidentally," he says, "Our program is one of priestly formation. We tend to avoid the term *training* since it has negative connotations, such as dog obedience. In time, you will learn that we constantly adapt. Furthermore . . ."

His voice trails off and then he says, "Forgive me. I begin a sermon. Best wishes, Thomas. If I can be of service or answer any questions, please call me. It is a privilege and duty I gladly accept."

I make a natural transition to seminary life. I learn to love God even more and thank him for his gifts. Yes, I begin to understand my parents and myself too. Sympathy replaces anger. Celibacy is a natural part of my life.

Even in my training, I minister to the disposables of our society, those who serve no purpose, and whose only aim is the absorption of drugs. I have no materials to seduce them, only the love of Jesus. Some listen when they have nothing else to do. Others tell me to fuck off. I read and agree with those who say drugs are the insulin of the addict. Decriminalization, medicalization, and harm reduction all make sense.

Yet I become detached, almost clinical. I feel no pain at their misery, only a duty to help. I offer spiritual help and wonder why they hurry to an early miserable death. Rarely do I shed a tear but remain thankful to minister.

Al remains my role model. For one glorious week each summer, Al and I go on holidays. Usually I spend a few days with Mom beforehand. Father is always at the mill and too busy to take time off.

"I hope you'll be active when you're a priest," Mom says. "More like Father Delorme used to be. He'd visit his people in their homes, hospitals, and jails. He even had the nerve to visit people at work. Now he doesn't have the energy."

"Well, Mom, we do that and more now. We reach out to the disturbed and distressed to help them, not only spiritually, but materially as well. I still maintain my goal to minister to drug addicts in the streets."

Mother is silent for a long while. "Well," she says, "If that's your mission, I won't try to dissuade you. Please be careful and don't catch anything. It's hard to imagine you as a male version of Mother Theresa."

At 8:00 AM, the distinctive sound of a Volkswagen penetrates the kitchen where Mom and I are having coffee. A youthful Al in shorts and baseball cap joins us.

"How would you like to visit the Canadian Rockies?" he asks. He is curious about my new life. "Do you still have curfew? Can you go out by yourself?"

"God, Al. It's not house arrest. We're trusted, and we can come and go as we please."

"That's good," he says. "It doesn't make sense to have a lot of controls and then be without them all at once. The only controls that really matter are internal."

Al flies. Driving is obsolete. I think he's trying to get to the Rockies before dark. "It's only about eight hundred miles. We should be able to make it."

We careen along that narrow ribbon that separates us from mountaintop and river. "What's the hurry, Al? It's getting dark, and we don't have midair refueling."

He actually slows and is silent for a while. Then, he says, "Do you ever have doubts about what you're doing? Is there anything that bothers you?"

"I believe, and I'm committed. There's no need for the luxury or aggravation of doubt. My calling sustains me. What about you, Al, are you steadfast?"

"Not as steadfast as you, Tom. But you're a special case. It's not everyone that God has touched personally. Am I steadfast? Yes. Have I doubts? Of course I do. Everything doesn't gel with everything else. Faith conflicts with reality and unless you live in a cave, it's a natural question."

"I don't get it. The church is truth. What more do you need?"

"I'm not sure. Sometimes I'm agitated and feel there's more. Yes, I visit the sick, counsel the distressed, do fundraisers, and visit jails. Anyone can do that. I feel like a concierge."

"Are you OK, Al? You sound depressed. Are you overworked, burned out, lonesome in your one-man parish?"

Al smiles a weak, wry smile. "Yes, to all of the above. It's depressing to see all my hopes dwindle away."

He sighs, takes off his cap, and runs his left hand over his bald head. "I've become morbid," he says. "This is no way to treat a friend. Let's take a break and become ordinary humans who are on holiday. We're tourists. Let's enjoy what we see."

We stop at one of those roadside motels that are illuminated by a flashing arrow. In the attached café is a counter with barstools. On the other side is a row of upright wooden booths. A waitress, still in her teens takes our order. Al smiles and asks her about her town and if she likes her work. Is it a summer job? He orders beer and a hamburger. He seems more cheerful after he's eaten and leaves an excessive tip. I say nothing, but he replies to the look on my face.

"I still work for a living, you know. It's still money that I've earned."

In the motel room, I reach for the Bible. After a while, I have a strange twinge of guilt and put it away. After all, we're tourists.

We continue our trip, but our conversation is muted and friendship changed. Eventually, we nearly get our old feelings back, nearly.

Over the next year, I invite Al to Seattle and offer to visit. He becomes elusive. Our letters are less frequent and less animated. I worry and pray for him.

A year before my ordination, he phones. "When's our next holiday, Tom?"

He sounds vigorous, energetic. Perhaps his doubts are resolved and his faith solidified.

"Where are we going?"

"How does the Grand Canyon sound?"

"It sounds wonderful. I've never been there."

Al looks charged, alive, gung ho. There is no talk of faith, doubt, or frustration. I love it. The old Al is back. I don't ask. We're tourists. He's hardly winded from a walking tour of the canyon.

We have no destination and by evening, blunder into Las Vegas. "It's getting late," Al says, "We'll have to stay in Sin City. Try not to save any one. We're still on holiday."

He thinks he's funny, but I assure him. "There won't be time after I get through with you."

We find an older hotel on the edge of town. Al orders a hamburger and Coke. After dinner, we're rewarded with a small stack of slot machine tokens. Al is excited when he wins and resigned when he loses the lot. I hand him my tokens and wish him a speedy trip to perdition.

This hotel room looks like any other. I refrain from reading the Bible and quickly fall asleep, exhausted from the canyon hike. After midnight, I'm awakened. Al is dressed. "Can't sleep," he says. "I'm going for a walk. Don't wait up."

He returns just before daybreak, fumbles the key into the slot, and bumps into furniture. I smell whisky and a faint odor of perfume. I say a silent prayer and close my eyes for sleep that fails to come.

Silence owns our return trip. Al drives like a normal human being. I cannot bring myself to ask, and he has no desire to explain.

A few weeks later, Rodriguez wishes to see me.

"I'm very sorry," he says. "It is most difficult, and I wished to offer you my sympathy. This letter that I have is self-explanatory."

Dear Thomas,

I am very sorry for the disastrous trip. My doubts persist and deepen. As you know, my behavior is reprehensible. I have discussed my situation with Bishop Rodriguez. I know you wish to help, but in your interests I will keep away from you at least until you are ordained.

Yours faithfully,
Al

Rodriguez unfolds his hands. "It is also my wish."

There is no discussion. He gives me his blessing, and I am dismissed.

II-PRIEST

CHAPTER 12

I am on the threshold to life everlasting. Purified, absolved, and clothed in white linen, I bow before the altar of my god, ready to be transformed forever. Sacred music surrounds me. Holy incense envelops me. In awed silence, I await the miracle. With my head bowed, I anticipate the mystical powers that are promised to me forever.

Beads of sweat gather on my forehead as my breathing escalates until nearly ineffective. Dizziness and faintness come over me. Trembling hands remind me I am also mortal, unworthy, but privileged to serve. Even though I am man, soon I will also be immortal. Before the altar of my god, I pray for strength and wait to unite with the mysteries I shall wed. Chosen by God and admonished to become perfect, I am within reach of eternal treasure whose reward no mere human can fathom.

A singer waits in silence, head high, and shoulders braced. Her hands are clasped. A white veil rests lightly on her auburn hair and shelters the beauty of her face. Motionless, disciplined, she also anticipates the miracle and is witness thereto. No lipstick hides the fullness or symmetry of her lips. From her neckline, a pale blue dress flows gently over an ample bosom. Long sleeves taper to her wrists and join embroidered gloves.

She inhales fully, exhales, inhales once more and begins to sing "Te Deum Laudamus." Her soprano voice, piercing in its beauty, impinges on the perimeter of her vocal gift. The aria soars to its apex, holds, and remains suspended near its shattering brink. My neck prickles. *Te Deum Laudamus* (God be praised). Silence applauds her. I am in the presence of God's creation upon whom his bounteous gifts are bestowed.

Grasped in my trembling hand is a lighted candle. Its flickering light guides my path. I am called to the priesthood by an unseen voice. My presence is acknowledged, "Thomas James Spanner."

Startled, I give the expected Latin reply, "Adsum."

At the altar, crowned with his miter, sits my friend and mentor, Juan Jesus Rodriguez, bishop of Seattle. I am privileged to kneel. This man who tested my faith and enshrined it with dignity now prays over me. "Let your teachings be spiritual medicine and your life a delight for the church of Christ."

Ashamed of my unworthiness and in need of divine assistance, I prostrate myself on the sanctuary floor and try to blot out my thoughts. I have too many and barely sustain the whirlwind of mind and emotion.

My bishop places his hands upon my head as I kneel before him. A wave of joy washes over me. Tears obscure my vision. *Hallelujah, the spirit of the Lord is upon me.* I am pure like a mountain sunrise on freshly fallen snow. But I am also ashamed at the fist of pride that intrudes against my humility.

"Receive the yoke of the Lord," Rodriguez intones, as he crosses the stole over my chest, "for his yoke is sweet, and his burden light."

Kneeling, I present my hands, little finger touching little finger, palms up. Holy oil anoints me. "Vouchsafe, oh, Lord, to consecrate these hands. That whatsoever they shall bless may be blessed."

Bishop Rodriguez extends his hands. "Receive the power to offer sacrifice to God and to celebrate Mass for the living as well as for the dead. In the name of the Lord."

Eternal power gathers unto me. I am another Christ, able to forgive sin and transform bread into the living Christ. I kneel and kiss my bishop's ring.

God saved my life at Raleigh's Canyon. Now he grants me a second miracle. I vow obedience to his might and kindness.

I join with my colleagues as we celebrate our first Mass together— concelebration. The body of Christ is in my hands and enters my soul. We recite the Apostles' Creed. Once again, I kneel before my bishop. He lays his hands upon me and says, "Receive the Holy

Ghost; whose sins thou shalt forgive, they are forgiven them; and whose sins thou shalt retain, they are retained."

From groveling on a wooden floor, I am rocketed spiritually to the power a mere mortal cannot comprehend. To transform bread into the living Christ, to forgive sins is a gift, awesome in its impact.

I scan the congregation and hope to see my friend, Al Maguire. There is no Al. My emotions sag. He cannot share my joy. A flicker of the perpetual flame attracts my eye. I say a prayer.

My parents are in the first pew. A flush of shame inflames my cheeks. Many times I have asked them to forgive me. Acid rises in my gullet and brings tears to my eyes. Eyes that now focus on the floor. Father holds my mother's hand, a gesture I have rarely seen. She leans her head against his shoulder. His massive hand engulfs hers, protectively. Her cracked fingernails and torn hangnails find safety. Tiny fissures from raspberry canes are filled with ground in dirt. No amount of effort from the brush can remove the tattooed soil from her battered hands.

Mother dabs her eyes. She wears my sister's kerchief, its orange-and-yellow stripes incongruous against her dress. I blink through the blur of my tears and see my sister's face. Julie is smiling. She blows a kiss and mouths the words, "I love you." Her forgiveness is unending, yet even now, I cannot forgive myself.

A corsage of white orchids decorates Mother's dress, and a wide-brimmed hat shades her eyes. Father sits erect, shoulders back, chest raised, and stomach held in check. I am amazed he can find some pride in his worthless son. He wears his only suit—pinstripe, multipurpose: funeral, baptism, Mass, and ordination.

Bishop Rodriguez opens his arms in prayer. "Dearly beloved in Christ, welcome to the greatest gift under heaven. Our god is merciful. Our god is a jealous god. Your priests have taken three solemn vows. Poverty is natural. Nearly all of us are poor. We can squeeze through the eye of a needle more readily than a camel can. Obedience is more difficult, but we are soldiers of Christ and, as soldiers, we obey. Chastity is most difficult of all. Body betrays the mind and logic falls in the face of desire. Celibacy is a gift to God.

Pray for your priests for they too are human. We preach detachment, but we all need friends."

He continues, and asks for support, community involvement, and personal commitment to the church. He seeks help for those priests who have committed all. Then he extends his arms and says, "Peace be with you always."

The reception is ruled by photographers. I am wedged between my parents, blinded by flashbulbs, and crushed by people trying to get close. My bishop has provided an open bar. *What better way to celebrate the greatest event in our lives?* Even strangers shake my hand and pat my back. Gloria Zielke, my confrere's cousin, surrounds me with her perfume, shakes my hand with hers, and its glued on crimson nails. "Oh, this is awesome," she smiles and hugs her large breasts against me. The phrase, eunuch for the church, flashes to my mind. For a moment, my mind envisions Moira.

Mother and I lean closer together to conquer the background noise. "I'm so happy," she says. "This is wonderful. I'm so glad for you, Thomas. It's marvelous."

Her cheeks are flushed. Hands flit from her hair, to her lap, to my hands. She fans her face with a napkin and then hugs my shoulder.

Father is less effusive. Droplets of sweat stipple his forehead. He grips a can of cold beer and washes away the wine taste of obligatory toasts. Mother offers a glass for his beer but he replies, "Spoils the taste."

His tie is in his pocket and the upper two buttons of his shirt are undone. His jacket, also undone, hangs loosely from his shoulders. He's frowning. It seems he doesn't share Mother's ecstasy. He grunts occasionally but is otherwise restrained. I wonder if he is a closet atheist. He shakes my hand, gently, careful not to bruise my fingers. My smooth white hand rests in his like a fragile egg. Father is restrained. No fingers are broken.

Mother smoothens Julie's kerchief. "Your sister would be so proud, Tom. I can see her smiling, hugging you, and tousling your hair. Then she would tease. 'You finally amounted to something— *Father* Tom, oh, brother.'"

Mother dabs her eyes, then raises a glass, "To Julie, our unending love."

I reply, "To Julie."

Father looks about, squints at his watch, and winds the stem. "It's getting dark. We got a long drive ahead. Besides, we don't know anybody here."

Mom pats his shoulder. "Just a few minutes more, dear."

He doesn't mind being the first to leave. I walk with them to the old Buick. All eight cylinders of polished pride gleam in the setting sun. He actually opens the door for Mother, buckles her into the seat, and mumbles something about stupid rules that forced him to get seat belts. "I'll just be a minute, Judith," he says, "I'm going to talk to Thomas, man to man."

He squeezes my arm and leads me aside to the shadow of an old oak. His grip tightens until my muscles ache. Caught in my own world, I stand beside him grinning like an anointed idiot.

"Well," he says, "I suppose you're pretty fucking proud of yourself, now that you're next to God, and still haven't done an honest day's work in your whole goddamn life?"

"Let go of my arm, Bruce."

His grip loosens. "Bruce is it? We're on a first name basis? I guess that makes us equal.

"Well, guess again. I just paid off the second mortgage for all the stuff you stole. You hid behind your mother and never made a real effort to pay me back. You fuckers talk about reconciliation. How about starting with restitution; or do you just forgive yourself, and everything is hunky dory?"

His expression darkens and metamorphoses to hatred. "Don't think for a minute that I buy any of this crap. You put on a dress, roll around on the floor, and then tell people you can turn a cracker into living meat. I was watching. The cracker didn't change. Some fucking miracle! Do a miracle for me; I've got a lot of metal washers in the garage. Turn them into gold, and I might just consider forgiving your sins.

"I'm not a total nonbeliever," he whispers, almost as it he was afraid to be overheard. "I always believed Julie ran out of gas. A while back, old hunchback Hal who looks after the car impound gave me the gas can that I usually keep in the garage. I believe I discovered the miracle."

He squares his shoulders and squeezes my neck. "Smile, you cocksucker, and wave to your mother. We've had our man to man."

The twin spires of St. James Cathedral cast their shadow on the courtyard. After a restless night and irritable day, I have my final audience with Bishop Rodriguez. Armed with God's grace and my psychology degree, I hope to help those enslaved to drugs. Perhaps in that interface between emotion and spirit, there is common ground where heart and mind find concert.

"Welcome, Thomas," my bishop smiles and opens his arms to embrace me. "You seem a bit down. Is it the letdown after an achievement? A deflation?"

"No, not at all. Father explained the facts of life from his perspective. He still wants repayment."

Rodriguez shrugs. "We've been over this, Thomas. Will money buy parental love? Would he forgive if the price were right?"

"I'm afraid not. Forgive is not in his dictionary. He despises me and thinks the priesthood is a sham. He's very angry."

Rodriguez winces. "Well, Thomas, you can't win them all. You must practice prayer, patience, and forbearance. Above all, have hope and forgive. You have important work to do. Put this behind you. It's been a long climb, Thomas, from the living dead to chosen of God. I have admired the innocence of your soul. *Cynical* is not in your dictionary."

"Thank you, Your Grace, these years have been the best of my life."

"No doubt, no doubt. You have been a model student, serious, dedicated, humble, obedient. We have no concerns about your sexuality, normal or perverse. No alcohol or substance abuse issues worry us, in spite of, or more probably because of your past. However, I wish the search for perfection were less onerous for you. I wouldn't mind if you had some small doubts, a little arrogance, or a flicker of illicit joy in your life."

"I'll work on that, Your Grace. Do you have a suggestion? And may I be forgiven prospectively?"

He smiles. "Of course, of course. I'm not here to berate you, Thomas. I have good news. You've been posted to a delightful parish. It's a nice farming community a couple of hours from Chicago. The town is mostly Catholic and has a school staffed by nuns. I hope you'll become an integral part, a role model."

I am unable to summon a grateful expression or smile a thank-you. Perhaps the sag of my shoulders portrayed my disappointment.

"You don't seem pleased, Thomas." His smile abates only a little. "It is an opportunity to serve God and your fellowman."

"I'm sorry to be disappointed. I'd just hoped that after my repeated requests, I'd be assigned to an inner city. I thought that with my experience, I could work among our modern lepers, the junkies, and hookers who discard their lives."

"This is not a burden we wish to inflict on you, Thomas. I believe there is one thing lacking in your life. That is something called *normal*. Johnsburgh is normal. It is a place where fathers love their sons and mothers have been known to kiss their boys in public. Observe and you will see what *normal* means. But most of all, I send an ordinary priest, one possessed of no special talent, no academic prowess, no spiritual insights, linguistically limited, and oratorically ordinary. I send a common priest for the common man. I send a priest who is both humble and obedient."

He unfolds his arms and invites my embrace. "Besides," he says with a laugh, "it's not a matter of choice. We are soldiers of Christ in God's army; we follow orders and obey our vows. I don't mean to be harsh, Thomas, but before you venture into that nether world, you need seasoning, maturity, and life experience. I think your heart will rejoice as you live in a community that loves and nurtures its own. Later, if you still want, I will reconsider."

I nod and think that I begin to understand. In my mind, I am again prostrate. He allows himself a small smile.

I drop to my knees. He blesses me. I cradle my bishop's fingers in my hand and feel the hardness of his ring against my lips.

CHAPTER 13

In the cathedral courtyard, guarding my luggage is a tall man in an azure blue Hawaiian shirt. His holiday shirt hangs loosely, and I look for lei around his neck. Beneath the undone buttons of his gaudy shirt, a gold chain glimmers against his hairy chest. Eyes hidden by dark glasses and sheltered by the short brim of a red hat survey me. Somehow, this ad for a travel poster is familiar, but I am unacquainted with any such gaudy figure.

This neon apparition engulfs me, hugs me. I smell his familiar aftershave.

"Maguire! It's you. Alive and well! You look glorious. Have you been transferred to Club Med? Or did the parish spring for a sun lamp?"

"You look wonderful, Thomas, penance and deprivation agree with you. It's good to see you," he says and slaps my back.

He removes his hat and glasses. A full overgrowth of hair, like moss on a boulder, covers his shiny head.

"I'm sorry," I say, "I didn't recognize the reverend hairy Maguire. And you're tanned as well. If not Club Med, what then, a nudist colony?"

"No, nothing like that. Rodriguez has given permission for you and I to resume our friendship. He asked me to take you on a holiday. He said you needed a friendly ear, a break. I'm to take you away from this for a while, relax, and play tourist and, act like a layman. We need to talk about the last few years. Hopefully, we can be friends."

"Sure we can, Al, why shouldn't we? We've always been friends and truthful with one another."

"I need to talk to you about the facts of life," he smiles and then adds, "But now that you're a priest, you may not need to know them." Then almost as an afterthought he says, "I thought we could take a spin down the coast and loosen you up."

He loads my luggage into the wrong end of the car. The VW is still alive. "New motor," he says, "Same body, different heart."

He is full of curiosity. I tell him about my father, Rodriguez. "Jeez. No kidding?"

He goes on: questions, prompts, curiosity. From time to time, he points to landmarks as if he were a tour director. This is not the Al I remember. This one obeys speed limits. The other would dart through traffic like a rabbit eluding a dog.

"Hold it, Al. I haven't seen you for a year. Thanks to your deal with Rodriguez. I get no letter, no phone call, no visit. You told me about personal doubts, vocation misgivings. Then you drop off the face of the earth. By holy command, I'm not allowed to see you. Don't be sociable, Al. Level with me."

He combs his new hair with his left hand and taps the wheel with the other. The car slows. "What's been going on in your life, Al? I know you're on holiday and you overdress the part. You look different, and you act strange, forced almost, I think. What happened?"

His knuckles blanch on the steering wheel as he frowns at the road ahead. For a long while, only silence is layered on the purring new engine. Almost painfully, he disengages his left hand from the wheel and slowly rotates his wrist so the knuckles face me. A wedding band encircles his finger.

It is my turn at silence. Numbness, irritating like Novocain spreads in concentric waves over my entire body. My mentor, my guide, has fallen to mortal flesh. Even in the slow lane, he slows. A semitrailer blasts its air horn. Al shifts gears and lurches ahead then begins the preliminaries to speech. He braces his shoulders, swallows, and clears his throat. I hold up my hand. "Not now, Al, not yet. Give me time." I want to say "Congratulations" but suffocate the cruel sarcasm.

Miles later he sighs, "I'm not asking you to forgive me. I haven't offended you, and it's none of your business."

I only shake my head. "I know, Al. Just give me time. I can't imagine how you can throw away the gifts that I've just received."

He continues, calmer now. "I'm not the first priest to fall in love. Nor am I the first to marry. Have you ever been in love, Thomas? Felt that need which bonds like eternal glue and holds one to another because without both there is none? Have you loved someone with all your will, loved her against your will, and in spite of your will? Of course you haven't, and I hope that in your sheltered existence you never will.

"I hope for your sake, Tom, it never happens. But if it happens, I hope that you find that person whose love is all encompassing, and that you are better prepared than I and the gut-wrenching agony of disobedience to the church will avoid you."

"But why, Al? You had everything, the love of God and life everlasting."

"I still do. And more."

"I don't understand. How could you turn your back on God?"

"I haven't turned my back on God. I've only challenged church rule, not that of God. He blessed me with a woman that I love more than heaven or the threat of hell. She is real and joined to me in body, mind, and soul. She is a gift to me from God that surpasses my gift to him. It's only my church who perverted man's nature. God said, 'It is not good for man to be alone.' Yet my church contradicts this message for its chosen priests."

"But, Al, it's only temporary, a few moments in the face of eternity. How could you give it all away?"

"What have I given away? I am still a priest. Priests were not always celibate. Other humans love and marry. Are we to be less? True, I am no longer a man of the church, but I am still a man of God and a priest ordained forever."

I shed tears for reasons beyond my ken. No prayer can soothe my turmoil. He spurns his calling for carnal pleasure, fleeting moments for eternity. Acid burns my throat, and I can only swallow.

My soul is mirrored in the front seat of a Volkswagen driven below the posted speed.

"Jesus, Al, I feel miserable. I'm sorry, but I can't help it."

He drives, more erratically now. Slowing in high gear until the car nearly stalls and then revving in the lower gears until the engine threatens to explode. A screech of breaks and tap of bumpers warns Al's driving is perilous. The Camaro driver raises his middle finger and utters his anger in words unheard but clearly understood.

"For God's sake, Al, pull over. Get off the road before you kill us."

He shrugs and coasts into one of those highway rest stops.

We face each other across a wooden picnic table, alone now except for the incessant drone of highway traffic. Incandescent lights shine through overhanging trees and streak Al's face in shadows. His forehead glistens. Hands tremble as if from too many coffee.

"I met her in my church," he says. "She was hiding from her husband. I found her cowering in the confessional. She relaxed a bit when she saw my Roman collar. She shivered, 'Help, Father, he's going to kill me.'

"A crash at the door froze my reply. The nose of a beige sedan penetrated my church. A short man with a roll of belly lurched out of the car.

"'Found you, Cassandra, you cunt,' he leered, 'now I'm going to make mince pie out of your pussy.'

"I confronted him, and he lunged at me with a hatchet. I evaded, barely, and with both hands crashed a candleholder into his temple. He collapsed, slowly like an imploded building. Watery blood tinged fluid seeped from his ears and nose. He twitched a few times, quit breathing, and died."

I am stunned. A picture of a dead man conjures in my mind. My heart pains for Al and his gentle soul. "It must be terrible to take a life when you've sworn to protect life."

"No," Al says, "it isn't. It was necessary. He would have killed me. But as he lay there twitching an urgent thought crowded my brain—last rites. I ignored that thought and condemned a stranger. That was terrible."

Al's eyes lock on mine. I start to speak, but he motions me to silence.

He shrugs, "She needed help. Her children, two sweet girls, aged two and four, whom I made fatherless, needed help too.

"Once each week, she sought guidance and prayed with me. One spring morning, in that gray light before dawn, Cassandra stood at the foot of my bed. I threw on my bathrobe and said, 'You shouldn't be here.'

'*Should* is a word with no meaning.' She said, 'I shouldn't even be alive. *Should* is a word that means guilt and duty.'

She knelt before me. 'Bless you, Father,' she sobbed and let tears fall on my feet. Then she hugged me to her, covered my mouth with hers.

"Have you ever been worshiped, Thomas? Been a god? Soared on that heady wine? In your fantasies, in your life, in some ecstatic drug-filled dream?"

I fortify myself with the sign of the cross. "This is blasphemy, Al. Only God is worshipped. How could you pervert this woman's gratitude and then deny your sins? It's sick."

My words make no impression. Al continues. "One rainy afternoon, I was in my den. 'Something really neat has happened,' Cassandra said.

"'What?'

"'I'm pregnant with your child.'

"My head spun, and I shut my eyes.

"For one sacrilegious moment, the word *abortion* sliced into my mind."

Al pauses. "What would you have done were you in my place?"

"I would have left her. The relationship was sinful and pathological."

"I'm sure you would have. The gifts of the heart mean nothing against your church. One quick hand wash, and all is clean. And what will become of my child? How will he live—bastardized and unclean? God in his wisdom allowed a temporal father for his son in the form of Joseph. Jesus had the lesser need."

"You're twisting it, Al, and I'm becoming very angry. You compare your child to Jesus. You've got delusions."

He laughs until his eyes are moist and then taps his forehead on the wooden table in mock imitation of a bow. "What more could I expect from a neophyte, a Boy Scout priest, not yet mature, and unacquainted with reality? It's not like that, Tom. I couldn't abandon her. She was on my mind every minute—laughing, touching, a vision in my bed. Obsessed, I loved her and in my way, adored her. Eternity became a myth. Soon our son would be born. We would teach him to be all things we were not. We named him Thomas."

Anger wells in me at his insulting words. "So you fell in love, Al. It's something that happened. It's beyond your control. Yes, a priest may love, but he may not be in love. You broke your vows. Don't whine to me, Al, because you've chosen the easy road."

I tap my watch.

"We'll go in a minute," Al says. "I thought you might be curious about how difficult it is for a priest adapts to normal life, how it feels to be laicized, to be deprived of sacramental privilege? Perhaps you'd like to hear modern positions on celibacy?"

"Not tonight, Al. I'm getting tired. Let's go."

a priest to adapt to normal life?

CHAPTER 14

Father Delorme and I become reacquainted. Mother has kept me in his memory. His eyesight fades. He is hunched, and I need to speak clearly near his ear. With a trembling hand, he pours two large glasses of port. I decline.

He sips his and smiles. "It seems only yesterday that I celebrated my first Mass. My parents and sisters were ecstatic. Of course, it was expected of me. Times are different now, but then, in a small Irish town, it was glorious."

He continues to reminisce: past glory, tradition, and keys to the city. Then he raises the second glass. "To you, Thomas, to the beginning of your priesthood and the end of mine. I pass the dwindling torch and pray it will rekindle."

In turn, I tell him of my training and journey toward God. He nods. "Yes, we always falter on the path to perfection. Sin is why we are here. Without sin we have no religion, no church, and no salvation. How many souls do you think we save over a life time's ministry, Thomas?"

"I don't know. How can you tell?"

"I believe it's all who confess." He is jovial. His second glass is nearly empty.

"Father Delorme, I'd be grateful if you would hear my confession in preparation for first Mass."

"Of course," he says and waves at the floor with his free hand. "Begin."

I'm taken aback. There is no stole, no confessional, and no privacy. He cocks his head. "It is still a valid confession, you know."

I kneel and confess my sins: righteousness and arrogance. I have judged and condemned my friend. I confess that I am mean of spirit. I would not be generous enough to leave my calling to nurture my child. Neither would I commit to another woman's children. I am weak and could not live with guilt or dare defy the God I serve in fear and awe and trembling.

I kneel beside this old man who barely hears me. After a while, he utters a small snore but spills no wine. At times he interjects, "I see. Yes, of course. Go on."

My confession is ended. I tap on his knee and look up. He waves a blessing. "Your sins are forgiven. For your penance, say ten Hail Marys."

My night before First Mass is filled with unholy dreams. Maguire, naked, intrudes into my sleep. His baldpate glistens. Cheeks are reddened. A faceless woman enfolds him in her arms. She whispers and he laughs at her words. I see the bulge of her breasts as they press on his hairy chest. "This is heaven," she says.

Even in my dreams, I am angry. What can she know of heaven when she is united with her accomplice, the deserter Maguire? They touch behind the altar where Al used to preach. Sacrilege compounds blasphemy. I ask God to forgive and close Maguire from my mind. In the dark, I rehearse the Mass. My thoughts turn to Christ on the cross. Other words fill my mind: suffering, evil, death, eternity, forgiveness, heaven, and blessing.

I am awake more than asleep. The square red numbers of the clock march slowly toward morning. I close my eyes but cannot shut my mind.

One half hour before Mass I am in the sacristy to reflect and pray. I wash my hands and ask the Lord to purify my mind and body. Its own prayer accompanies each vestment. I ask for strength and purity.

Mother does her best to ensure my first Mass is memorable. The church is less than half-full, much less. Mr. Wilson sits beside her. Father is at the mill attending to an acute emergency.

Mrs. Wilson and her children fill the first pew. The aging ladies of the church are in attendance. I see no one from my high school. Several rows back is a newspaper reporter. *What did I expect, trumpets, red carpets, rose petals?*

Yet the miracle of the Mass remains eternal, and I am awed at
the power that enables me to turn bread and wine into the body
and blood of the living Christ.

In my sermon, I give thanks to the God who saved me. I tell of
my journey from the streets and God's call to the priesthood. I
thank my mother for her love and constancy. The message of the
church also remains constant. She is here to save sinners from the
sin we inherited from Adam and Eve, and those sins we commit.

I'm sure the words of my Mass are the same words that Father
Delorme recites each Sunday. I dismiss the congregation—go in
peace, the Mass is ended.

Mother has the reception at her house. Side by side on the
living room wall are two portraits, one of Julie with her orange-
and-yellow kerchief, and one of me wearing the Roman collar. The
reception is short, but I am thankful that even a few came.

I stay for a few days to keep Mother company, but soon we are out
of topics. I spend time on the seashore watching waves and kicking
sand.

My arrogance returns to haunt me. "Judge not" is a neutered
phrase. I judged my friend, condemned him, and banished him
from my life. Yet I seek comfort in my church. She is more valuable
than those who defy her and will last forever. As it was in the
beginning, is now, and ever shall be world without end. Amen.

One afternoon, I sit on a boulder, just below the railway tracks,
at the edge of the beach. I hear the screech of seagulls carried by
the wind, and when their noises halt, natures might remains. To
myself I say, *Well, Thomas, who do you think you are?*

*I am an ordinary priest, newly ordained, and possessed of no special
talent—just as my bishop noted. My spiritual insights are limited, but
adequate. I have not the ability to arouse emotions or inflame a crowd.
I readily obey and accept my lot as a worker in the vineyard. It is my
nature to follow and manifest leadership only under duress.*

Fortunately, my thirtieth birthday occurred a week before my
ordination. I hesitate to use the words *celebrated my birthday*,
certainly not in the same context as *celebrated the Mass*. Yet, I am

happy to be thirty for my first assignment. Twenty-nine sounds young, a connotation like the baby father.

Fortunately, or otherwise, I am still a virgin and hope to remain so. It is a state of being that occurred fortuitously rather than by design and in spite of my efforts. Yet I consider it a small point of unearned pride. Of course, I discount the results of a roving hand or manually aided fantasies. Even the inept groping of my awkward youth leaves my status intact. Nevertheless, my orientation is heterosexual, and I try to understand the homosexual variety.

From my place on the rock, I return to the question, *Well, Thomas, who do you think you are?*

The answer is clear; of myself I am nothing.

CHAPTER 15

I am blessed with the penitential midnight flight from Seattle to Chicago, and from there to a peaceful community in America's midwest. The economy flight sets a moral and fiscal example. It would be unbecoming for a priest who espouses poverty to fly first class during normal hours.

I suffer beside a snoring fat man who claims my window seat. At times, his head falls forward on a wad of chin and obstructs his breathing. Strange, his chest moves but he turns blue, then gasps and snores until he regains a lighter shade of blue. *Perhaps I should rouse him? But then what would I do?* Not only does he occupy my seat, but has the audacity to remove my armrest and overflow to my side. I forgive this incursion. Nevertheless, he could have asked. Perhaps I forgave too soon. My legs are numb from the weight of his torso. Paralysis threatens me. I shake him to wakefulness and explain my state. He appears annoyed even at this minor inconvenience.

With bifocals perched on the end of his freckled nose, the aisle seat passenger pretends to read. Secure between the buttresses of his armrests, he ignores the world and barely notices as I climb over him to grab the overhead luggage compartment. My numb legs barely sustain me.

A crisp, alert voice assails me. "Are you all right, Father? You look a bit distraught."

Even at 1:00 AM she is fresh: white teeth, blond ponytail, and rosy cheeks. Dark emerald green eyes look into mine. Concern forms wrinkles on her brow. Beneath a pair of silver wings is her name, Linda. Her ample bosom attracts my gaze, but I refrain from more than an occasional glance. I explain, "It's very crowded in my seat, and my legs are numb. They've also become quite weak. That's why I'm hanging on to the overhead compartment."

She suppresses a smile, then speaks to the reader who answers with an unsure frown. She marches to the front of the airplane and in a few moments returns. Book reader rises reluctantly and stretches lazily in the aisle. Two small boys perhaps eight and ten years old bounce past me. Each clutches a five-dollar bill as they share the seat and a half beside the fat man. Even their chatter cannot wake him. I now have a seat of my own in first class. Earthly comfort suits me. Luxury is a full stretch of my legs.

Linda smiles. "Isn't money wonderful? But I guess you're not supposed to know that?"

She pats my shoulder. "Have a pleasant trip in the friendly skies."

How long has it been since a woman touched me like that? Coffee and my mind alert me. I cannot read or doze.

A tangerine fireball fills the eastern sky. Flight 099 has devoured the night and streaks to the sun's molten core. We bump along the runway and taxi to the sky ramp just left of runway two. Linda stands demurely at the exit, hands clasped at her lap. Her smile dazzles. "Thank you for flying Western."

Somewhere between Chicago and the Mississippi river, among a thousand lakes, many unnamed, is a place called Johnsburgh. I have visions of frozen winters and mosquito-infested summers. An uncomplimentary thought intrudes. Perhaps Johnsburgh is another name for Hicksville.

I carry my luggage across the tarmac and ascend the ramp of a waiting plane. Its twin propellers idle slowly, barely moving the humid air. A smiling man in blue jeans and a Chicago Bears cap greets me. He wears no uniform and seems younger even than I.

I'm the only passenger on this trip to nowhere. My two suitcases, with the remainder of my worldly goods, are already in the cargo bay. I can stand erect in the center aisle and when seated, my knees are clear of the seat ahead. A small contradiction crosses my mind. The smaller plane is roomier than the larger jet. *Perhaps I can use this in a sermon on humility?*

The lone stewardess serves coffee. She too wears blue jeans and a Chicago Bears cap. Around her fourth finger, she wears a ring.

No fat man intrudes on my territory, and no small boys receive five-dollar bribes.

Land and water in equal parts form splotches in an endless view. We approach Johnsburgh. Only one runway serves its needs. Our two-prop plane touches down and glides to a stop, using only a fraction of the runway.

A staircase is wheeled to the opened door of the airplane. Humidity clashes with air conditioning to generate a cloud of fog. My hand slips on the railing; and even before I reach the terminal, my shirt sticks to my skin and sweat trickles from my armpits.

A committee of three welcomes me. No banners or balloons announce my arrival, and no trumpets herald my presence.

One of these, a nun in full black habit, stands quietly with her hands hidden inside her sleeves. She appears unaffected by the oven blast heat of a Johnsburgh morning. Perhaps, like desert nomads, she is acclimatized. An unadorned metal cross dangles from a silver chain around her neck. Level with the cross is a pair of half glasses suspended from a plain black lace. Her white headdress hides her wrinkles more effectively than any surgeon's scalpel. Sagging upper lids nearly encroach on her vision, while her cheeks indent over a thin lower jaw. A slender hand speckled with brown spots reaches toward me. "I am Sister Mary James, principal of Sacred Heart School."

Her voice is even, unaffected by the vibrations of age. Not so her eyes when her gaze meets mine. An opaque ring, unkindly named arcus senilis, forms a barrier where the white abuts on the dark brown of her eyes.

I take her hand, surprised by its firmness and aware of its restrained power. "I'm Thomas Spanner, your new priest."

"Welcome. We are overjoyed to have a priest in our midst. It has been too long."

Only her eyes move as she inspects me from top to bottom and left to right. Finally, she stares at my Roman collar. A slight momentary shiver surprises me.

"I am pleased," she says without intonation, "to notice that you wear your collar, the declaration of our faith. You wear it even while you travel."

"I've never considered not wearing it, except when I exercise, but then it still is a very new blessing."

"Of course," she says, "as with all things, time will reveal."

Then turning to the tall man beside her she says, "This is Peter Krantz. He is the grand knight of the Knights of Columbus. He and Willem DeRooy, the knight's chaplain, have dedicated themselves and worked hard to maintain meaningful Catholicism while we had no priest."

She returns her stare to me. I feel an urge to apologize for my tardiness and explain that ordination was a requisite.

My eyes are level with Peter's collarbones. In spite of the heat, he appears relaxed, almost cool. A light brown tailored suit flows easily with each movement. His grip is firm, friendly. A white shirt with gold-and-diamond cuff links protrudes with his extended hand. Interspersed among his boyish haircut are a few specks of gray. He smiles with his entire face, eyes crinkle at the corners. His teeth are a natural white but not perfect in symmetry.

"Let me add my welcome," he says. "We're honored to have a priest after two years of begging and lobbying. It's been difficult without one. None of us ever realized how much we needed direction and sacraments bestowed upon us."

"I'm happy to be here," I reply. "It's a little early for honors. I am, as you know, very green, but I'll do my best to serve."

Peter smiles, and the early crow's feet softening his face even more.

Almost as an afterthought, he turns to the quiet man at his side. Willem DeRooy appears to be in his fifties. Reddish sideburns protrude beneath a fedora that keeps his face in shadows. He remains quiet, as if drawn into himself; faceless and self-effacing. Peter turns to me. "Father, I'd like you to get to know Willem, our spiritual guide and our knights chaplain. He won't tell you, so I will. He's held us together spiritually. Our beloved Willem was nearly a

Benedictine monk, but he felt unworthy a weeks before his ordination."

Willem hardly moves. His head, slightly bowed, gives no response. Then, in a quiet tenor voice, he says, "I am pleased to meet you, Father, but with some trepidation, I pray that my teachings have not strayed from the church. If they have, I ask your forgiveness and guidance toward the true path."

I'm not sure what to make of this and wonder at its sincerity. Nevertheless, I respond, "I'm grateful to meet you, Willem. I'm sure there is much that you can teach a novice priest."

He bows slightly and then surrounds my offered hand with barely a touch of his. He almost smiles his greeting.

Peter loads my two suitcases into the back of his Ford Explorer. I ride in the front. As we drive toward Johnsburgh, he says, "Welcome to our little corner of heaven. To the right is the mighty Marsalaat. Note our heat and humidity—a natural greenhouse for an abundant harvest."

He is silent for a moment, almost pensive. Then he smiles and points across the river. "It only looks like the Red Sea in autumn," he says. "That's when acres of cranberries have been flooded. Marvelous, the ripe berries float to the top and are scooped up. Berries aren't supposed to grow this far north. A little luck and some basic natural selection make it possible."

Willem interjects. "God answered our prayers and allowed us to live within our community so that we could grow in grace and wisdom. When you meet our people, you will grow to appreciate their progress."

"It sounds as if you've had some input into their growth," I say.

"Of course," he says, "some."

"Forgive me," sister interrupts, "this is no time for modesty. Willem is our mainstay. He ensured our morals, kept our children on the straight and narrow, and made sure no undesirables corrupted our community."

Willem raises his eyebrows. "It wasn't my doing. It was a community effort. We all had the same goals."

I am curious and wonder what goals? How were they achieved?

After a few moments of silence, Peter points to a white steepled church at the end of a winding road. "Your new home. Just like in the postcards."

Surrounding the churchyard is a three-foot high box hedge, broken intermittently where dogs and children took shortcuts in their haste. Attached to the church by a closed-in walkway is a house whose architecture blends with the church. A secondary walkway connects with the school.

"You'll love that walkway in winter," Peter says. "When you're snow bound in a forty below blizzard, you can visit in your church or beg tea from the sisters."

Sister Mary James carries my suitcases. She insists. "This will be the one and only time."

Across the kitchen cupboards is a six-foot banner. WELCOME, FATHER SPANNER. The school children have signed their names in crayon. Sister smiles. "School project."

She opens the fridge. There is enough food for a month. One shelf is half filled with iced tea.

Sister commands. "It's time for you to get some sleep. We'll call you this evening and help you get settled."

For a moment, I think she'd tuck me in, then she turns abruptly and ushers Peter and Willem out.

Time in bed is useless. I can't sleep. A cool shower revives me. Not to full alertness, but to grogginess that simulates it. I stumble into the kitchen. The coffee maker is armed and ready. Emblazoned on a white coffee mug are red letters—Father Thomas Spanner OSB.

CHAPTER 16

Dressed in blue jeans and a plain gray shirt, I explore the town. *How better to get a natural feel for a new place than to be ordinary and wander like a tourist?*

The streets are clean, sidewalks swept, and buildings painted in subdued colors of white and beige. I am somewhat surprised. There are no hotels, restaurants, or video stores. Even the sidewalks are made of cement. Somehow, I expected boardwalks. The roads are paved and neatly washed. The usual No Parking and One Hour Only signs are absent. Expenses have been spared; no parking meters line the streets. Strange. There are no stop signs.

I did, however, find a gas station, hardware store, supermarket, clothing store, and sporting goods shop. The clerk at the convenience store is polite. He calls me sir and passes my 7 Up. I look about but find no surveillance cameras. No beggars dot the sidewalks, and no staggering drunks accost me.

Even the alleys are washed and clean. Each block has a series of recycling containers: glass, paper, plastic, organic, other. I am impressed and uneasy. Everything is tidy, regimented, and clean. It's unnatural.

I can imagine the contents of the paper and bottle container, but the one marked "other" intrigues me. I lift the lid to examine its contents and am jolted by a large hand that clasps my shoulder and spins me around. A craggy face with a gray mustache says, "You're under arrest for vagrancy and loitering."

"I'm not a vagrant. I live here."

"No, you don't. I've never seen you before. Show me some ID."

I reach into a pocket, then into another. My wallet is missing.

"I don't have any with me."

"You're a vagrant. Why else would you be looking in the garbage?"

"My ID's at the church. I'm the new priest at St. Joseph's."

He smiles. "That's rich. I've never heard that one before." He puts an arm around me. "That's a good one. Real good."

He rolls back my sleeves and gives a grunt. "Looks like you're clean, but let's take a ride and find out who you really are."

I see him more clearly now as the afternoon sun slants beneath his trooper's hat. His eyes are hidden behind dark glasses. It's only the reflection of myself that I see in the lenses. His jaw is set, not given to idle chatter.

"Hands against the wall," he commands, "feet apart."

He helps me attain the position by giving me a painful kick against the inside of each ankle with his steel-toed trooper boots. He pats me down and cuffs my wrists behind me, then rams me into the backseat of the cruiser. It is uncomfortable, but I remain silent. Nevertheless, I'm sure he's seen the tears in my eyes. Each sudden start and forceful stop causes the handcuffs to bite into my wrists.

This is my first escorted tour of downtown Johnsburgh. I am impressed by its neatness and hanging baskets. I can see my church near the dike but I see no Anglican, Baptist, Lutheran, or any other churches. On the opposite side of town, we reach a cinder block building with bars in its small windows. I'm reminded of those jails in old Western movies.

The hulk of an officer yanks me out of the car by grasping the handcuffs that are still fastened behind me. He raises my wrists above my shoulders. My eyes water, and I feel that my shoulders are dislocated. I restrain myself and stifle a scream. It would not do for the new priest to be seen as a wimp. Nevertheless, tears trickle down my cheeks, and blood flows from my bitten lip.

The young policeman behind the desk springs from his chair. He appears to be at least sixteen years of age with blond wavy hair, blue eyes, and an unnecessary shave. He knocks his coffee onto the floor and reaches for his hat as he attempts an awkward salute. "What's happening, sir?" the kid says.

"Never mind that formal crap. You've been here long enough. Call me Rudy. Now let's find out who this bum is, Billy, and how he got here."

Billy nods his head and moves toward the camera.

"Let's get the prints and send them off to Chicago," Rudy says, "This guy looks like a pipsqueak, but you never know, sometimes they're the worst. They'll suck up to their victims and then stab them in the back. Once we know who this bum is, we can charge him, and run him out of town, or if he's a real bad ass, we can give him swimming lessons."

My black-and-white mug shots are not flattering. The one in profile is much too dark and would be enhanced by color. The ink on my fingertips looks permanent.

Rudy pushes me into a cell. "Here you go," he says. "Cool your heels. When it's dark, we'll go sightseeing."

"Officer," I say, "I'd like to make a phone call."

"Oh, right." Rudy passes the telephone. Its cord dangles freely to the floor. In my mind, I pray—*Forgive him, Father, he's a dodo. Too much muscle not enough brain.*

"I can't make a phone call with a disconnected line. What you're doing is against the law."

"Really? Well, for your information, I am the law."

I keep quiet for some time. He obviously won't listen to reason.

When darkness nears, I say, "What's for lunch, Rudy? I thought this was room and board?"

"How'd you like a knuckle sandwich, asshole?"

I assume the question is rhetorical and decide to have a nap. After a while, I am jolted to wakefulness. Peter Krantz's voice shoots through the office door, commanding, precise, and dominating. In the background, Rudy is whining and subdued.

"You do know how to welcome our priest. Does he look like a bum? Does he dress like a bum? Does he talk like a bum? Has he lived in those clothes for weeks and stink?

"I'll have you in front of council, Rudy. You can show cause why we shouldn't fire you. As of now, pending a hearing, you're suspended. As for you, Billy, I want a transcript of everything that happened here. I want it in my office by six, just the facts. Don't stick up for Rudy. Accomplices too are liable."

Peter, grim faced and apologetic, enters my cell. "I'm really sorry this happened to you, Father. It's inexcusable and unacceptable."

He hands me a manila folder. Inside are my photos and fingerprints.

Peter drives me to my church in his Explorer. Again he apologizes for Rudy and then hands me a small cardboard box. "Midnight snack," he grins. "You'll need it. I can always pick up another one."

As I eat my sandwich, a biblical phrase comes to mind—*I was hungry, and he fed me. I was in prison, and he visited me.*

My first night in Johnsburgh is restless. My shoulders throb when I lie on my side. During the night when I lean on my elbow, I am jolted by lancinating pain in my shoulders. Beneath the bruises on my ankles, a steady throb reminds me that the man chosen to protect me has assaulted me.

I am awake at sunrise. Stiffness overwhelms my body. Perhaps exercise will get me back in sync. My running shoes need a workout. After a few stretching exercises that are more painful than usual, I jog on the dike. The Marsalaat is quiet, barely flowing. Humidity persists even in the cool of morning. On the other side of the river, men in waders skim red berries.

Running works out some stiffness. Because of the humidity, I sweat and compound nature's dampness. Soon the pains in my joints ease, and I run even faster. Perhaps my endorphins are kicking in. I return home, invigorated. After a shower, I read my breviary and thank God for a safe end to my minimisadventure. As an afterthought, I say a prayer for Rudy and try to understand his point of view.

After a few days, the *Johnsburgh Herald* runs my picture on the front page. Not the jail picture, but a presentable one taken at my ordination. Alongside is a short article.

JOHNSBURGH WELCOMES NEW PRIEST

The fulfillment of our Catholic community's prayers came to fruition with the arrival of Father Thomas Spanner. Recently ordained, he comes to us from Seattle, Washington.

He was welcomed by the spiritual guardians of our peaceful community: Sister Mary James, principal of our school; Mr. Peter Krantz, our grand knight; and Mr. Willem DeRooy, chaplain of the knights and our de facto priest as far as he was able.

It appears our priest possesses an unusual quota of stamina. After an all-night flight and morning shuttle from Chicago, he was still vigorous enough to explore his new surroundings without supervision. Unfortunately, our stalwart police mistook him for a vagrant and duly incarcerated the criminal, since he failed to prove his identity or address. Mr. Peter Krantz became aware of Father's predicament and intervened.

Our Father Spanner is not disposed to turn the other cheek and forgive. He is not so much disturbed by his arrest; however, he alleges police brutality and denial of a phone call at the hands of Chief Redekop. He also maintains that he was not informed of his rights. To this end, he has lodged a formal complaint to town council. He asks, "If I, as your spiritual leader, don't receive justice, what justice can others expect?"

What he does not understand is that we are unique. There is no conventional legal system. We resolve and mediate our offenses and compensate accordingly.

We have interviewed Chief Redekop, and he regrets the inconvenience to Father Spanner. However, he reminds the citizens of Johnsburgh that he is mandated to safeguard the community. He also asks that we remember the anarchy of this community, when it was the site of a halfway house that was virtually unsupervised and attracted criminals.

I am depressed and fear that there are no limits to Johnsburgh law. To whom shall the police account? Who shall police the police? Will it be the paymaster, city council?

Next afternoon, I am at my desk and prepare for my first sermon. I aim for diplomacy and dedication. Furthest from my mind is any hint that I prefer parasitic addicts to the productive law-abiding citizens of Johnsburgh. A rattle of the screen door interrupts my thoughts. Outlined against the screen is a figure shaped like Santa. He wears a blue striped shirt with the top two buttons undone.

"Thank you for seeing me, Father," he says, with more than a trace of Polish accent. "I am Michael Grizkovich, editor, owner, and delivery boy for the *Herald*. I'm sorry that I didn't talk to you earlier. I didn't want to bias the article with any views other than my own."

He pumps my hand vigorously as if seeking my vote. "Welcome to Johnsburgh. I'd like to do a feature on you, Father. We've been without a priest so long that some of us have forgotten what he is and what he does.

"Also, tell me about yourself so that I may tell everyone else." He grins hugely, and then adds, "That's my job you know.

"So, Father, what about you? Spill the beans."

I tell him about my life. I have nothing unusual to say. The chronology of my education and milestones on the road to ordination are really public knowledge.

"My goodness," he says, "this is all so ordinary. Have you no desire to tell me of your addiction, the death of your sister, Rodriguez, or Al Maguire?"

I am stunned. *Who is this man to delve into my personal life? How dare he exploit me?* I turn to Grizkovich and say, "I hardly know you. You have no right to violate my privacy."

"Ah, Father, many would argue that you are a public figure and have no private life or rights."

"But I have the same rights as every other citizen. I think even Christ was entitled to privacy, and I'm sure God is. Do you think he tells us everything?"

Michael holds up his hands. "Peace," he says, "I do my homework, but I print only that which the subject permits and that which is public knowledge."

"Well, that's a relief. I thought you were going to describe my underwear."

He laughs, then frowns, suddenly serious. "I'm glad you have a sense of humor. I doubt you know what you're up against. If I told you, it wouldn't matter. You wouldn't believe. This place is too Catholic. The challenge is to make it human. Become a stonemason and remove the bricks one by one. That's your challenge."

I'm puzzled. "Could you be more specific? This is all much too vague even to consider your challenge."

"Of course I could be. But there's no need, since you've already been drawn a picture. Stick around. You'll have a whole album before you're done."

CHAPTER 17

The people of Johnsburgh welcome me with warm enthusiasm. My house is like a bus station.

Some call ahead. Others drop in: "Oh, I was just in the neighborhood, Father." "I just dropped in to say hello." "It's so nice to meet you." "Sally sent over some warm soup. She says you aren't used to cooking. She had a cousin in the seminary that was always hungry. You look like you could use a few pounds yourself." "We'd like to have you over once you're settled." They shake my hand. Some pat my back.

Later in the evening, the phone rings. A quiet voice, young and female, says, "The Sisters of the Naked Cross wish your presence for tea tomorrow afternoon at 3:00 PM. Do you accept?"

"Yes, I would be pleased."

Each nun is introduced in turn; and in turn, each delivers a miniresume. Of course, I won't remember much of this. They are too polite for name tags.

Sister Mary James presides at the head of an ornately carved walnut table. I know it's the head, because only her chair has armrests. Inlaid at the table's perimeter is a band of ivory carved tigers, elephants, and lions. The chairs are upholstered a rich red. Their wooden frames elaborately carved. Absent-mindedly I trace my finger along the inlaid ivory.

"It is a gift," says Sister Mary James, "to the convent. It belongs to the convent in perpetuity. We, like you, are rid of material possessions and strive to become spiritual beings."

A young nun, she could have passed for sixteen, head bowed, pours tea and serves cookies.

Sister Mary James begins. "Bless us, Lord, for finally sending a priest to our parish. We may now partake of your flesh and blood and renew the life in our souls, now and forever, world without end. Amen."

"Amen," we echo.

"We know nothing about you," sister continues. "How shall we work together in God's garden?"

"There is not much to know. I am an ordinary priest doing God's extraordinary work. I believe in the church and promulgate her teachings. My mission is to bring souls to God. I have no special talent or unusual calling. In humility and gratitude, I serve."

"I think that's wonderful," she states. "We have an ideal priest. Our parish is aptly named, St. Joseph the Worker. Our new priest may not be a saint, but he promises to be a worker."

She smiles. "And to the second part of the question? How shall we work together?"

"It is not something I've considered, we are the church and the way to God is through the church. I don't think it should be a problem, sister. We follow Christ, share in his suffering, and in the end rejoice with him."

"Excellent," she says. "We pull our wagon in the same direction."

"We need to meet," Peter states. "Much has occurred in the last two years. We have seen to our spiritual needs as best we could. The knights have also preserved the integrity of the material church. We are not complaining and are willing to supervise the fiscal aspects. However, should you wish to assume these duties, we will happily relinquish them. Do you have any thoughts on this, Father?"

I don't understand what he's saying and display my ignorance with a question. "Would you please elaborate."

"I'm talking about money, Father. Someone has to look after repairs, taxes, upkeep. We've been doing that. But if you want to, we'll step aside."

"I'd need more details. Of course, if it's my duty, I'll do my best."

"I'll ask Greta to show you the ledgers. You'll have an idea of what's involved."

Next morning, I visit Greta. This is not the dowdy church secretary I envisioned. She's pretty, in a wholesome sort of way.

She is alert, self-assured, but not overbearing. Were I not ordained, I would think her more than attractive. Her office is a jut out from the enclosed walkway. From the open door, I see the river and her desk that faces it.

"Come in," she says, "You're not on holy ground. Here we deal with filthy lucre. Welcome to a materialistic island in a sea of sanctity." Then, with a mischievous grin, she rises to greet me. "Peter tells me you've come to see how I cook the books."

I like her instantly. Her eyes, dark blue, crinkle as she suppresses a smile.

"I'm just trying to get familiar with the state of the parish," I say, "Finances weren't high on the seminary curriculum."

She points to her workbench.

"Pull up a chair, Father. The first ledger is for the last two years. The second ledger is for the two years prior to that just so you can compare. If you need to know anything, sing out."

I look at the first ledger and think I understand it. There are columns and rows—money in, money out, balance. The second ledger is computer typed and titled, *Johnsburgh Catholic Church Corporation (in trust)*. It is filled with foreign words: adjusted cost base; capital cost allowance; dividend reinvestment; Class A, B, C, D shares; disbursement; retention; financial statements.

I am ignorant and throw up my hands. "Ms. Simpson, I don't understand this ledger. Is it possible to have a translation?"

She pulls a chair beside mine. I sense her perfume, faint, alluring. Her arm touches my sleeve as she points with a pencil.

"The first set," she says, "is like any straightforward ledger. You can see that the church is always broke and begging."

I glance toward her, note the graceful contour of her eyebrow, and then quickly look away.

"This second set," she says, "is complex. You won't understand it without an accounting course. Peter created it. It saves the church a bundle in taxes. There are land grants and leases, government money for the cranberry initiative, water rights, and tax credits."

"It's overwhelming," I say. "How did a small parish ever achieve this?"

Greta takes a breath. "Computerization and the global village." She pauses for a moment. "When we had no priest, Bishop O'Doul asked the knights to manage the church finances. Peter put it all together. As you can see, the church is solvent and accrues from its investments enough to supply the needs of the church."

"Does this mean the church no longer controls its finances?"

She smiles. "Very good, Father. The answer is yes and no. To understand, you'll require a translator to interpret the contract between Bishop O'Doul and the church corporation. The simple answer is, the knights have formed a management company to administer church assets. Also, these assets belong to the diocese, not the parish. In other words, finances do not affect you."

Somehow, I feel cheated. I haven't even earned my poverty.

She reads me. "You seem off, Father. It's out of your league. But you're in good hands and will never need to worry about how you'll fix the leaking roof or fix your run down car. As Peter likes to say, 'The clergy looks after our souls, and we look after the clergy.'"

I should be more pleased. "It sounds quite liberating," I say.

Greta's smile is enigmatic. "Yes, Father, it can be."

I close the books.

"Coffee's on, Father. I think you need a cup."

She leans back in her chair, flicks her wavy hair over a shoulder, and sips her coffee. "This must be quite a change from the coast. Wait till winter."

I have never been adept at social small talk, so I say, "Have you always lived here?" She refrains from smiling at the inane remark.

"Just about," she says, "except for college and working in Chicago while I was married. After that, I came back to look after my sick father."

"May I ask the nature of your father's illness?"

"He has Parkinson's."

"Perhaps I should meet him. The church may offer hope and comfort."

"Perhaps, perhaps not. He lost his faith and has become quite depressed. He's my dad. I do what I can and that's what keeps me here."

"That's very noble of you. Many people wouldn't do that."

"I don't do it all for Dad. Peter made me an offer that was better than I could get anywhere else. He told me it was for as long as I wanted. The only request was that if I left, I should train my replacement. Do you know how long that would take?"

I'm saved from further conversation by a knock on the door. Peter comes in, as though it's his office. "Good morning," he grins. "Are you rested, Father, and has Greta shown you all you need to see?"

"I'm sure she has, but I may have wasted her time. Most of it's beyond me."

He laughs that low mirthful chortle. "It's easy, Father. You look after the parishioners and leave the rest to the knights. We'll provide a stipend and more to meet your needs—bishop's orders. It's something like obedience," Peter laughs. "Let us corrupt you further. Here are the keys to the Chevy parked in your driveway. Relax. It's not yours. It's only for your use."

Greta's lips pucker into a mock pout. "Why can't I get a deal like that? I'm poor too."

She pauses. "I know, it's too easy for Father. It's too comfortable and deprives him of the need to suffer."

"Well, if it's suffering he needs, we can recall Rudy."

As I leave, she taps my shoulder with her fist. "Buck up, Father. We'll try to make it miserable for you."

I return to my rectory, thankful and uneasy. On my desk is an envelope. A note says, "Initial stipend. You might want to spend it on clothes." I am taken aback. *How many clothes will a thousand dollars buy?*

CHAPTER 18

The sisters request my first official duty. "They've been baptized," says Sister Mary James. "Many have not been to confession. We've prepared them as best we could and rehearsed. Would you be kind enough to give a talk on the importance of this sacrament?"

The children sit cross-legged on the gymnasium floor. Boys in their light blue shirts and navy blue shorts. It is still warm. They won't wear trousers until October. The girls too are in uniform, plain dresses, the same color as the boys' shorts. Each clean face stares at me, concentrating as if my words were those of God himself. The sisters are on folding chairs behind them.

I smile and begin. "Blessed children. It is my pleasure and duty to be here and tell you about the sacrament of confession. Some call it reconciliation. I'm sure the sisters have taught you about this sacrament. It is necessary to confess one's sins at least once per year, if possible, because it's a church rule. You probably all know what sins are. A sin is when one breaks the rules of the church or the commandments. Even without knowing the rules, you can tell if you've done something wrong, or injured another by word or action. God loves you and wants you with him in heaven. That's why we have confession, to remove sin from your souls."

I look about. They are not yet restless. I continue. "The sisters have made sure that you are all baptized. Any one can baptize and remove the stain of original sin from your souls. It is not necessary to have a priest. The good sisters have made sure that you can go to heaven."

I think even Sister Mary James allows herself the beginnings of a smile. The others nod slightly and exceed her smile.

"But more than that, confession prepares you for the ultimate miracle, Holy Communion. In this sacrament, the living body of

110

Christ is given to you. It is a miracle which you can only feel in your heart and soul and neither touch nor see."

My confessional is clean, scrubbed, aired. I was expecting a dark and musty closet, damp from years of misuse. Around my neck is a new purple stole, a gift from the sisters. Even my bench is padded. I can deal with misery in comfort.

By her voice and expression, I estimate that my first penitent is a girl of about six. "Bleth me, Father," she lisps through the gap in her primary teeth. "This is my first confession. I got picked, because I'm the youngest in grade 1. I did some bad things. I stole my brother's penknife. I got mad at my mother when she wouldn't let me sleep over."

"Please give back the knife and say you're sorry. Since you didn't sleep over, you obeyed your mother. Everybody gets mad. That's the way we are. Now tell me of the good things you do?"

"I help Mommy make supper and set the table. I don't do dishes, 'cause that's Billy's job. Also, I baby-sit Andy, my brother."

"I'm happy that you're a good girl. Is there anything you want to talk about?

"Nope."

"Very well, if you need to talk, come and visit. For your penance give back the knife."

"Thankth, Father," she squeaks through the grill holes. I imagine a set of pigtails and freckles bouncing through the church with not a pause to genuflect.

The second sinner is much older, a boy. "Bless me, Father. I got some stuff to confess. It's kind of private."

"The confessional is private, and no one will know what you say here."

He blurts. "I jack off and think of naked women. I know I'll go to hell if I don't stop, but I can't."

"Have you tried to stop? How have you tried?"

"I don't know. I just try."

"One can only do one's best. Console yourself that your sin hurts no one else, unless of course you're married. Are you married?"

A muffled "no" greets me. "Well, sin is a part of life. That's why we have confession. Pray, turn your mind elsewhere, and do your best. You will stay out of hell. Is there anything else you would like to talk about?"

"No, thanks, Father. I feel better now."

"For your penance, draw pictures of Eskimos on the ice in their warm parkas. Pretend you're one, and then imagine yourself naked in the frozen arctic. Also pray for strength. Your sins are forgiven. Go in peace."

A litany of normal behavior is filtered through my grill, venial sins at most. The children seem well behaved. None stay long. There are many who wish to confess.

A curious pause—both sides of the confessional are empty. Perhaps the sisters have scheduled a recess. Not so. I hear a rustle on my left and see an adult outline as I open the grill.

Sister Mary James stands with both hands leaning on the wall. "What," she hisses through clenched teeth, "do you think you are trying to do? We have feedback from the children. You treat sin as a joke, dispense laughable penance, and make no mention of how sin killed our Lord and Savior. I will send no more children until you seek adequate amends for their evil deeds."

I am outraged at this intrusion into the children's lives and my sanctum.

"This is a confessional, not a talk show or public forum. Do you wish to confess?"

"I most certainly do not. I will have no part of this mockery. I only came to warn you."

"You place yourself in grave danger, sister. My confessions are valid. It is blasphemy to interfere with them. To deprive others of access to the sacrament is in itself a serious sin. I will wait for ten minutes; if there is no resumption, I will leave this box and inform your superior of your actions. We all hold different views, and you are not qualified to be my judge."

She leaves with a bang of the door and in three minutes returns.

"Bless me, Father," she says, "I have sinned, but I did it in the children's interests. I ask forgiveness for my outburst and for depriving the children of the opportunity to reconcile. I think we need to dialogue so that we may find a common front for the children's best interests."

I forgive her sins and prescribe her penance. "For the next week, at every opportunity, practice humility, place the other viewpoint ahead of yours, try to be a follower, and know that a leader is not always right—only for a week, sister."

I recognize Sister Theresa's voice, young, almost pubertal in tone.

"Bless me, Father," she begins. "Through no fault of my own, it is two years since my last confession. I wish forgiveness for my sins of anger and sexual daydreams. I'd like to detail, but there are many who still wish to confess."

"Very well," I say, "as your intent is true, you are forgiven. Say the appropriate penance. If you wish to discuss feel free. Go in peace."

Confessions continue. Nuns confess their conflicts, deprivations, and trials of faith. *What do I expect?*

My replies are standard. "Bless you, bride of Christ, sacrificial lamb who has left all for the church. Laity would not believe your confession as sins. You are special among women and exalted before God. Go in peace."

Both sides of my confessional are empty. No one waits in the pews. I squint and rub my eyes. As I pass Greta's office on my way home, she greets me with a Coke and sandwich.

"Miller time, only eight hundred sinners to go before Sunday Mass."

I feel revived even before my first sip. "Thanks, and when is it your turn?"

"Oh, I don't know. My father's been trying to unconvert me. I'll wait until I have enough sins to make confession worthwhile."

"I'm Mary Stuart, chairman of the church committee," she says and squeezes my hand excessively. Her straight gray hair hangs loosely in a short cropped style. Her stare is direct. She wears one of those loose unbelted tentlike dresses, the kind women wear to hide their shape when they have no shape.

"We've always celebrated Mass in the Latin rite. We believe that we, as well as our priest, should face our Christ on the cross. All the children learn Latin and most of us do too. We mean no disrespect of Vatican II. The traditional rite just sounds more real to us."

I am puzzled. "How can you possibly object? The essence of the sacrament remains immutable. Liturgical reform only makes the Mass more understandable and modern."

"Many people and several popes would agree with you, Father. We think there is an element of faddism in this reform."

"Please excuse me, what bothers you about the modern Mass?"

She inhales, sighs, and begins counting on her fingers:

"One. We think it is disrespectful to stand and look God in the eye during Communion. He gives himself to us and expects humility in return. We prefer the humility of kneeling. Two. We are used to the host being placed on our tongues. It seems irreverent to hold God in our hands. Three. The secularization of the Mass into the vulgar vernacular and local custom brings disunity to the church. Four. We feel the priest needs respect and trading genuflection for the peace sign diminishes that respect. He is not the president of the assembly. Five—"

I hold up my hand and shake my head. "Enough. I'm familiar with the arguments and counterarguments. This is a matter that we need to discuss and resolve. The core of the Mass is intact with either rite. Both masses are valid. In the meantime, since I have no missionary beliefs on the subject, I offer a compromise. I will begin with the Latin Mass. During the next week, I will introduce a change at the church committee meeting. We will do it democratically, and I will try to convince you of its benefit."

She nods her head, and the corners of her mouth rise. "Thanks, Father. On behalf of all of us, we are relieved. We didn't know what we'd do if you had insisted on the new version."

I too am relieved and smile. "I wouldn't know either. But then it's not a matter of faith or morals. It's rite, not dogma."

I keep smiling, but a random thought intrudes. *My church? Or theirs?*

In the sacristy, my vestments are displayed in order and selectively layered from the gold chasuble to the amice. I pray for purity as I wash my hands. Again, I pray to be cleansed as I wear the alb, white in its symbolism. As I tie the cincture, I pray for chastity. I accede to the parish and place the maniple over my left arm. When I place the stole around my neck, the prescribed prayer emanates from my mind, *"Lord, restore the stole of immortality, which was lost through the collusion of our first parents, and unworthy as I am to approach thy sacred mysteries, may I yet gain eternal joy."*

Gratitude overwhelms me. My church is full. *Keep holy the Sabbath.* The sisters occupy the first pew, kneeling and standing in unison, like soldiers. In the second row are the Knights of Columbus in full uniform. The remainder of my people are scattered throughout the church, jammed against each other. Even at 10:00 AM heat and humidity intensify. Occasionally, an infant's cry and hush interrupt the quiet.

As I celebrate my first Mass at St. Joseph's, I am blessed with two well-rehearsed altar boys. I must confess to a little stage fright.

As agreed, the Mass is in the Latin rite. In some ways, the ceremony is more real in this ancient language. At times I feel a tingle akin to that of an opera sung in a foreign tongue. When my congregation responds correctly, I am thrilled. Obviously the Mass is alive. What vernacular phrase can upstage traditional words as: *mea culpa, Miserere nostri, Kyrie eleison, laudamus te, credo in unum Deum.* In that moment, the culmination of the mass, when I place the body of the living Christ on a sinners tongue, I am fulfilled to hear my own words, *Corpus Christi* (body of Christ).

What shall I say in my sermon? I am overwhelmed with the kindness and help I have received. I begin, "I have been in Johnsburgh only a week. Already you are dearly beloved. It is with gratitude that I thank you for your kindness and help. Already I feel part of your community. I am overwhelmed. Thank you for taking me into your hearts.

"For my part, I am a priest of the Catholic church. My function is to bring souls to God and to bring the Mass and body of Christ to the people of Johnsburgh. My purpose culminates in the ultimate sacrifice of Jesus Christ. It is to that end his body and blood are freely given to those who believe.

"I hope to increase your love for one another, show you the way to holiness and the path to life everlasting."

After Mass, there is a reception in the school gym. I am introduced. People ply me with juice and food.

"We thought of name tags, Father," she says, "but they're no easier to remember than a face. I'm Stella Jones, Father, I'm so happy to meet you. It's not often a pillar of this community gets arrested. Do you have a rap sheet?"

In a strange way, I welcome her jibe. "As a matter of fact, I do have a rap sheet. Some day, I'll tell everyone about it."

"Just kidding," she says, "only trying to make you feel at home."

CHAPTER 19

Town council meets every Monday at six. There is no mayor. Spokesmen rotate, and like the Supreme Court, a majority of the five members decides. I recognize four of them, now out of Knights uniform, their faces serious.

About twenty people, most talking to each other, are seated in the audience. Fragments of talk drift to my ears—so young, doesn't understand, needs training, ears are wet, a little big man.

The council spokesman, Charles Wilson, is a short dapper man. He extends a hand in welcome. His nails are manicured, the cuticles trimmed precisely to reveal the light lunule. Even his ear and nose hairs are trimmed. He smells of soap. "During the day, I'm the banker," he explains. "At night, I go to meetings. Tonight your concerns are at the top of our agenda."

Rudy is seated opposite me. He appears relaxed, at ease. He wears his uniform but does not flaunt it. No dark glasses hide his eyes. It makes no difference.

I wear my suit and Roman collar. There are no lawyers, no advocates. "This isn't court," Charles Wilson says. "We're all friends and can sort this out. There's no need for complications."

Turning to me, he asks, "Is there anything in your affidavit, Father, that you wish to amend?"

"No," I say, "these are the facts as they occurred."

He looks at Rudy. "Any comments?"

Rudy stands, faces the audience, and stares a few in the eye. "My job," he says, "is to keep this community safe. That's what council asked me to do, and that's what they pay me for. I work to keep druggies who would infect the community away from here and stop people with no visible means of support from stealing. When I first met our priest, he had no ID, no money, no fixed address. By all appearances, he was a vagrant, and I had a duty to arrest him.

"When he lipped me off about room and board, I responded in kind. My intent was to drive him to the highway, flag down the bus to Chicago, buy the ticket, and give him fifty bucks as a token of good intention.

"I apologize for any inconvenience or trauma I've caused, but these are my directions from council."

Charles interjects. "I know, I know."

To me he says, "Let me explain—we have a unique situation here. You see we have no judge and no real court system. There's only one law firm, and they mainly handle real estate transactions. We must and do resolve most of our disputes without rancor."

My mouth drops open. "What are you saying, Mr. Wilson? Because there is no formal legal system in this town, it's all right for the police to assault people and carry out their own justice? Is it also just to arrest someone who has committed no crime and run them out of town? What about freedom of movement?"

Wilson says, "You know this will never happen again. Some of the onus lies with you. Had you identified yourself properly, all would have been well. You must admit that it's strange for a priest to rummage through garbage. In that way, you actually entrapped our police."

I am dumbfounded. Rudy is now the victim.

"Council will recess to talk this over," Wilson says. "We'll be back when we're done."

Five minutes later, they return.

"You're legally right, Father. You weren't Mirandized, there was no phone call, and you were threatened. If you want to pursue this, you'll have to do it in Chicago, I guess. We don't know how to do it here. Why a man of the cloth would be vindictive escapes me—no harm's been done, and Rudy's already apologized.

"In regards to you, Chief Redekop, times have changed. It is council's directive that you modify your procedures. Council will form a task force to this end and welcome input from concerned citizens."

He smiles and surveys the audience. "Questions, comments?" I have none. *Did I gain anything for my parishioners, or for me? Have faith, I say to myself, time will tell.*

Charles Wilson stands, smiling broadly. "What we have here is a win-win situation. Father now recognizes our concerns, and Chief Rudy can mellow out. We'll see to that. Meeting's adjourned."

Rudy taps my shoulder. "Welcome aboard, Father." He grins. "Sorry about the initiation. No hard feelings, I hope."

I grasp his extended hand. "By tonight, they'll be gone. You're forgiven, and I won't ask you to kneel."

Mike Grizkovich lumbers from the spectators' section with a notepad and pencil in hand.

"How do you feel about the result, Father? Any editorial thoughts?"

"No comment," I reply.

He looks me straight in the eye and nods. "I see that you're a quick learner."

The next morning, I'm surprised to find Grizkovich on my doorstep. "I was thinking," he says, "you just got here and aren't used to us yet. You've had a rough ride already too. But there's nothing like going fishing to get away from it all. I'd be happy to take you, if you like—even though you don't drink."

What does he want? I wonder. Curious, I accept his offer.

Two days later, I rise at daybreak and read my breviary. By five thirty I've finished my coffee and banana. I'm excited, actually. I'm also embarrassed. I've only been fishing in my dreams.

Grizkovich pounds on my door. "Wakey, wakey. The fish are biting. Pretty soon they won't be hungry. Goin' to take you to my favorite lake," he says. "Big mouth bass. I've seen some where the mouth is bigger 'n the fish."

"I've never seen that in a *fish*," I reply.

He guffaws as he gathers the inference. "Now I see why Rudy figures you lipped him off."

Boat and trailer in tow, we bump along a pair of ruts called a road. Grizkovich shifts into four-wheel drive. Suddenly serious, he says, "So what do you think that meeting the other night accomplished?"

"Well, isn't it obvious? Council knows how Rudy operates, and they're going to have him change his procedures." He gives me a quick sideways look but, except for a slight grunt, does not reply.

He backs the old boat and trailer into the lake. Once we are afloat, he pull-starts the ten-horse Evinrude. The five-horse spare for emergencies sits with its prop high out of the water.

A few minutes later, we've agreed on a good spot to start. I sit in the middle of the boat and reel out about a hundred feet of line. Behind me, Grizkovich lets a baited line run out from each side of the boat.

"Fishing imitates life," he says. "You always need a backup, an alternate plan, Father. Insurance."

"What do you mean, Mike?"

"Well, just look at the water. It's peaceful now, but in a short time, it can blow up and capsize a small boat. So you learn to stay near shore, unless you've got a fast boat—or like to take risks."

He grips the rudder with one hand and drinks coffee with the other. I often check my line for a fish. After about fifteen minutes, there's a zing of the reel. Grizkovich turns the boat away from his line and jumps toward me.

"Let him run," he prompts. "Then reel him with just some tension on the line—not too much, or he'll snap your line. That's it, that's it. Pull, ease up."

Eventually, with the help of his coaching, I net the bass. Grizkovich slaps my back. "Looks like a five pounder," he says. "Really nice."

I am thrilled and have a fleeting desire to take a picture and send it home. Grizkovich inspects my line, baits the hook, and resumes the vigil at his own line.

"Fishing is a game of patience," he says. "It's one of the seven virtues."

Later, he hooks a fish and reels it in. To my amazement, he can drink his coffee, operate the reel, and use the net all at the same time.

"Let's go," he says. "We got enough fish for a while. Let me give you a tour of these lakes and show you the signposts. There's a way to get clear to the Mississippi—if you're smart, lucky, and real careful."

He points to markers, trees, land points, and streams. "You gotta know the signs, or you'll get lost for sure. Remember that, Father."

I give him a questioning look. "You'll catch on," he says, "one way or another."

I am soon too busy with priestly duties to spare a thought for Grizkovich and his snippets of advice. Mass, confession, baptisms, and teaching religion to children fill my days. From time to time, I also anoint the sick, perform marriage ceremonies, and bury the dead.

Like any good priest, I make house calls and visit the sick. Most are women of a certain age, living with chronic pain, futilely seeking help from doctors, chiropractors, herbalists, and even magnetic mattresses. They have resorted to prayer and find a new source of hope in me, Johnsburgh's neophyte spiritual healer. Some even manage a smile as I climb their steps.

"Thank you for coming, Father," they say and discreetly swallow assorted pills and capsules. I look into their long suffering, freshly made-up faces, and think of Mother.

My weeknights too are heavily booked—only Monday and Friday are free. On Tuesdays, it's the Catholic youth, on Wednesdays, bowling—a compulsory activity during which I'm a source of laughter.

Thursdays are for my adult discussion group. We meet in the school gymnasium and sit in a circle. Dress is casual. Our sessions last one hour and fifteen minutes, and I prefer to facilitate rather than talk the whole time. After all, our purpose is to exchange ideas, inform each other, and expand our minds.

But at best, they are hardly a talkative group. Nods and a "yes" in unison are their only responses to my question, "Am I my brother's keeper?"

I decide to challenge them. "Why have we not eased poverty throughout the world? You need only watch TV on Sunday to see children in garbage dumps and families in shacks. What are we doing to ease their suffering?"

"We donate money so poor people in Africa, Central America, and Latin America can buy food," one of the younger men says. He's rushed straight from work and still wears coveralls. "But often the money's intercepted by local government. And there are so many children. Not like here, where we limit ourselves to one, two, or three, then practice restraint."

An overweight middle-aged woman nods her agreement. "I think the problem is ignorance and lack of discipline. But we do what we can to help."

"Are you suggesting birth control?" I ask.

"Of course," she says, "naturally and natural. It works for us."

Her sister is beside her. Same look, different clothes. "Don't mistake our intent. We adhere to the church and to Humanae Vitae. But you still can't help wondering if the nonbeliever's solution would in fact be more fitting for believers."

"I don't think we should interfere with nature," says an older man, a retired farmer. "Just look at Africa. They're getting' knocked off with AIDS, and a lot of them are just little kids and not even homos. That's natural birth control if'n you ask me."

The meeting ends on the hour. "Thanks, Father," they say. "That was worthwhile. We're looking forward to next week."

I return home and brew tea. A cup of hot water, six dunks of a tea bag, no cream, no sugar—I go through the motions like an automaton, troubled by tonight's discussion. They are *so* Catholic.

Between home visits and group meetings, I soon discover that the parish has a seemingly endless supply of cookies and sandwiches. After Mass each morning, I make my first priority an hour of exercise and running. Were it not for this I would need to add a new notch to my belt. Even so, I am beginning to show the results of a perpetual round of lunches, teas, and dinners. I look in the mirror and fear that someday the name "Thomas the Fat" will suit me well.

Willem, the Knights' chaplain, sometimes joins me for a run. Unlike me, he never seems to feel the weather. On this morning in late October, the trees are golden. Frost paints the grass, and along the Marsalaat, spicules of ice extend from the shore. Willem is wearing shorts.

He's also in better shape than I am and finds it easier to run and talk at the same time.

"How are you fitting in so far?" he asks. "Any surprises?"

"No, I don't think so. Everything seems pretty conventional middle-of-the-road Catholic. It's sin and forgiveness and redemption."

"Sounds pretty dull. Don't you ever wish you could spice it up, light a little fire in your life?"

The cold air stings my throat, and I gasp as I answer. "I preach constantly so people can avoid fire in their lives. I'm not about to search for it for myself. The Scriptures and church have been constant for centuries. There are no surprises."

"Really? There are changes you know, Vatican II, for instance. Pope John and Paul were progressive. Who knows, after this present stick-in-the-mud pope, we may have one that's with it."

"What would you like to see, Willem? What would make the church more relevant?"

"Oh, it's very simple," he says. Tiring of my slow pace, he lopes ahead and looks back at me over his shoulder. "I would like to see a church that serves its people. The people have served the church long enough."

CHAPTER 20

The winds of November howl from the north and funnel arctic air into a bunkered Johnsburgh. Only a few parched leaves cling to barren branches. Ice in formation, like frozen fingers, points from the shores of the Marsalaat, builds and joins at midcurrent. My face reddens as I march along the dike. I have decided not to jog ever since my throat seared with the intake of each frozen breath. Perhaps I have an underdeveloped sixth sense. My night is quiet, strangely so. All those meaningless and unidentified nocturnal noises are absent. By morning, Johnsburgh's roads and landmarks are blurred by a drifting swirl of snow. Fat horizontal snowflakes cling to the sides of my church, making it nearly invisible, like whitewash over a painting that the artist now despises.

A flicker of the bedside lamp and flash of the clock get my attention. We are on auxiliary power. I light the fireplace and wood furnace in the basement and prepare to become cozy. All duties are suspended on power down days.

Sister Theresa knocks on my door. She smiles, like someone playing hooky. "I just wanted to remind you that we won't be at Mass today. I doubt anyone else will be either. And," she grins, "there's no lunch either. We're snow bound and the little darlings are stuck at home. We love our work, but it's nice to have an EDO—extra day off."

I'm snow bound too. It's a new sensation, one I've missed in the northwest. *What will I do for exercise?* Running on the spot is boring. Perhaps I could charge along the walkway from my house to the school and back.

I glance out my window. A figure clothed in parka and backpack approaches on snowshoes. It's Greta. She sees me and waves. I'm in my jogging suit, still trying to figure out a winter exercise, when

she knocks on my door and breaks into laughter. "Going jogging?"
she asks. "Better wear gum boots. The track isn't shoveled."

"Funny," I say and explain my dilemma.

She is suddenly serious and frowns. "It's a problem all right."

"Come in," I say. "Coffee's on. Maybe you've got an idea."

"I can't stay long. Peter's handed me the paperwork—again.
I'm to put the best taxation face on farm labor now that the Mexicans
have gone home to spend their hard-earned dollars. I'm to find a
way of getting government grants from Mexico, Illinois, and
America because we helped the poor starving Mexicans. Any ideas,
Father? Give me a hand. You're tax free."

"Oh, that's easy. I'm a charity case. Even the money I spend isn't
my own."

"Nice work," she says. "I'm going to find a sugar daddy that
let's me spend money that isn't mine."

She laughs, a low feminine rumble from deep in her throat.
Then like a darkened light, her face changes. She is suddenly serious.
"I know you've only been here a few months, Father. But how do
you like it so far?"

"Well, it wasn't my first choice. In the church there isn't a
choice. Everybody's been wonderful to me. There's nothing that I
need. People are believers. They accept me, invite me into their
homes, and make me part of their community. In the Christian
sense, I am showered with love and am one with my brothers."

"That's great," she says, "how wonderful for you. Well, I'd love
to stay and chat, but I have a paper mountain to tackle."

At midmorning, I knock on her office door with a cup of coffee
in my hand. A disheveled Greta shakes a knotted fist at her computer
and utters a phrase which I'm sure is an Anglican expression. She
bids me enter with a wave of her free hand.

"That's great," she says. "Maybe it will stimulate my mind to out
smarten this computer. Just put the coffee here, Father. I don't have
time to stop."

Snow continues. Nothing moves. Even the brash discontented
crows have disappeared. By noon, Greta has shut down her computer
and taps on my door.

"I'm leaving now," she says, "but I'll be back tomorrow. Is there anything you need?'

"No thanks. This place is well supplied. I think I could survive a year."

Then she hesitates. "Coffee, please," she says and sits on my favorite chair.

I like her company and enjoy the freedom of her demeanor. I like to be close to her and at times, I would like to touch her. No, I am not one of those closet womanizer priests who hides the fantasies of his mind behind a cassock of sanctity. I just want to touch her. Not in a sexual way, not a fraternal pat, and not as an invitation. No, I just would like to touch her.

We talk in those generalities that are meaningless in themselves but make us less than strangers. Yes, she likes it here. It's safe. Living with her invalid father isn't always easy, but it's something she needs to do. I tell her that my mother is also unwell. Father is away a lot. He works in a sawmill.

She finishes her coffee. "I'd better go. I'm talking to a priest like I would a normal person. If it socks in, and I'm stuck here with you overnight, it would be really bad for my reputation."

I laugh with her.

"Well," she says, "see you around. Try not to get lonesome."

"Oh, I don't get lonesome. In my teens, I used to go on hikes by myself for a week at a time. I loved it."

She was suddenly serious. "You don't know how happy I am to hear that. Your predecessor, Father Barnes, needed constant approval, company, and the human touch. He craved that touch. It was his cross, his addiction, and his undoing.

"Have you any idea what happens to a parish when its only priest becomes intimate with its wives? Surely, you must have been taught in preacher school? How do you think the men react? And what do they do if he's not transferred? That is the how the church operates. Isn't it? What recourse have the women who are blessed by his attentions?

"I've heard it said, Father," she continues, "that the best way to get to know someone is to be alone with him. Perhaps in a boat or a hunting trip.

I nod my agreement. "I've been fishing with Mike Grizkovich. And not long ago Russ Thompson, the Vietnam vet, took me deer hunting. What a high. We actually got ourselves a buck."

Her expression is unreadable, her tone flat. "Yes, I've heard the talk around town. You're a man's man. A real crack shot."

She shakes her head as if addressing a child. "You might consider the good old boys just want to get to know you and find your weak spots. Of course, once they get to know you and pronounce you clean, they're friends for life."

I am silent for a moment. "That sound pretty cynical and ominous, Greta. I pose no threat to their wives or children."

"That's good, because they're just making sure. Barnes jeopardized not only family but also finances when he incited the Mexicans to equal rights."

She pats my shoulder and turns to leave. "I don't mean to rain on your parade, but I'm not part of the chorus."

Snow continues for several days. Fat flakes layer on each other. No wind swirls them about and all sound is absorbed in the whiteness. A field of snow bars my view of the river, but I know the river still runs at it's deepest current. Faith.

Phone lines heavy with ice snap under the weight.

I don't mind being alone in my den. I'm warm, cozy with plenty of food and drink. Even the TV has quit. Its portrait of snow depicts the winter. I enjoy these days of isolation. Sometimes I say morning Mass alone. At times, there's token representation from the sisters. They too wish to enjoy their isolation. It is a time for reflection. Perhaps I'm a social isolate. I don't miss confession, discussion groups, and I could even dispense with daily Mass. The sisters are perfectly capable of teaching catechism and have no need of my presence. Teas and dinner are not an essential part of my diet.

After the storm, Peter is at my door. He's amused and cannot quite restrain a laugh. "The knights discussed you at our meeting last night," he says. "We think you're snowbound and suffer from exercise withdrawal, endorphin depletion. You need to get out more. So we've brought some exercise equipment."

He watches as I unwrap my present, a pair of snowshoes and matching boots. My eyes water. "I'm overwhelmed, Peter. Everyone is far too kind."

"Nonsense, Tom. We're happy that you're not perfect. If you were, you might expect the same from us. Besides, you provide us with a source of entertainment. I hope we're laughing with you."

"I'm glad no one here is perfect. Just the same, I expect everyone to be working on it."

He is serious for a moment. "Since I had a lot to do with bringing you here, how are you doing so far? Are you comfortable with what's happening?"

"I couldn't be happier. Every one is kind. The community is morally exemplary. And that's the part that worries me. My job is to eradicate sin. If there is none, I'm superfluous."

"Oh, stick around. You just haven't looked in the right places."

His crow's feet crinkle and his boyish face softens. I feel secure in the presence of this man that I've grown to trust in only a few fleeting months.

He looks at his watch. "I have an appointment. But I've asked Greta to give you lessons."

A clear sky warms the fallen snow to form droplets on its surface. In the distance, a crow caws, flaps its wings, and glides away, outlined in sharp black against the purest blue.

Greta faces me. She wears dark glasses, toque, and leather gloves. "Listen up, Father. There's really nothing to it. You put your feet in the harness and strap them on. Then you walk with your feet apart. Don't slide. Lift step. It's harder in soft snow like this. Out in the woods with a little crust, it's fun."

I'm not having fun. I wipe the sweat from my brow with the back of my hand. Greta puts her hands on her knees and laughs. "It's child's play in a kiddie playground."

I lunge at her and fall face first into the snow. Another laugh. "Getting up's the hard part."

She reaches toward me and helps me to my feet. "Let's try it again. No sudden moves. On your feet and distribute your weight equally. Just pretend that you're walking. Keep moving. There's less time to sink that way."

I persist and Greta encourages. With repetition, I begin to master the technique. Eventually, Greta's satisfied. "I think that's enough for one day," she says. "You just need to do it to get the hang of it."

As if I were an invalid, she helps me to my door and undoes my snowshoes. In return, she accepts the offered coffee. "Warm," she says and stares into my eyes a little too long. Then touches my hands, "cool hands, Father, warm face, and warm heart."

Feelings, long suppressed, bubble within me. My mind reverts to Moira, her tenderness forever in my mind. I place an arm around Greta's shoulder and give a fraternal squeeze. "Thanks a lot," I say, "snowshoes could even be better exercise than jogging."

She smiles again, and my spirits lift. She drinks her coffee black and purses her full lips as she blows steam over the rim. "Well, Thomas, I hope this job is right for you and that you're happy here. It can be very lonesome with no attachments."

"Thanks for worrying, Greta. It's not just a job or a career. It's my reason for being."

She seems less animated for a moment, and I return to the present and the vows that I have made. After she finishes her coffee, I gather myself and thank her again, more formally, for the lesson.

She pats my shoulder as she leaves. "See you around, Father."

I am disconcerted and take a moment to pray. All during my college years, I was aloof, thankful to my god for my rescue. It was just God and I back then. I close the portals of my mind and secure my feelings behind my inner door.

CHAPTER 21

Thankfully, I resume my duties: baptism, marriage, funerals, Mass, confession, Communion. I anoint the sick, visit the healthy, and have an endless round of teas and dinners.

The parishioners love me. They invite me for cross-country skiing, snowshoeing, skidoo rides, and ice fishing. Everything seems perfect. It is unnatural, and I become uneasy. They have no needs, no wants. My congregation presents me with no problems to solve. I am an ornament, a figurehead.

Winter becomes Christmas, and we celebrate the birth of Christ, triumph over evil and redemption of our sins. But as the church teaches, we go on sinning; no matter how many times I change bread into the body of Christ. Our sins were forgiven on the cross. We repeat them. What else shall we do when our sins are forgiven in advance?

Willem remains distant, withdrawn like a silent monk from a cloistered order. I approach him tentatively. "Willem, I would be grateful for your views and your advice. Some days I feel superfluous. Every one here seems fulfilled and not in need of my ministry. I'm ready to fight sin, but I can't find any."

He folds his arms, places his hands around his shoulders, and bows his head.

"It's not easy, Father, to respond to what you say. By nature and training, I am reserved. It is even more difficult to expound on the sins of the people, when the sins of the clergy are vast and public. I was conscripted to be spiritual leader after Father Barnes died. It was not my choice. I always kept my religion private. Do you know how hard it is to do a job that you're not qualified for? I did my best, but it's not in my power to transmit divine forgiveness. So we, and I mean the community, improvised by consensus.

"Father Barnes preferred lust and alcohol to God and perfection. You don't know how hard we tried to help him. Nor will you ever know the lengths we went to keep him functioning as a priest. He had the power that led to salvation and the keys to our redemption, so in his sober moments, we asked his blessing.

"We also pleaded with Bishop O'Doul to remove him and send us another. Peter lobbied but to no avail. The church had other priorities. We thanked God for his divine intervention after Father Barnes fell in the river and drowned."

"He drowned?"

Willem lifts his head and now looks straight at me. "You look startled. Did no one tell you?"

I shake my head.

"Well, no matter, it was a tragic accident, but it's behind us now. As for sin," he went on, "the greater the sin, the more it's hidden. Some sins are very, very private. Others are hidden because we refuse to see. There is sin in Johnsburgh, Father. Perhaps more than you would like to guess."

"That's pretty general, Willem. Couldn't you clue me in a bit more?"

"I could and I won't. Valid truths are discovered. They lose their strength when told. If you are astute enough, and tolerant, in time, you will find our greatest sins. If you are exceptional, there is a slight chance that you can reconcile and forgive."

He folds his hands and bows as if retreating under his cowl. Then turns one hundred and eighty degrees and leaves. The conversation unnerves me. *Have I turned the latch on Pandora's box?*

By tradition, the children's Mass is at 3:00 PM every December 24. I recall a passage from the Bible. "Suffer the little ones to come unto me so that in their innocence, I may bless them." I was honored to baptize them and remove the stain of original sin from their innocent souls. I am fortunate to tell them of the one true church of heaven. I will say the Mass and let them leave without much ceremony.

"Father, a word with you before you begin." Sister Mary James is stern, commanding. "I don't know your views on the subject, but in our school, we teach honesty and have no interaction with deception, no matter how harmless it may seem."

I'm unsure of her drift. *Could she be referring to the tooth fairy?* I am about to ask but bite my tongue.

"You seem puzzled," she continues. "I'm referring to Santa Claus. We place him in the same category as Snow White, Cinderella, and the Three Little Pigs. It is important to separate fantasy and reality. Don't get me wrong, Thomas, we are not against gifts. After all, God gave us his son at Christmas. All I ask is that you be honest and not partake of the rampant commercialism that despoils this blessed season."

Life is serious, even for the young. No more asking, "What did Santa get you for Christmas?" In Johnsburgh, Virginia, there is no Santa Claus.

We sing songs of hope, and joy, and love. I pray all have a happy childhood that prepares them for happy adulthood. I bless them and remind them of God's love for them so they may also love one another.

In the true spirit of her own Christmas, Sister Mary James intercepts me after Mass. "You're a patsy, Thomas. You're all love and mush and gush. You ignore the meaning of Christmas. Christ was born so that our sins could be forgiven. He was born to be killed. You do no one a favor by denying truth and dipping pickles in icing sugar. We crucified him, Thomas. That truth frees us and truth is respected more than a candy passing preacher."

I am astonished at her vehemence and the effrontery with which she assaults me. Quietly, I say to her, "I know why Christ was born. Shall his sinners have no joy?"

There is a custom in Johnsburgh that only relatives spend Christmas together. No one invites me for Christmas. It may have been an oversight where each person thought the other had invited me—as with the lost Jesus of the Bible where each parent thought he was with the other. Perhaps I would be an intruder to intimate family events, disrupt the bond. Inadvertently, I might mention Santa Claus.

Sister Mary James indicated that the nuns have their own prayers and ritual and would not see me until midnight Mass.

This is my first Christmas alone. Even when I was on the streets, I had company. The Salvation Army provided meals, clothes, and for once omitted it's sermon. All the love and generosity that I'm surrounded by has not included me. I try to be philosophical. Yet my feelings are hurt. In a cynical moment, I think they love me not for who I am but for what I do. I allow myself to wallow for a moment and then thank God for his gifts.

After Mass, my congregation returns to their homes. I remove my vestments and return to my home. Greta is at my door, smiling. "Merry Christmas, Thomas. I brought some contraband, a crassly commercial Christmas card. I hope this outlawed piece of sinning won't lead you to perdition."

"Of course it will, Greta," I reply. "But I'm already past redemption for mentioning Santa Claus and his evil deed of giving presents."

She takes my arm. "I'll only stay a moment. Dad's asleep for Christmas. He must be an atheist to do that."

Greta smiles and hands me the card. "I made it myself. You can't buy one in town."

I open the envelope and take out the card. There are no pictures and no words.

"It's a card of Christmas hope," Greta says. "Whatever you wish, it says to you. Whatever you want, it draws for you. It's something like faith."

I shake my head and thank her. "I've never had a card like this."

"Now you have," she says and kisses me on my mouth. "Merry Christmas, Thomas."

She turns to leave. "I'd like to stay, but I have to go."

I am discomfited, more upset than aroused. Not yet guilty and far from repentant. I shrug off my feelings and think of Christ. *Nothing else matters.*

I have no wish to dance at the edge of eternity, fracture my vows, and fall into an eternal abyss. I resolve to tell that to Greta.

Of course, I also understand. She's lonely.

CHAPTER 22

One evening in early February, I rock in my easy chair while outside a northern wind howls and piles snow against my back door. The storm door rattles, as if winter too, needed warmth. I lean back and dream of mountain meadows stroked by a warm Pacific breeze.

I read for a while, then go to bed and continue my dreams. At 3:00 AM, I'm rousted by the irritating jangle of the telephone. On the first ring, I knock it over and fumble in the darkness, finally reeling in the receiver by its cord. A breathless, urgent voice that I can't recognize accosts me. "Hurry, Father, she's dying. We've sent a vehicle for you."

"Who's dying? Who are you? What's this about?"

"No time to explain. Please hurry."

I stumble into my jeans and T-shirt and grab my emergency kit. Snow is piled against my house. I am unable to get out and need to raise the garage door to gain an exit. Slaps of wind drive my collar against my face. As I leave, snow drifts into my garage propping the overhead door ajar.

An old maroon all-wheel drive pickup truck idles outside my house. Its wheels reach past my waist, and I nearly need a ladder to reach the cab. In the back of the truck is a load of sand bags, presumably for traction. Behind the black metal front bumper is a winch whose cable ends in a metal hook.

The passenger door is open, and I climb in. Hunched over the steering wheel is a stranger. He appears to be about eighteen years old and greets me with a few mumbled phrases.

"I'm Fred York," he says, "I'm s'posed to come and get you and take you to the farm."

I ask him for details, but he is silent now and picks at a pustule while he plows through the snowdrifts. No road is visible, so he aligns himself six feet from the utility poles. He misjudges and the truck lists precipitously. He is unperturbed; and while I cling to the door, he shifts down and careens sharply to level ground.

In the distance, a glow of lights appears on the horizon. From a farmhouse, subdued orange lights project from the window, and incongruously, remind me of a Halloween pumpkin.

Fred slides his truck to a full stop and jumps out to open the truck door for me. "This way," he says and propels me by my arm.

Death has an aura. The stench of dying defines itself. Decay assails my nostrils, and I swallow against my rising nausea.

Pale and sallow faced, a young woman is propped on a narrow bed. Black rims circle her sunken eyes that raise themselves tentatively toward me, then fall away with the effort. Each breath begins heavily, then truncates before it is full, impeded by the pain in her gut. Her face, the color of cold, gray porridge, reminds me of a starving prisoner. She nods on the verge of sleep. Neck veins fill then collapse in synchrony with every shallow breath.

She tries to moisten her cracked lips, extends her hand to me but collapses with the effort. In the dimness of candlelight, her pupils are black, dilated to the whites of her eyes.

I am stunned and call out, "Somebody get an ambulance. She needs a doctor. She needs to be in hospital. She needs oxygen, an intravenous."

There is no response. They look at me as if I were a lunatic, out of contact with reality.

"Well, if you don't do something, I will."

I lunge for the phone. Willem's hand immobilizes my wrist. Softly he whispers. "There appears to be a misunderstanding or at least a paucity of information. Christine, our sister in Christ, suffers from a terminal illness. She wishes to be anointed before her passage. She is of age and wishes no further medical intervention. She has a living will. We respect her wishes. Her lawyer and doctor are present."

Kneeling in the darkness at the foot of Christine's bed are two bowed figures with their hoods pulled over their foreheads. Side by side, the knight advocate and knight physician pray for the sinner. One knight holds a crucifix with both hands, and the other advances the beads of his rosary. His whisper is audible in the quiet room. He prays, "Hail Mary full of grace."

I feel like an ignorant fool and mumble, "I'm sorry. I didn't know."

From the deathbed, the girl's eyes glance toward me, and her lips move in a barely heard whisper. I hear the words. "Bless me, Father . . ." Her hand reaches toward me, and then falls under its weight. I pick up her dropped crucifix and replace it into her hands. Slowly she clasps her fingers around the cross. My eyes sting from the smoke of a hundred candles.

I motion others away from the bed, out of earshot, as she seeks to be reconciled to life everlasting. Final confession is to God alone. A tear trickles down her cheek. My eyes mist as I absolve her. With a trembling hand, I place the body of Christ on her parched tongue. Holy oil anoints her, and I pray that she is pleasing in the sight of God. My hand shakes as holy water sprinkles on her like rain on desert sand.

All is quiet; until her rasping breathing escalates for a few moments then yields to a final gasp and stops forever.

Her mother, who has been constantly at her bedside, embraces her child and with her tears anoints her; tears more holy than any oil that I possess.

Willem and the two knights are at my side.

"You can go now, Father," Willem says. "We'll look after things from here. There is nothing more you can do."

Anger wells within in me. I maintain my voice just above a whisper. "Who do you think you are, Willem? Are the parents to be abandoned in their need? Shall I not try to bring the blessing of Christ to them? I'm not the wash machine repairman who's hired to do the job then dismissed. It is my duty to help—and my privilege. Move aside."

I take a step toward Christine's father. Roger York's shoulders are bent in defeat. The inevitable has marched over him and engulfed his will. "Thank you for bestowing the sacrament, Father. We don't wish to talk now. Her dying, in the end, was inevitable. Please visit us another time. Thank you for coming."

From the edge of my vision, I see Sister Mary James move toward the corpse with a basin and washcloth. She lifts a naked lifeless leg and begins. Wilma springs from her chair and pushes sister aside. Water splashes on to the floor. Wilma's face is contorted in anger. She points to the door. Sister leaves. Her head is held high, and she stares at me too long as she takes her exit.

Roger York sees me to the door and helps me climb into the idling truck. Fred York forges through snowdrifts in his monster truck. I try to make small talk: "Do you go to school?" "Do you work?" "Did you build this truck?"

I am answered in short words: "Yup." "Yup." "Nope."

He plows through snow drifts and finally halts beside my garage. As I leave, I say, "I'm sorry—."

He interrupts. "Me too. She didn't have to die." With those words, he drops the clutch and aims his truck toward home.

My night is spent in turmoil. Fred York's words unnerve me. *Is it from anger that he speaks or is there substance? No one gives me answers. What was her illness? Where was she when the church could comfort her? Could I not have counseled her, prayed for her soul, and eased her burden?* I try to imagine her in health, in the joy of life. I cannot. A skeletal mask obliterates my imagination. No one asked for prayers on her behalf. Now, in the hour of her death, she seeks the Church. I can understand. Fear is often the portal to God. Much good is accomplished in the eleventh hour.

CHAPTER 23

Winter's whipping blizzard abates overnight and surrenders to a brilliant morning sun. The peaceful shores of the Marsalaat beckon, and I indulge myself in a miniretreat. Sunglasses and light clothing are all the equipment I need. Peter's gift of snowshoes is now comfortable on my feet, and I've mastered them on a horizontal surface. As I trek across the snow and ice, I need to remind myself that the river, now hidden, still flows below. A slight breeze cools my brow. Snow and drifts have a sculpture of their own. Like in clouds, I see shapes and faces and amuse myself with this childhood pastime. Nature lifts my spirits. I offer a silent prayer for Christine York and return to my home.

It is my duty to comfort the bereaved, and their right to receive comfort from the church. Mounds of pushed up snow, like giant furrows, outline Johnsburgh's streets. I drive the old Chevy to the York farm. *What words can I say that have meaning and have not been said before?* I discard them all—the Lord giveth, mysterious ways, rewards in heaven, God's will. *What can I say to ease their pain?* Nothing.

Roger and Wilma rock in the two-seater swing on the verandah. Slowly, with excess effort, they rise at my approach. Eyes, still red from weeping, look into mine for a moment, and then look away. Roger's trembling hand reaches toward me. Wilma too shakes my hand with a grip firmer than Roger's. He points to a chair with a listless wave of his beefy hand. He still wears yesterday's work clothes and suspenders. The gray stubble of his beard attests to physical neglect.

Wilma raises her eyes and glances briefly in my direction. I clear my throat and begin to express my sorrow. "Before you go on, Father, please read this," she says.

She hands me one sheet of paper, unfolded.

> *I, Christine York, am of sound mind. I have a fatal illness.*
> *It is my wish as an autonomous human being that I receive no*
> *medical attention to alter the natural course of my disorder. I*
> *wish no painkillers, antibiotics, blood transfusions, or any other*
> *medical intervention.*

"Forgive me, I am ignorant. What was her illness?"

Wilma clenches a handful of hair in both her hands. She continues, quiet now, her voice barely a whisper. "My daughter was pregnant. We never knew the father. She said that he was very important and promised him that he would not reveal his name. She was a stubborn child and faithful to him. She tried for an abortion, impossible in this town. Tried it herself, botched it. We pleaded with her to get medical help. Offered to take her to Chicago. She refused. Stubbornness became intransigence.

"Christine turned to her former teacher. Sister Mary James counseled her while Willem DeRooy prayed for her soul.

"Christine became entrenched. She vowed to endure the consequence of her actions and place her faith in God.

"The sisters and knights were constantly at her bedside." Wilma's tears well at the memory. "All my prayers and supplications were like water on sand. She ran a terrible fever and became delirious. My child bled from her lacerated womb and burned in her private hell that the gushing of her blood could never quench."

Roger sighs. "Willem DeRooy was immovable. 'It is God's will,' he said. 'She prepares herself for a high place in heaven.' There was nothing we could do."

Roger holds his head in his hands and watches his own tears splatter on the floor. His wife is dry-eyed now and watches with a pained expression. Someone has kicked her in the guts.

From the far side of the porch, one obscene word intrudes. "Bullshit." Fred York, the son, the brother, spits the word through clenched teeth. "Bullshit. It's all bullshit. My sister didn't have to die. You could have just taken her to Chicago before Sister and that pervert DeRooy got to her."

Roger knots his fist. "I'll have none of that in my house, buster."

The son's eyes clash with his father's. "It's our house, and I hope I never get sick here." He turns and marches into the house. In a few minutes, he returns with his travel bag and winter jacket.

"I'm leaving," he hisses. "It's too easy to die here."

From the driveway, his monster truck growls to life and hurls shards of snow and ice onto the receding house.

I search for words of solace and find no printing on the page. Roger takes my arm and guides me to my car. He opens the door, and helps me to my seat, with a gentle arm across my back.

Slowly, I return to my home. I have no balm to ease their pain. Their grief's so strong that words cannot describe. Fury is so deep that it chokes expression. Rage burns and holds the tears that I might have shed for them.

I kneel before the altar of my god and bow before his might. I pray for understanding, of the kind that brings wisdom after prayer and meditation. I pray but cannot find the answers to an assisted suicide, that's forbidden by my religion, and the feelings of my heart.

Dressed in white satin and a wreath of flowers in her hair, Christine York holds a bouquet of freesias in her hand. Entwined among the flowers is a rosary of crystal beads and agate cross. Serene in death, she lies in her coffin. It's velvet lining comforts her on this her final journey. What transformation has occurred? Christine's face, at peace, seems youthful. Eyes are closed as if in sleep. The scent of freesias wafts toward me, almost unearthly in their perfume.

A procession files past. Some dare not look, and others stare at the floor as they pass by. Some pause, bow their heads, and some touch her in a final goodbye. Roger stands and watches his tears wash over her hands. He stoops to kiss her forehead and gently strokes her hair. Beside him, Wilma whispers a prayer and kisses her daughter's lips. At the end of the procession, Sister Mary James places a naked metal cross over Christine's heart. She does not touch her and does not stop to pray.

I recite the funeral Mass by rote. Christine's unnecessary death, imposed by excess piety and religious zeal, robs my words of meaning. *Lux perpetua* (perpetual light). *Requiem aeternum*—eternal rest grant unto her O Lord. I continue, "I am the resurrection and the life. She that believeth in me, though she were dead, yet shall she live: and whosoever liveth and believeth in me shall never die."

Sorrow is a contagious emotion. My parishioners weep and have no wish for consolation. On their knees and with bowed heads, my people pray. I am unable to pray with them and in my fury, I address them.

"Dearly beloved, does it require the darkness of death to see the light? Are you so blind that the luster of your souls lies buried beneath your vision? Christine died in the bloom of youth. Her very name—*Christ*ine, implies suffering, sacrifice, and devotion. She died to pay for what she perceived were her sins.

"I have her parents' permission to say she died as the consequence of a self-induced abortion. She sought counseling from Willem DeRooy and Sister Mary James. Both advised her to avoid medical help and let nature take its irrevocable course.

I scowl across the pulpit. "Willem and Mary, is this true? Are these statements accurate? I have no wish to cast you in a dark light. Speak now. Defend yourselves. Show us that you are human beings whose welfare for one another eclipses rigid doctrine."

I stand down from the pulpit and wait. Neither Willem nor Mary advances. They meet each other's gaze and exit the church.

For a few moments, I wait and face my silent congregation. "I believe that we are all accountable for our sins. I believe that sin requires forgiveness. Human failing does not always require punishment. All of us are weak. Shall we be beaten for our weakness?

"There are legitimate medical means to deal with the aftermath of attempted abortions Sir Knight, the doctor, knows full well. Where these means applied? No. Willem and Mary intimidated Christine. She became frightened and submitted. Sir Knight the lawyer is witness to her will.

"Christine need not have died. The whole practice of medicine is to delay death. Shall we deny our God-given intelligence? Shall we deny life to a young woman in the bloom of her future and condemn her to an untimely death?

"I ask you to love one another, to forgive, to comfort, and console. Death comes for us all in it's time. We all hope to live forever in the kingdom of God. No one has the right to hasten this."

I pause and look about. Do I expect an answer? "In the meantime, what are you prepared to do with your sorry plight? Will you continue to absorb this abuse? If you do nothing, you deserve what you get. Start. Do something."

I hammer at them, love one another, help one another, be kind. Sin requires reconciliation, not punishment. We all fail. Failure is not a sin."

There is a hole in the snow that leads to a hole in the ground. Christine's frozen plot of earth lies in wait to absorb her earthly remains. The sun shines in brilliance between dark clouds.

I seek out Willem at the school. On Mondays, at 9:00 AM, he reads Bible stories to the children. A child of about six holds a book while he sits on Willem's lap. The others are seated on the floor in a semicircle around him. On my entry he places a finger across his lips. He reads from a realistically depicted book. Jesus in a brown robe has found the sheep that is lost.

"Trust in Jesus," Willem says, "and pray to him." His soft hypnotic voice has the children's rapt attention. "When you don't know what to do, he will show the way." He closes the book. On its leather cover gold embroidery highlights the title, *Bible Stories for Children* by Willem DeRooy.

I think he is finished and say, "Good morning."

He holds his hand, palm toward me. "Please be patient, Father. We have more stories to read and talk about. Children too deserve undivided attention, even when adults are inconvenienced."

He continues with his stories. I'm sure I saw a slight smile play on his lips. After the children are dismissed, he takes my arm. "Come, Father, after your misguided tirade, we need to talk. Sister Mary James is expecting us."

She rises, and without greeting me, comes to the point. "Each of us has free will. It was Christine's choice to accept martyrdom as payment for her sins. Most of us are not blessed with that option. She, like the crusaders, offered her body for the absolution of sins. Hers was an act of bravery. I am dismayed that you belittle her faith. I fear that you are becoming secular."

I am appalled by the harshness of her stance. "Yes, Sister, each of us has free will. Slow suicide is also a choice, and so is assisted suicide. She need not have died. Kindness and human counsel could have saved her young life and modern medicine would help. Are we now so holy that we believe the wages of sin is death? Have you no compassion, or do you tread the razor edge of homicide."

Sister reddens and spittle gathers at the corners of her mouth. "You're a green pup, Thomas. She was brave and is an example of Christian valor. We seek to build strength in our community. She was a martyr. You have a different view than ours. We have the right to what we believe, and you have not the right to impose yours.

"Perhaps you are unaware of our mission. We support fundamental Christianity, no compromises. Christ died cruelly for our sins. We share his pain and offer it for the forgiveness of our sins. Our mission is to teach this lesson to the world."

I shake my head and say, "Invincible ignorance at best, sadism at worst."

Willem is calm. "We have the children all week. Rant and rave for twenty minutes each Sunday. We can undo your best, and worst."

Indeed, I rant and rave at every opportunity that comes my way. I preach Christian charity, ordinary charity. Love one another. Help one another. Catholicism is not a test of strength. It is measure of how much we love one another and help the weak. Even in our weakness, God sent his only son to save us. He did not ask that only the strong enter the kingdom. Love, forgiveness, charity, prayer, and help, these are what I have to offer.

Does what I say make a difference? I hope so.

My faith is lifted. An unexpected source supports my cause. On the front page of the *Johnsburgh Herald* is an editorial authored by Michael Grizkovich.

> Father Thomas Spanner has demonstrated a grasp of the obvious. Something's rotten in Johnsburgh. In a brave and naïve confrontation, he challenged the Knights of Columbus. Challenged, where it matters most, their spiritual foundation.
>
> Yet Spanner's concerns reach beyond the spiritual. He points out that we are first and foremost human. He is adamant that our joy, our focus, and our duty is to love one another. After this all else is easy.
>
> His generous approach clashes with the Johnsburgh tradition that man is evil, sinful, and must suffer to be redeemed.
>
> To what end this suffering? Is there more too it than spirituality? Where is the grand knight? Has he nothing to say? Or is he too involved with fiscal matters to address our concerns? Has he delegated the spiritual and neglected to hold accounting?
>
> If this were only religious debate dancing on the pinheads of ineffectual religious, it would not matter. But it does matter. The community suffers. Were it not for excess zeal, there is an excellent possibility that Christine York would be alive today.
>
> On a wider scale, could this tragedy have been avoided by effective birth control and access to legal abortion? Access is readily available in Chicago, one hour by jet, but not here.
>
> Spanner is wedged between a medieval Catholicism and humanity. Is the church more important than its members? He can expect no help from the sisters, the knights, or his church. Where can he turn? There is only one place, the flock that he cherishes.

CHAPTER 24

Routine once again enters my life. At morning Mass, the sisters sit in the front row. A few elderly people are maneuvered into the aisle seats by steadier hands. I preach no sermons at these times. It is traditional. My people come only for Mass and Communion. Often I walk along the aisle and watch the old folk as their folded hands shake. I place the host on trembling tongues and say, *Corpus Christi* (body of Christ).

After Mass, I too have my routine. There are no senior's homes in Johnsburgh. It's relatives who care for the ill. I visit the frail and infirm in their houses. I am free to make clerical house calls and bring the hope of salvation and body of Christ. Many are too frail to leave their homes and ask me to say a morning Mass. I say an abbreviated but valid version.

After my visits, I return to my home and find my desk littered with folded paper and crayon decorations. A kaleidoscope of colors greets me: bright red, blue, green, and yellow. Written on the cards are greetings—"We love you, Father. Happy Valentine's Day, because you're nice." I know the sisters organized this. Nevertheless, I'm touched and read my cards again. There are more cards in a day than I've had in a lifetime. Sweet.

I look out my window. Winter, aided by low cloud, asserts its presence. Usually no children are allowed in the playground for lunch and recess because when they return, their wet clothing makes puddles on the floor. Today, two boys, about eight years old, stand at attention with their hands behind their backs. Neither wears a shirt. Do they think snow is sand, and the sun will turn them brown? I hurry toward them.

"What do you boys think you're doing?"

Neither speaks or moves. I take them each by the wrist and lead them to the school. They dig in their barefoot heels. "We're not going."

"And why not?"

Sister Mary James steps in front of me. The boys again stand at attention.

"Billy, you can go in now," she says in a matter of fact tone. "Sid, you've got ten minutes more."

She turns to me. "You can go back to your room, Father. This has nothing to do with you. It's a matter of school discipline."

I feel like yelling but maintain control. "It does have to do with me. I am their shepherd also. This corporal punishment smacks of child abuse."

"Very well," she says, and shrugs her shoulder. She remains cooler than the winter air. "I suppose we'll have to talk about this. 6:00 PM., my office."

She grinds a heel into the snow as she turns to leave. "Ten more minutes, Sid."

Words from the past come to my mind: short words, four letters, five max. I am furious. My jaw muscles twitch, fists knot, heart races. I've been dismissed like a school boy: "Go to your room." Arrogance. My afternoon is spent recalling the scene. I become more agitated, miss lunch, and drink coffee.

At six, Sister Theresa shows me to the conference room. Others besides the sisters are at the table.

"I've decided to clear the air once and for all," Sister Mary James scowls. "The entire school board is here. Mr. Lewis is our leader. The rest are duly elected members. As you can also see, the entire teaching staff is present."

Lewis stands, his hairline has receded to mid scalp. As if compensating, his sideburns are overgrown and reach below his earlobes. His fingers are stubby, and the nails are filled with ground in dirt.

He calls the meeting to order. Then, peering at me, he says, "Father, I'm quite reluctant to be here on such short notice. The sisters are upset and insist we meet. They feel you interfered with the disciplinary function of the school and virtually accused them of child abuse."

"There are other means of discipline that do not include shirtless boys standing at attention outside in the middle of winter. It is inhumane."

"Of course," says Lewis, "that's your opinion, and we respect that; but there are other opinions. Let me refer you to chapter 17 of the school constitution."

The knot in my stomach tightens. Lewis hands me a paper. "This is Sister Mary James version of this morning's events. Do you have any comments?"

Lewis continues, "I quote, 'Our teachers are free to discipline our children in a manner they deem appropriate, providing no lasting injury ensues."

Sister rises, "Perhaps Father is unused to our ways. We take actions that make an impression. Our aim is to build character through discipline. It may seem harsh. However, we have near-zero alcoholics, little mental illness, and only one drug addict in living memory."

She glares at me. "Besides, Father, school discipline is not your jurisdiction."

She hasn't touched me, yet I feel like I've been spanked.

"I don't know why we even had this meeting," Lewis says. "The school mandate is clear enough. We have to go by the democratically drawn charter. And we just can't change it when somebody disagrees. You should know that, Father."

Sister sits with her hands tucked into her sleeves.

"Does anybody want to say anything?" Lewis asks. "Or can I go home for a late supper?"

I repeat myself. "There are other means of discipline, more effective, more humane, and more sound psychologically. Violence only perpetuates itself."

"Yes, yes, Father. We know your views, but this is hardly violence. If you wish to change the system, please present your brief to the school board. I'm going for supper."

The room empties as if on cue. I am alone, and my mind has only one word for company, *shit*.

I return home and slither past Greta's office. She's working late, and her door is open. She stares at her computer and gnaws on her pencil.

My ego still smarts, and I feel the need to talk. I tap on the door. She replies with one hand in the air as if stopping traffic. In a few moments, the noise of the printer tells me her task is complete. A wisp of hair dangles on her forehead, and she blows it into place with an upward current. She stretches, places her hands behind her head, and yawns. I note the swell of her breasts against her blouse as she inhales.

"Well," she says, "how did it go?"

"How did what go?"

"You know perfectly well what I mean. How was the meeting with the school board and the sisters?"

"Awesome," I say. "How could you know about that already?"

She stands, folds her arms across her chest, and frowns. "People tell me things, Thomas. Tell me things that don't sit right. Tell me things they tell no one else. I'm nondenominational. I don't ask for penance. I don't blab. I don't advise. But that's not why they tell. They tell because they have a need, a need to get words off their chest, off their mind. Things seem less threatening once they're said. Things they can't tell their wives. Things they won't tell their pastor."

She pauses, rotating her neck to ease the tension. "So, Thomas, how did it go?"

I meet candor with candor.

"It went very well," I reply. "I never knew castration could be so painless."

She laughs and says, "Is that so bad for a priest?"

Her deep blue eyes penetrate mine. For the first time, I notice flecks of a lighter blue that pattern the dark. I look away and laugh, "I thought I was supposed to hear confessions, not you."

She sighs, stretches her arms, braces her shoulders, and looks at her watch. "That's enough for one day. You look like you could use a drink, Father. I could too. Can you make iced tea?"

She makes herself at home in my home, sits in my easy chair, and kicks off her shoes. "So," she says, with a trace of a smile. "What do you think of sister now?"

I exhale. "She's a tough nut. She spanked me with a book of rules. Reluctantly, I admire her expertise. If this were the army, I'd do push-ups and salute her. I just don't agree that harshness begets kindness."

Greta smiles. "Welcome to Johnsburgh where it is not enough to be merely holy."

She closes her eyes for a moment and sips her tea. "You're a good bartender, sir. I should come here more often."

"You're welcome as often as you like," I say, and then add, "I'm sorry, that's so trite and hackneyed."

"Don't worry, Thomas. It's supposed to sound like that coming from you, but thanks anyway."

I am embarrassed. I think I actually blush.

"Have you been working here for a while?" I ask.

She laughs that alluring rumble from deep in her throat. "Oh, I love it. That's even better than do you come here often?"

Greta yawns then slips on her shoes. She hesitates a moment, smiles wanly, "Give me a hug, Thomas, and I'll leave quietly."

CHAPTER 25

Morning Mass brings only the few who prepare themselves for the grave. *What has happened in their lives that they so vigorously pursue sanctity?* No sisters attend. None will break ranks.

I'm still fuming. It is unfair. The premises are false. Punishment is inhumane for so small a deed. One boy called the other a homosexual and received a punch in return. The talker got fifteen minutes in the cooler; the puncher, thirty.

I prepare my Sunday sermon. Sunday Mass is mandatory. Sister Mary James has not yet won. I have a psychology degree and am not totally defeated. I begin. "Dear Christians, believers in Christ, followers of Christ, find for me anywhere in the Bible where Christ caused another to suffer, humiliated another, or struck him. I defy you. Yes, he even cast the moneychangers out of the temple with words.

"Kindness breeds kindness. If I have a dog that loves me, pleases me, and follows my wishes, I have no need to shout or beat him with a stick. It is natural for him to obey and love me in return. If I have another dog and beat him when he ignores my commands, or shout when he disobeys, should I be surprised that one day he bites me?

"If I have a child who punches another, what will he learn if I also punch him? Perhaps, it's better that I show him he lost a friend, and help him to mend the wound. Or shall I banish him to the cold?"

I pause and stare at Sister Mary James. My mind plays tricks. I see the middle finger of her left hand rise in the air and a smile on her lips. For a moment, I lose the thread of my talk.

"Dearly beloved, I have a degree in psychology from the University of Washington. All that I've learned and all that I know say kindness begets kindness. Retribution begets retribution. Let us pray for understanding and compassion. We are created in the image of Christ. Christ did not cause us to suffer."

I continue with the Mass. The custom at Communion has been to place the host on the sister's tongues. Today, their mouths are shut, and they hold out their hands to receive the body of Christ. I'm distressed at their stance, yet gratified that I still serve my function—to dispense the living body of Christ to their souls.

In the afternoon, I put on my snowshoes and trek across the frozen Marsalaat. There are times I just need to get away, to exercise and clear my mind. Snow is clean on the other side. There are no tracks and no dirt. Here the cranberry fields lie buried. In a few months, dead branches will bud and yield in abundance.

How shall I make peace with the sisters? Obviously, we cannot continue this low-grade war. In the afternoon, I phone Grizkovich and invite him for dinner.

"Why dinner?" he says. "You know you can't cook. I know you've been freeloading every Sunday, and even sandwiches are beyond you. You can't even boil a hotdog."

My face reddens. "I'll have you know that I'm quite capable."

"Sure, sure," he says, "but I've got a problem. I've been ice fishing, and I don't want to freeze everything I've caught. There's nothing tastier than a winter char—fresh, firm, delicious. Why don't you pop over?"

Gizkovich lives in a shack on the river, upstream from town, a mile from his nearest neighbor. Snow hides moss-laden shingles. Icicles hang from the eaves and point freely to earth. No eaves trough blocks their path. I look for a rusty stovepipe protruding from the roof. Incongruously, it's a granite chimney that extends beyond the gable.

Old wooden-framed windows, each with a central latch, are recessed into walls lined with vertical boards. I knock on the door and avoid the splintered sun-beaten plywood. I shrug and wonder at Mike's income bracket. Perhaps he spends too much on fishing gear.

He opens the door and shakes my hand. "Welcome, Father. I'm so glad you make house calls."

He closes the door and clicks it shut with a large latch. My mouth refuses to shut. Plush Persian carpets cover polished oak floors. A floor-to-ceiling granite fireplace with a rounded front occupies the northwest corner. *Elegance* is the word for his kitchen. Intriguing. The den boasts computers, fax, telephone, and strange electronic arrays. Indicator lights of yellow red and green blink like a miniature traffic display.

"God," I say. "Jesus. Holy smoke."

Mike just laughs. "Did you think I was a bum? I run a first-rate newspaper and need to know what happens in the rest of the world and relay it to the locals."

I nod my head in agreement. "From the outside, it sure looks like a bum lives here. From inside, it's quite cozy."

"It's nice here." He smiles. "And it's fire proof and bullet proof. It's hard to believe, but there are actually people who don't like me. And I bet there are some who don't like you either. If you need to hide out from the sisters, phone me and come running."

"So you've heard?"

"Of course," he says, "it's my business to hear. There'll be a small editorial in tomorrow's paper."

I look around. "Why do you need all this?"

"Some of it is because of hunters. They'll break in, or shoot the place up or light it on fire. I've got a lot of expensive electronic equipment, and I don't want it destroyed by shotgun pellets. I'd be grateful if you wouldn't tell anybody about the décor."

He opens the fridge and takes a beer for himself. I get a can of Coke. "So," he says, "what's on your mind? Are you losing the power struggle, or would you like to run for school board and have me endorse you?"

"They're so archaic and practice poor psychology. There's no need for this. I suppose they still use the strap too."

"Would you like to send a letter to the editor and outline your position? Have you anything to add to your Sunday sermon?"

I shrug and sip my Coke. He swigs his beer, thankfully not Coors, but Heineken in little undersized green bottles. He puts another log on the fire and sits in his armchair.

"You know what I think, Thomas? I think you've lost a useless war in a teacup. Let it rest. You've alienated the sisters by telling them how to do their job. So how are you going to solve this dilemma?"

He stops for a moment, opens another beer, and lets out a deliberate belch. "If I were you, I'd be patient and lose this little difference of opinion. Roll over like a dog. Kiss a bit of holy ass. It's good humility training. You need the sisters. Besides, he laughs, wait till the wetbacks get here. You'll have enough human rights and equality issues to piss everybody off. But do yourself a favor. Talk to me before you ride off with a lance on a white horse."

I'm taken aback. "You want me to capitulate?"

"No," he says, "not capitulation. Try diplomacy and manipulation. Confrontation only breeds entrenchment. Why be assertive when you can't be effective?"

On my way home, I ruminate. I will endeavor to ameliorate sister's harshness.

I request an appointment with Sister Mary James. "I'd like to meet with you so that we can resolve this issue."

"There is no issue, Thomas. We act according to our democratic directives and in the interest of the children. There is not even a point of compromise or discussion."

I am unable even to save face. I follow Grizkovich's advice and roll over. "Is there anything I can do to repair the damage?"

She smiles. It is the first time I have seen her teeth.

"Why, it's easy. What you say in public, you rectify in public. Just say it so you don't appear wishy-washy. You are, after all, our spiritual leader."

I begin my sermon. "Give into Caesar those things that are Caesar's and unto God those things that are God's. Also give to the school board and teachers the right to teach their children. While I am entitled to my opinion, majority decision must prevail. This is not a matter of faith or morals. Since I have exercised my rights to no avail, I have decided to cease and desist."

I assume my words were satisfactory. I'm invited for afternoon tea. Chocolates are passed. On a plate beside my tea is a cardboard cut out of a crow and a saltshaker. Beneath are the words—*you do it so well.* I look about sternly. It is no use; we join in the relief that laughter brings us.

Puddles form on the slush-covered Marsalaat. Near the shoreline, black earth absorbs the sun's rays and forms a rim of clear water.

Across the river, still buried below a protective blanket of snow, cranberry fields lie dormant and await their resurrection. Spring and the Mexicans bring warmth to rejuvenate a new crop. It seems a long journey from the Gulf of Mexico, then northward against Mississippi current to follow lakes and rivers to Johnsburgh's shores. Grizkovich tells me the route is easy if you can find it. Mostly, it seems, the wetbacks just appear about the same time as the bushes green.

Wetbacks live in their own world on the other side of the river. Only men work the farms. Families are Mexican and belong in Mexico. People tell me, "They've got it good, you know. They get a free ride to and from Mexico and have a barrack with bunk beds and a kitchen. The farmers make sure they're warm and fed and dry. In some places, like in California, they sleep under cardboard or under branches. We even have latrines built by the community. And they're paid real good by Mexican standards."

I have heard the litany a dozen times. It is plausible. Yet somehow I have reservations. Above all, it becomes clear to me that "living in their own world" means not welcome to mix with our world. By some pact with the devil, Mexicans are barred from Mass.

In my mind, it is not right to deprive those in the fold of the sacraments. They too are part of the human family and have a need to reconcile their sins. Everyone is entitled to partake of Christ's body and blood. I will take Christ to the workers. It is my mission.

But first, I seek advice from Grizkovich. "I hear you. And that's all I have to say about that. Size it up. Shut your mouth and watch your ass. I won't help you get yourself killed."

I decide to ask Willem for help. He harbors no rancor for my outburst at Christine's death. He stands in my den, warms his hands at the fireplace.

"Funny," he says, "it's spring, but I still enjoy a fire. Have you noticed how it can be warm in the day and still freeze at night?"

This chatter surprises me. Until now, Willem was distant, at times antagonistic. I am happy he's talking.

"Don't you find it strange," I ask, "that you and I have had only a few meetings." Willem's face is placid, not so much as a raised eyebrow. He fidgets with his hands.

"I don't know if this is a good time to bring it up, Willem, but I wanted to talk to you about the Mexican problem."

He smiles, a sort of rueful, half smile. "Now is not a good time. There is no Mexican problem; no problem at all unless you choose to create one."

I choose to create a problem. On Sundays I have everyone's attention and deliver my sermon. "I am privileged to be part of this community and serve your spiritual needs. On a larger scale we are all a part of the world community. This includes those itinerant workers from whose labor we profit and who enhance our material well-being.

"We are all equal in the sight of God. From many of you I've heard reference to the Mexicans. I have yet to meet one, and none have attended our church. Brothers and sisters in Christ, I would be grateful if you'd bring your workers to Sunday Mass so they too may reap the benefit of Christ's sacrifice. Please extend our hospitality to others of the human family."

I look about me. A fly in the church attracts more attention than my voice. Two children play in the aisle. A woman stifles a yawn and nudges her hat over her face. Another is not as polite. Even from here, I can see the fillings in her back teeth. Some of the men stare at a spot on the ceiling. I doubt it's a holy image.

During Communion, they are humble and dutiful. At the end of Mass, the church empties rapidly, like gravel from a dump truck. Today, they seem reluctant to socialize.

Sunday after Sunday, I preach brotherhood. "I know some of you must speak Spanish. Ask our Mexican brothers to partake." Nothing happens. In my church, it's only the farmer's faces that attain a brownish hue. None are a natural brown. I am angry and determined to minister to God's Mexican children.

III-MISSIONARY

CHAPTER 26

I drive to the Mexican side of the river only to be blocked by a barricade and sign—Private Property. No Trespassing. I shift into a lower gear and crash through the barricade. One hundred yards farther, Rudy's police cruiser blocks my route. Since drainage ditches parallel the road, there's no room to get around. Rudy and his deputy are cheerful. Billy removes his hat and gives a half-hearted wave.

Rudy stands with his hands on his hips.

"Mornin', Father," he drawls. "Great day for a drive."

"Yes, it is. Would you please move, so I can get by?"

"You must have missed the sign, Padre. It says, No Trespassing. So turn around and go back."

"I'm here on God's business. I'm going to say Mass for the Mexicans."

"Well, ain't that special," Rudy grins, "I don't recall that God has a seat on council. Aside from that, he never comes to meetings. Not even DeRooy has his proxy."

"I suppose you think that's funny, Rudy. Move aside, you're starting to piss me off."

He laughs and doubles over in enjoyment at my crudity. Billy too thinks it's a joke. Rudy takes a step toward me.

"You must have taken a wrong turn. Mexico's the other way. Now swing around or I'll arrest you. I have a witness. I'll read you your rights and arrest you. When we get to the precinct, you'll get your phone call and due process. If you can't afford a lawyer, one will be assigned to you."

I refuse to move. "Well," he says, "you can be like Christ or be like Gandhi. But I still have a job to do. The law applies to everybody."

He reads Miranda and places handcuffs around my wrists. Hands in front this time, gentler as well. He pushes on my head as

I slide into the cruiser. This time there is no Peter on a white horse charging through the iron bars and granting me salvation.

I make my one phone call. Grizkovich laughs as I tell him my predicament. "I'm your lawyer," Grizkovich says, "what now, Thomas?

"Get me out of here."

"Sure. Have you got bail money?"

Mike talks to Rudy who phones Peter. Rudy opens the cell and points to the door. He has a smirk on his face as he looks forward to another round.

I sit beside Mike in his beat-up jeep. He's still laughing. "Guess you lost that round," he laughs. "This is going to make a juicy article in tomorrow's paper. Can you see it? CHURCH VERSUS STATE. Score: State, 1."

"I'm glad you think it's funny, Mike. Why are they so determined to keep me from the Mexicans?"

"Who are they?

"The farmers of course."

"Are you sure about that? Why would they object to a priest who teaches obedience, humility, give unto Caesar and turn the other cheek. You're perfect, Thomas. Your church espouses subservience. Why would any farmer object?"

"You're toying with me, Mike. There's something I don't know. So why don't you quit screwing around and spit it out."

He still grins, lopsided like a Halloween pumpkin.

"Well, I guess, the community had one negative experience. You're hired as their priest. They pay you and house you. Let me spell it out—Mexicans are here to work. Not to become American citizens with the help of a bleeding heart preacher."

The Mexican issue frustrates me. I cannot understand the community's resistance. I've vowed to be apolitical, but they don't believe me. I talk to Grizkovich, Greta, Peter, and even Rudy. Rudy is blunt. "Barnes tried to unite the countries, put ideas into their heads, and made them think they were entitled to everything American. Then lawyers and immigration got involved, and we nearly went under. I think you'd do the same thing, 'cause you're a pussy like Barnes. That's why you're going to keep away from the Mexicans, and that's over my dead body."

I ask Peter. "How can I minister to the least of these if I am denied access?" He is unsympathetic. "Why don't you move to Mexico, Tijuana, perhaps? You could get your fill of sin and corruption, perhaps even a dose."

"I'm getting a dose of obstruction here," I reply, "I don't have to move for that."

He laughs. "Very good, Thomas. The answer is still no. The reasons are obvious."

I return to my room. It is difficult to pray in anger. Instead, I plot and scheme. But nothing comes to mind. I am outnumbered and outmaneuvered.

I think Sister Mary James has given me a reprieve. From time to time, I'm invited for tea and scones. I hold the delicate china cup between my thumb and finger. The fragile porcelain is painted with pale pink oriental blossoms. Lightly veined leaves blend subtly into the background. I place the cup in its saucer, carefully since I want no chips. If only my question to sister could be phrased as delicately.

"I'm curious, Sister. I've been inviting the Mexican farm workers to Mass for three weeks now, and none have appeared. I don't understand. Is there an explanation?"

"Yes," she says, "there is. There are probably several. Some are plausible, some facetious, and others rude. For one, you haven't asked the Mexicans to attend Mass. You've only asked others to ask in your stead. You haven't deigned to do missionary work."

"That's a problem. I don't speak Spanish."

"Are you incapable of learning? Are there no audiotapes, videos, computer programs, and no people to talk to? Surely someone in Johnsburgh speaks Spanish and would be happy to tutor."

Her lips move in suggestion of a smile. "On the other hand, the Mexicans may not wish to attend your church."

"They are Catholic, aren't they?"

"How do you know? Perhaps they're Anglicans." She pauses for a moment." More tea, Father?"

I understand. There is a lesson in the question she asks, and the answer resides in the question. I nod. "Thank you, Sister."

Her smile is wider now. "Ignorance is not always invincible."

She pats at the corners of her mouth with an embroidered cloth serviette and folds her hands on her lap."

"I must quit teasing you, Thomas, even though it's so easy and so much fun."

I have an inane desire to chew my fingernails. My zeal and righteousness are stuck in neutral. I thank sister for her kindness and advice.

She agrees. "I've been kind, Thomas, but I've given you no advice."

Of course, I haven't done my homework. Now I am determined. I learn Spanish, the Mexican version—no lisp. I've obtained a keypad translator, tapes, books in Spanish, and correspondence courses. In a few weeks, Sister Mary James stops me after morning Mass, "Buenos dias. Como esta usted?"

"Muy bien," I reply.

"Well, it's a start. We've decided to offer our assistance, Thomas. Each morning, after Mass, one of us is willing to tutor you for an hour, before breakfast, while you're still hungry."

My head nods in agreement before I find words to reply.

I am an enthusiastic pupil and apply myself religiously, if I may use the word.

Why can't I leave well enough alone? Must I unsettle the order of things? I know that most Mexicans live across the Marsalaat, in a shelter of sorts. I am not easily deterred. It is not in my nature. Obstacles serve only to fuel my determination. On Sunday afternoon, I become devious and pretend to go on my jog. I have ceased haranguing my flock and no longer accuse them of bigotry. Also, my futile efforts at a triumphant march into Mexico have come to a halt.

I jog on the riverbank and continue unnoticed. In my backpack are the tools of my trade: chalice, wine, hosts, stole. In my missionary heart, a mounting excitement gathers. Two miles downstream a fallen tree spans a narrow part of the Marsalaat. I follow tracks and find the Mexican's dwelling. It is an army barracks with cots, shower, and kitchen. Outside is a trench latrine.

My stole and collar are the beacons I carry. I hear voices from the barracks and enter uninvited. At first, they move from me until I address them in Spanish.

"Brothers in Christ," I begin. "I am Father Thomas Spanner, and I have come to share the miracle of the Mass with you."

I hold out my arms like Christ on the cross and invite them to partake of the miracle. A short leathery-faced worker comes near and kneels at my feet. Others embrace me and kiss my hands. In unison, they kneel before me and wait for me to begin. Just before Communion, I announce, "God has given me the power to forgive your sins. If in your heart you are contrite and seek forgiveness, you are now forgiven. As you are forgiven, you may now receive communion."

I am elated as they kneel to receive their god. I place the host on their tongues—*body of Christ*. I turn from the last communicant. Tears of joy still fill his eyes.

A tall Mexican marches toward me. He raises an angry voice to the workers. Then points at them and yells something in Spanish. They scurry out en masse. He taps my shoulder, points to the door, and leaves.

It is the pinnacle of my life. The Mexicans hunger for the Mass, and thanks to God's grace, I have delivered the sacrament. My mission is successful and I hope, again, to bring them the miracle of the Mass.

CHAPTER 27

I retrace my steps to the fallen tree. It lies in midriver where I cannot reach it. A few miles north the bridge spans the river. The center span is raised. It must have occurred spontaneously, since there is no attendant.

I know there are no houses on this side of the river. The idea of asking the Mexicans for shelter does not appeal to me. By tomorrow, at the latest, someone will come to my rescue. In the meantime, I sit by the river and offer up this minor inconvenience. Behind me the sun turns orange and bloats in its descent.

Nights now are above freezing. I am fortunate to have the opportunity to meditate, pray, and give thanks. But my attempt at prayer transmutes to anger. *Who dares bar Christ from his people?* Sister has given me part of the answer in general terms. *Who now directs the orchestra?*

I sit on the banks of the Marsalaat, hug my knees to my chest, and brood. Uncatholic words traverse my mind. Near dark I become aware of another presence. A canoe glides effortlessly along the Marsalaat and angles into shore. A voice assails me. "How! Me Pocahontas. Who you?"

Greta waves at me through the darkness and begins to giggle. "Need a lift, Father, or shall we just light a fire? I saw the bridge up," she adds, "and saw you leaving with your backpack. I put two and two together and launched my own rescue mission."

Awkwardly, I find the center of the canoe. "Sit in the middle," she says. "Hang on to the sides and just breathe."

She paddles smoothly upstream to my church. "Here we are. Time to get off. Good night, Father. There's more to this than you know. Perhaps martyrdom appeals to you. How do you like the title—Saint Thomas of the Cranberry Fields? You're getting to act like the late Father Barnes."

I, God's anointed, am unused to criticism. It is not a priestly pastime. I leave her canoe and return to my home. Sleep evades me, and I scheme of ways to say Mass for the Mexicans. It is their right. It is mine. I don't wish to be obstinate. I have found a mission beyond the mundane of routine Johnsburgh. I even fantasize of martyrdom and Mexican sainthood.

After next morning's Mass, I walk past Greta's office. Even at seven she is working. The door is open, and the smell of coffee greets me. Peter sits beside her at the computer. As he reaches for his cup, I notice for the first time that he's left-handed.

Greta waves at me to come in. Peter rises and greets me with his enthusiastic welcome smile. "How would you like your coffee, Father?"

"One cream," I reply. "You're certainly at work early."

"We're trying to project our cranberry yields, ensure our market, and estimate our labor requirements."

"All before breakfast?" I ask.

Greta slams back her chair. "Don't be a smart ass, Father. You've stirred up enough for one weekend."

Peter raises an eyebrow, and Greta says, "Saint Thomas, the wannabe wetback found his way to the Mexican shelter yesterday. With delusions of duty, he was set to recite Mass a la Eric Barnes. After Mass, the Mexicans disappeared. They knew better than to repeat history. Somebody raised the bridge, and our hero was stuck on the other side. I came paddling out of the sunset and rescued him."

I assert myself in righteous tones. "They are also God's children. *It is my duty.*"

Peter says, "You have choices. All choices have consequences. You can choose to integrate into our community and learn from its history, or you can choose to ignore what we've learned from bitter experience at the hands of a perverse priest. I know to you it's a matter of social justice. To us it is too. But to us it is also a matter of survival. Extend your mind, Thomas, to immigration officers, legal fees, compensation, flights to Mexico, hotel rooms in Chicago while an extended trial goes on. The cost would annihilate every farmer in this community.

"You can work with and for the community, or you can incite revolution. You can thank us for inviting a naïve priest into our hearts and community, or you can assert your priestly authority. We are willing to extend our Christianity to a recovering junkie and aid him in his continuing struggle. Priests are scarce. We house you, feed you, provide you with a generous stipend, and allow you the use of a car. In return you endanger our community."

For a moment I am speechless. Then anger supervenes. "Forgive me, I thought these gifts were born of generosity. I never dreamed they were bribes or reward for good behavior."

I turn and leave. In a few moments, I return and place my accumulated stipend on the desk. "Here it is, Peter, all of it. I don't need it. Give it to the Mexicans."

I reach into my pocket and toss the car keys on the money pile. "I don't need the car anymore. I'm sure my parishioners know where to find me."

I find my runners and jogging suit. Even though I'm running, I feel a chill that exercise won't erase. Soon I slow to a walk as my mind sifts this morning's encounter. In a few sentences, Peter has placed my life in perspective.

I wander upstream and follow the Marsalaat as she twists like a writhing snake. I pray for persistence and resolution. I pray that my duty to all of God's children will be fulfilled. Also, I pray that my flock will open their hearts to their brothers.

Everyone has choices. Every choice has consequences. My choices are thwarted. When I comply, my actions are praised. At other times, I am ignored. I wonder if this is obedience training.

During my ruminating, I've wandered to Grizkovich's shack. His boat, the *Santa Gordo*, is pulled up on the bank. I see his bulky frames as he squats on the river's edge. A small puddle of guts and blood floats away from the fish that he's cleaning. He wears one of those Tilley hats that stay on his head no matter how fast he moves. I don't see him immediately. The sun is in my eyes, and the boat shadows his bulky frame.

I am startled by his gravelly voice. "Watch where you're going, Mack."

"Oh, sorry, Mike, I didn't see you here."

"Well, lucky I saw you first. Since you're here, how'd you like to come in for breakfast? We can talk about your search for sainthood over a fresh coffee."

Onion and oil smells fill the kitchen. He dices yesterday's potatoes and browns them until they have a crust. I sip my coffee and say, "Thanks, Mike."

"What's with you? Can't you talk anymore? What kind of a preacher is lost for words?"

I tell him of my encounter with Peter

"Bless you," he says. "Now you have no money and no car— and you think you've won. I wish I could help you, but religion isn't exactly my field."

Somehow, I am not deflated. "It's the price of freedom, Mike, and a step toward independence."

Next Sunday I am still fuming. "Not so dearly beloved," I begin. "I am very annoyed at the lack of charity displayed by this community. The Mexicans too deserve to attend Mass. Examine your conscience. With some exceptions, my life here, thanks to your generosity, is all I could ever ask. My bishop assigned me here. My duty is to the church and the people in it. There is a misapprehension that since I was hired by the parish, and am housed, clothed, and fed by the parish that my primary duty is here. And like any hireling, I am bound to follow the orders of those that hired me.

"Not so. My duty is to God and my church and my fellowman— even if he is Mexican. Every attempt to minister to him has been blocked. I think, at this point, no avenue is open to me. From here on, I will say very little. I only ask that you find a way for me to minister to the Mexicans who are also your brothers. Examine your conscience and act on it."

Miracles still happen, but not in Johnsburgh. My days are quiet now as summer approaches. I no longer teach catechism, the youth group is otherwise occupied, and the discussion group has exhausted its topics. Confessions are trimmed to one hour a week. Daily Mass maintains its status quo. From time to time, I am invited for tea with the sisters who say, "We do not entirely disagree with your position on the Mexican issue. However, we feel there are nuances and implications, which you have not yet grasped and are to this juncture unaware of. These will become clear in due course."

They play with me. Test my patience and forbearance. Talk down to me. Yet I refrain from using words I learned on the street.

On the following Sunday, I am deliberately late for Mass. I'm dressed in my jogging clothes. "Good morning, my less than beloved people who cannot extend their love to Mexican workers. As you know, we are all equal in the sight of God. There will be no Mass today or any other day until all are treated as equals. At 7:00 AM next Sunday, I will be in your church, dressed in my liturgical vestments. I will expect a ride to the Mexican side and I expect to say Mass for them. I am sure I will be received as God's emissary. If there is a Mexican Mass, there will be a Mass here at 11:00."

Excited and apprehensive, I leave my church and begin to jog. My mind is filled with possibilities. I place my faith in God and pray.

On Monday, at precisely 9:00 AM, my telephone rings. "Good morning, Father Spanner. His grace, Bishop O'Doul, wishes to speak to you."

I am actually afraid. I feel like I'm in the principal's office and about to get the strap.

"Father Spanner," O'Doul says, "is it true that you no longer celebrate Mass for the people of Johnsburgh?"

"I celebrate Mass equally for all of God's people and wish to include the Mexican workers."

I explain my dilemma and its solution, but he remains inflexible. "Thomas, I can have you defrocked for denying the sacraments to your flock. I order you to resume your duties."

"Certainly, Your Grace, as soon as my flock assumes theirs. Should a church enquiry occur, I believe I have a defensible position."

"Don't threaten me, you insolent junkie. You have vowed to obey. Do your duty."

I am silent for a long while. He threatens me. Finally, O'Doul says, "I want an answer."

My guts tie in knots, and I sweat. Nevertheless, I answer. "I will say Mass for all who are equal in the sight of God."

Within the hour, Peter barges into my den. "I have no wish to engage in a Mexican stand-off. You know my concerns. I won't have a repeat of the Barnes fiasco. Bishop O'Doul has authorized the following: You have permission to say Mass for the Mexicans every Sunday. There will be no confession and no sermon. Mass only! We will have no repeats."

"This is pretty harsh, Peter and not in the Christian spirit."

"Take it or leave it. Screw with it, and we'll get you a bus ticket."

Next Sunday, I am dressed in my liturgical robes. At 7:00 AM, Roger York opens the passenger door for me and drives me to the Mexican shelter.

CHAPTER 28

Greta, it seems, has decided to acknowledge me again. Her door is open, a signal that she relents. She interrupts her work and waves to me. "Come in, Thomas, and close the door."

Her hands clasp, loosen, and clasp again. "I'm so worried about you, Thomas." For a while, I thought you were in real danger. If you know what's good for you, you will stick to the letter of Peter's peace plan."

Suddenly, she shuts down her computer. "Come on, Thomas, buy me a drink. Your place. We've got stuff to talk about."

I make an attempt at humor. "OK, but my place isn't much, and there's no other watering hole in town."

She sits on a kitchen chair and folds her arms around herself. "I'm glad you can back off when you can't win. These people have their own ideas about life and destiny. There's no formal legal system here. How do you think this place runs?"

In my den, she kicks off her sandals, puts her arms around me, and whispers, "Oh, Thomas, I'm so glad you're safe."

She sits back in my easy chair, as if it was hers, and raises the footrest. Her forehead remains wrinkled, tight. Her eyes are moist with the wetness that comes before tears. "Scotch, please, Thomas. Make it a double. Loosen my tongue. You don't have to torture me. I'll tell you everything."

"I don't think I have any scotch."

"Oh, you do. I stocked it for you—in anticipation. It's under that pullout shelf. Typical male doesn't know what's in his own cupboards."

She closes her eyes and inhales scotch fumes. Eventually, her face relaxes and smoothes, while the tension in her shoulders eases.

"Once upon a time," she says, "a very clever man named Peter Krantz discovered a fertile valley through which coursed a small creek that connected two lakes. In time, soil surveys and climate analysis were done. Geological surveying near the creek was intense. Peter formed a corporation and bought a twenty-by-twenty mile piece of land. As if by magic, engineering transformed the little creek into a river suitable for irrigation.

"But while the economy here was developing, so was a problem. The town's holy man became nonfunctional and a moral disgrace. He drowned in alcohol and, then, literally in the river, some say with help.

"Mr. DeRooy, the almost monk, converted people to his brand of religion—those who consumed God in Communion became part God. Heady stuff, Thomas, you are what you eat".

It's a concept that I haven't heard. In a way it's logical, in another it's blasphemy. I nod. Greta sips her scotch. "So you see, Thomas, you're valuable. To become God, they need a priest—any priest. You, Thomas, are the chosen candidate—young, inexperienced, guilt ridden, impressionable, gullible. They bribe you and mold you because you're wet behind the ears. Sorry, but that's how they view you.

"The Sisters of the Naked Cross also believe that within them is the living god. They are enthusiastic supporters of *Domestic Missions*. Their numbers grow. Money, power, and politics are their earthly goal."

She slouches in my chair and extended her glass. Swirls it to indicate the ice has melted. Her face is pale, its color drained, her hair disheveled.

"Don't you think you've had enough?"

"Not quite," she says, "pour me another half, and I'll tell you the rest."

I pour a bit more scotch. She closes her eyes and continues. "Peter is very smart. He organized the blueberries and cranberries. Of course, he has connections. It's expensive to send kids to college. He found cheap reliable labor. We prospered. Peter is committed to *Domestic Missions*. It's a long-term program that trains for positions of influence in places of power. Are you getting the idea?"

"Yes," I reply, "the light is a little less dim. This may be a bad time to ask, but how are you involved in all this."

She waves her hand. "Not now, Thomas, later I'll tell you. Just make me some coffee then I'll go."

She puts her arms around me. "Hold me a while. I need to be touched to ease my pain and so, Thomas, do you?"

We cling to each other, more out of need than desire, and find comfort.

CHAPTER 29

In the fading light of autumn, a man in blue jeans and T-shirt searches the galvanized garbage can behind my house. He sees me, jumps backward, and takes a boxer's defensive stance.

I raise my hands, palms up, and face him. "I'm unarmed," I say, "and harmless. Come in before you freeze. I just want to deposit my garbage."

He enters warily. His eyes dart around the room, and he tilts his head for house noises. He has an ink tattoo of a poorly made cross between thumb and forefinger. Old tattoos disfigure his knuckles. A teardrop is etched at the corner of his eye. He appears to be in his early thirties.

I don't feel threatened or afraid. I've seen many such cons on the street. They wear the marks of society's abandonment. Somehow, I am comfortable in his presence.

He combs his shoulder-length hair from his face. Scarred and knotted veins line his forearm.

"Who are you?" he snarls.

"I'm the parish priest, Father Thomas Spanner."

"O, yeah, where's Barnes?"

"He died two years ago."

"Too bad. Listen, there are some things I need from you. One, keep your mouth shut. You never saw me. I need ten minutes to find Barnes's hip waders and raid your kitchen. Have you got a backpack? I'll need a jacket. I'd tell you I'm innocent, but it's no use. So is every con I ever met."

I agree to his demands. After all it's my duty to help the helpless, and I feel a latent kinship with this man.

He returns in a few minutes. "I'm going now. Just shut up, or I'll have to shut you up"

I shrug at his bravado and do as instructed. I sit in my recliner and sip my tea. The TV volume is increased so that noises are inaudible. *Wheel of Fortune* is on. It's my regular amusement. Sometimes, I'm almost embarrassed as I vicariously enjoy the happiness money brings. It has become a pastime, like candy, but I've told no one. I raise the volume again, lift the foot piece on my easy chair, and try to solve the puzzles before the contestants do. When I solve the puzzle first, I yell encouragement to the contestants.

The con's timing is impeccable. The winning contestant starts the final puzzle when a large hand clasping my shoulder startles me. I nearly drop my teacup, but it's rescued by another hand. Rudy smiles at me, "Really, Father, *Wheel of Fortune*. No wonder you didn't answer when I knocked. Volume's up to the roof."

I flushed.

"Oh, relax. It's not like I caught you jacking off."

My face reddens a bit more.

"Congratulations," he says, "while you've been watching others make a fortune, you've been robbed. The thief cut the screen door and helped himself to supplies from your kitchen. I've just come to warn you about him. He's an escaped con from Strachan Meadows. He got sent up about three years ago for killing the town's only hooker. Said it wasn't his fault. Somebody slipped Peyote into his drink and made him hallucinate.

"His name's Ted Stone. You can't miss him if you see him. He wears the uniform, long hair, tattoos, and scars for veins. He got ten years. Lucky for him, she was only a hooker or he would have gotten a lot more."

Again I bite my tongue. Rudy goes on. "We thought he might come by here. Preachers are such an easy mark."

Rudy hands me a wanted poster and says, "If you see him, let us know and don't have any misguided ideas about helping the helpless. This guy's a mean cocksucker."

Then, pointing his index finger at me, he says, "There's a jail term for harboring a fugitive. You'd do a lot of kneeling jail. They'd just love fresh meat like you."

I begin to worry at my actions. *What right have I to break the law and harbor a fugitive? Is the safety of my parish subservient to my ego? Oh, he's long gone,* I say to myself. I've helped him and harmed no one. I have rationalized my behavior. Nevertheless, I'm haunted by dreams of death and blood and torture.

In early September, when the plague of flies and mosquitoes begins to decrease, Rudy stands at my screen door.

"This is going to be a social visit," he says, "at least for starters."

He waits for me to unlatch the door and steps across the threshold. He has a grin on his face. "Just checking up on folks," he says. "Got a coffee—black?"

He sips, squints at me over the brim, and says. "Sounds like you're fitting in really well here, Father. The parish likes you, and the men must too if they take you hunting. I hear you're a good shot. We like that, not just a book preacher but one of us."

He grasps the cup and warms his hands. I'm not expected to reply.

"I've got something that belongs to you. Been meaning to give it to you for a while," he says and dumps my backpack on my carpet.

I become anxious, but my feelings of guilt are not proof.

He grins widely. "The way I figure it, Teddy helped himself while you were watching the *Wheel* program and split before we got here. He got in by cutting a hole in the screen door.

"Sure was hard to track. Knows these parts. Those waders he was wearing changed the scent."

"Course," he says, "I could figure it another way. But I won't just yet. I'll just say this makes us even for your reception to this town. I figure Teddy was smart enough to cut the screen and make it look like a solo effort. But from now on, Tommy, don't fuck with me. I guess you're not using any more. I always say junkies are like alcoholics. Once and always."

My mouth drops. I have no secrets.

"Have a nice day, Father," he says and gently closes the door as he leaves.

In my own eyes, I am diminished. *How shall I redeem my lost integrity? Does Rudy know I aided a criminal?* Of course he does. He lacks only proof. So readily, I aided my own kind, automatically, unthinking, naturally. I am authority, yet I defy it. I don't even follow my conscience. My ego reigns supreme.

I am beset by *what ifs. What if Stone killed? Took hostages? What if he raped Sister Mary James or Greta?* He has a history. *How would my parishioners feel if they knew I betrayed them, rendered them vulnerable, exposed?*

Yesterday's happiness eludes me. I feel miserable, dirty, depressed. I need to confess, to reconcile my sins, and right my wrongs. I don my cassock and enter my church. I hope my god will acknowledge me if I appear in uniform.

On my knees, I bow before his might and mercy. I ask forgiveness and understanding, and I ask him to make everything right, just like it was before. To whom shall I confess—certainly not myself. I don't feel qualified today, but I'm the only show in town. I confess to God and avoid his intermediary. I stare at the altar light until haloed circles surround it.

I examine my conscience and list my sin. Pride. In my smugness I have become superior. I bear false witness by failing to divulge Ted Stone's presence. I lie by omission. I am still a junkie. I haven't used for ten years. *Is it so hard to admit?* Alcoholics do it daily.

And when I first came to town, I could have accepted Rudy's apology after he arrested me. But no, I acted like a punk and yelled, "False arrest, I know my rights, police brutality, I want a lawyer." I, a man of the cloth, would not forgive. In spite of this my people love me. I am humbled. I am in need of counsel. *How shall I right my wrongs?*

After next Sunday's Mass, I seek Willem's advice. He is, after all, the knight's chaplain. I decide against Peter.

"Well," Willem says, after I tell my tale. "It's difficult for a layman to advise the ordained. I can only tell you what I used to do and leave it to your better judgment."

He looks uncomfortable. "I may be wrong," he says. "When we had no confessional, we confessed to each other. We did so with honesty and consideration. We compensated the injured, apologized, and reconciled. We also imposed a penalty by mutual consent as a strategy for deterrence.

"For instance, on one occasion, a grower siphoned about 20 percent of a neighbor's cranberries. In our small community, we had no ready legal recourse. After discussion, we settled on the following. Farmer Smith admitted his guilt and gave back what he stole plus an additional 10 percent in penalty.

"In your case, Father, it's easy. Be honest and apologize. There's been no harm done. Your people are very forgiving. They don't hold grudges."

CHAPTER 30

During the next week, I agitate myself. Each sermon that I write is edited and rewritten. I talk into my tape recorder and practice in front of a mirror. Instead of sleep, I rehearse my lines in an alert frame of mind. Willem's words echo inside my skull. "Confess to those you've injured. It's really not that hard."

Until now, I've confessed to God alone, in secret and in the dark. Willem's simple words and casual advice unnerve me. Confessing to the injured is outside my training.

Next Sunday, I begin the Mass and recite by rote. The chalice nearly slips from my damp palm, and the host is soggy from sweat. The order of Mass has changed. Today, the sermon will be at the end.

With shaking hands and quavering voice, I begin. "People of Johnsburgh, you have welcomed me with kindness and generosity at every opportunity. I am overwhelmed and truly grateful. Today, I stand before you and confess my sins. My past is part of my present. I was a drug addict. Rather, as my alcoholic brethren would say, I am an addict. I haven't used for ten years. When Chief Redekop arrested me, I responded like any other junkie. Later, I had not the charity to forgive and sought redress at council.

"Mostly, I regret that I endangered your community and aided Ted Stone's escape. As in my youth, I again defied authority and aided the criminal. The phrase, 'what you do for the least of these,' is no smug comfort in the face of possible murder, hostage or rape at the hands of a desperate criminal. Because of my pride and deceit, you are vulnerable.

"I am thankful for the gifts of your heart but don't deserve your kindness. Neither do I deserve forgiveness. If it is your wish, I am prepared to leave."

My eyes seek the floor as I turn away. With sinful deeds, I've repaid their kindness and acted like a traitor that is fit only to be ravaged by an inner city. Faith, love, and honesty are paid in betrayal. My guts knot to push a bolus of acid into my throat. I, chosen of God, slink away. Vestments cling to me like an unshed skin. I am not worthy.

Willem's tenor voice stops me. "Please, Father, sit for a moment. Hear us."

He helps me to a chair, gives me a sip of water, and speaks to my people, casually, as if over a cup of coffee.

"We've been through a lot worse than this. An honest man makes mistakes, which he deeply regrets. Did anybody bring stones to throw? This is a two-way street. Father forgives us, and we forgive him. It's fair."

Turning to me, he lowers his voice and says, "We know your history, Father. Bishop Rodriguez actually came and talked to us. He assured us that you weren't a womanizer, pedophile, or alcoholic."

Willem faces the congregation, extends his arms, looks toward heaven, and scans each face. "What Father Spanner did is very brave. A junkie would have hidden behind his needle. Father has confessed and done penance. Look at him. You know it must be true. Pray for him. Let him know that he's always welcome in our hearts. And above all, let us help him reconcile himself with himself."

Perhaps there is wisdom in my parish that I've not yet tapped. I am left alone. No one tries to console me or make me feel better. I am relieved and apprehensive.

In the late afternoon, I hear a thudlike knock at my door. Mike Grizkovich is outlined against the fading sun. "I won't stay," he says. "I just want a few words with you."

He seems agitated, knots his hands into fists, and then releases the knots. "I don't mean to bother you, but why talk about the past that you can't change? What have you accomplished? Now everybody knows you're a junkie and a bleeding heart."

"I don't do this for myself, Mike. I want a clean slate, honesty, and mutual respect. Besides, there are other words that you may not understand—forgiveness, love, caring . . ."

He holds up his hand. "You're hung up on words like intangible, invisible, faith, duty, sin. Every man has secrets. It's his private life. Now you're in everybody's pocket. You are too innocent, Thomas. How will you protect yourself? Did you learn nothing on the streets?"

"I don't understand, Mike. I am open with my people and lead them to God and purity."

He shakes his head. "And that's the other thing."

The door remains open as he leaves.

I resume my duties. I anoint the sick and visit the healthy. I have an endless round of teas and dinner. My parishioners love me. Everything is perfect. I am uneasy. They have no needs, no wants, and present me, with no problems to solve.

One morning over breakfast I say, "This is a very peaceful community. I'm unaware of any major sins, criminal activity, or violence. Sometimes I think confessions on an annual basis would be sufficient. Everyone seems at peace with his neighbor."

Sister Mary James squints in my direction. "Are you obtuse? The community confesses to God those sins, which are against God. Neighbors confess to each other those sins against themselves. We began this when Willem led us and it continues today. Did he not tell you the parable of the cranberry fields?

"And did you not join us in public confession when you told us of your sins. You were the same as we who had no priest we could kneel before. Obviously, confessions in the open have merit."

"Obviously. Just as obviously, every sin is a sin against God. It is forgiveness that enables us to enter heaven."

"I agree with the catechism," she smiles, "but the church has no monopoly on forgiveness. Are you suggesting that we can't forgive each other in the manner we choose?"

I thank sister for breakfast and enlightenment. Perhaps I am obtuse. My natural impulse is against public confessions. However,

I find no reason to ban them. Are they a threat to the church? Do they render unto each other rather than the Church?

I read and pray. However, there is no objection in print. Maybe it's just that I don't like competition. Especially, when the competition is winning.

CHAPTER 31

Greta weighs heavily on my mind. My attraction to her has grown steadily, and I have begun to imagine her as part of my persona. Sometimes I think "we," rather than "I."

My soul still aches over Al Maguire. Al introduced me to God and the priesthood. In response, I shunned him when he succumbed to worldly love.

Greta and I are friends, nothing more. I must set her straight. For my part, I have no wish to follow Al's footsteps and court disaster. *I won't betray my calling.* If I do, I won't be as angry with myself as I was with Al. The judgment was much too harsh.

Some afternoons, I lie back in my easy chair and dream of Greta. I see her smile, feel her touch, and delight in the pleasure of her kisses. I turn my mind to other thoughts but always they return.

Sometimes I walk past her office when there is no need. I bring her coffee. After work, she taps on my door—just to see how things are.

At night, I lie awake and pray for strength. Pray that I may excise desire from duty and ask for control that the Grace of God can bring. From the darkness, I imagine sister's words. "Your predecessor was a lot like you." I see her smirk. "He preached painless salvation and unearned redemption. It didn't work. Eventually, he drank too much and fell in the river."

To divert my fretful mind, I recite the Mass inside my head. A few hours before dawn, I fall asleep, only to be wakened before I'm ready.

My vestments are donned automatically. Today, no altar boy accompanies me. I light two candles. I am not surprised, only the sisters and a few elderly people attend. I am honored Willem DeRooy is in the third row. He follows the Mass and gives the proper response. At Communion, he approaches the rail, kneels, and sees my questioning face. "It's all right, Father," he says. "I've been to confession in Chicago."

When the Mass is ended, Willem walks stiffly to the altar. "The Knights of Columbus would be honored by your presence at our meeting tonight. Perhaps, in our zeal, we have drifted from mainstream. You could address us and if need be, help us chart a new course."

That evening, a transformation descends on the school gymnasium. Its walls are curtained in black and red. Dimmed lights absorb into the fabric. A burgundy carpet soften our tread. In the glow of incandescent light, Peter Krantz stands and waits for silence. He is enfolded in a royal purple robe and mantle with a white collar that extends over his shoulders. His knight's anchor emblem is suspended from a ribbon that hangs from his neck.

Willem DeRooy stands near the wall—chameleonlike. His black robe melds with the shadows. From around his neck, the emblem of the black cross blends with his robes. There are other men. Various robes and emblems denote their rank: chancellor, treasurer, warden, lecturer, and advocate.

Peter welcomes me. I am treated to a recitation of good works performed by the knights. The list is lengthy: scholarships; helping the poor; service to church, country, and fellow man. The knights support prolife, Catholic education, and defense of the priesthood. Peter pledges the support of the knights to the church, its commandments, and precepts.

I have no quibble with the desiderata of these lofty ideals and nod in agreement. Peter continues in his melodic narrator's voice, now hypnotic. "Our new priest has displayed his love for our community by confessing in public the wrongs he has done. What braver act could he portray? What greater example of humility could he show us? Indeed, Father leads by example. In return, we can be an example to Father Spanner. Tonight, we extend a formal invitation for him to become a more deeply committed member of our community and partake in the fellowship of the Knights of Columbus."

Peter closes the meeting with a prayer, and we exit the gymnasium. I am flanked by knights and swept along. A half-moon hangs low on the horizon. My shoes dampen in the evening dew. Each knight carries a torch to the river's edge. The Marsalaat is at its autumn low, meandering, awaiting winter ice, and then to flow submerged until resurrected by the light of spring.

Willem whispers, "We thought it best to show you rather than describe. We believe sin presages evil. Sin needs punishment. A few pitiful prayers won't suffice. Sin also needs restitution. The sins of one affect us all. To this end, our confessions are public. As is the righting of wrongs."

A young girl, perhaps fourteen years old, dressed in a light blue robe emerges from the shadows, and stands in the light of the torch flames. Her robe is cinched at the waist and accentuates her pregnancy. Downcast eyes fixate on the rosary in her folded hands. Her parents, heads bowed, stand beside her. Her mother is bent and gray. Her father's beefy hands are clasped at his waist. Near the top of his head is a white line where his hat blocked out the sun.

Beside the mother is a motionless cowled figure in a white robe. She speaks, "I am the sinner's advocate."

My curiosity gives way to despair. The speaker is Sister Mary James. Already the accused is condemned.

Willem raises his hood. His features flicker in the flame. I shudder. He blesses the girl and makes the sign of the cross over her, like a priest at Mass. From within his robe, he finds a vial and anoints her forehead.

His voice is a low murmur. "Alice Mary Carlson, are you here of your own free will?"

Only silence greets Willem. He repeats the question.

"I guess so."

"What brings you hither?"

"What?"

"Why are you here?"

"My mom and dad brought me."

"Are you willing to ask forgiveness and repent?"

"I didn't do anything," she replies.

"What sins have you committed? What evil brings you hence?"

"I didn't sin. Somebody got me pregnant. Wasn't my fault."

Willem projects his voice. "As all can see, this ignorant child is with child. In her naiveté, she indulges in the marriage act outside the blessing of marriage. In lust, she has broken God's commandment, shamed her parents, injured them, and cast doubts on their worthiness."

"Who did this to you, child? Who impregnated this child?"

The girl's eyes seek the ground. She is mute.

"Come now, sinner," Willem says. "We wish to help but cannot if you won't help us."

She remains silent. Willem again insists.

Finally she answers, "I don't know who got me pregnant. Maybe it was a dream. I dreamed, somebody kissed me, but I don't know who it was."

Willem's jaw muscles contract, once, twice. Then he smiles. "How noble of you to protect your accomplice. In law, it is called withholding evidence."

I am furious. *What right has he to interrogate?* This is not a court of law. He is presumptive in his arrogance. I step forward.

A firm hand over my mouth muffles my shouts of protest. A sting in my buttock weakens my resolve. Soon I am unable to stand. Breathing is difficult. I pant like a winded dog. A loud voice announces, "Father Spanner has fainted."

Gentle hands move me from the circle and prop me in a chair. I still see and hear the ceremony. My mouth falls open. I cannot swallow, and breathing is more difficult. Two thumbs reach below my ears and shove my jaw forward. It is quite painful. My eyes tear.

Willem stands erect, folds his hands, and continues in measured tones. "Alice Mary Carlson, you came here to confess to Almighty God in the presence of, and with the help of your community. Our prayers are for your benefit, and the benefit of all those who are stained by your sin."

He raises his voice almost to a shout. "Will you deprive yourself and disdain all others? Who is it?"

She falls to her knees, body hunched to the ground, and sobs. "I dunno. It was just a dream. Wasn't anybody I knew. He sang and stroked my hair. I sat on his knees and drank some pop."

"Describe this man."

"I dunno. He's just a guy, tanned, nice looking."

Sister steps forward and waits to be recognized.

"I have prior knowledge. I've known of this itinerant Mexican farm worker. Alice told me about him. He spoke passable English and entertained with magic tricks. The Carlsons liked him, invited him into their home; something no one else was foolish enough to do. Like all itinerants, he dreamed of a green card and haven in America. Would this girl leave the door ajar?

"Please don't blame this naïve child. She has no evil intent. She was beguiled, seduced, and entrapped. Ask yourself what was in the pop? Giving birth will be penance enough for Alice Mary. Let us rally around her and her family, pray, and support them. Show them we are community, invite them into our homes and hearts, and love them as Christ loves us."

I am confused. *Is sister schizophrenic? Where is the punitive warlock that impugned my confessions?*

Willem DeRooy surveys his audience. "Does any one wish to speak?"

Roger Carlson lifts his head, clears his throat, "My wife and I would like to thank everyone who has been caring for us, and I don't know how to say the way we feel, but . . . ."

Willem places a hand on Carlson's shoulder. "It is very difficult, but it is for the good of us all. Also it is very brave of you. Go in peace."

Go in peace. Words from the confessional. How presumptive. This pseudopreacher is an affront. I make a mental note for a future sermon.

The circle parts to form a gauntlet. A man, taller than most Mexicans, his hands bound, is pushed forward by the crowd. His shoulders are straight, not bent from endless labor like many Mexicans. His eyes rove and dart to hidden faces beneath knightly hoods.

Willem moves toward him. "What is your name?"

Silence.

"I believe you are Enrique Espinoza. I believe you are the father of Alice Carlson's child. Do you wish to confess?"

Enrique stares at Willem. Not quite hard enough to burn his hood.

"We can help you," Willem says, "Confess, do penance, and we will redeem you. Do not, and you will pay dearly for your sins."

Enrique spits in Willem's face. Two knights grab him.

"Unhand him," Willem says, "He too has free will."

Two knights, hooded and silent, drag me home to my bedroom. They undress me and tuck me into bed. My strength returns gradually. I can breathe and swallow. Soon, I lift my head from the pillow. Anger invades my home. I've been assaulted and silenced. Yet I am resolved.

Sleep escapes me. After the night, I shower and prepare for Mass. Every muscle aches when I move. Even my eyes hurt. I don my vestments, light two candles, and begin.

Like a second-rate rerun, Willem again nears my altar. I ignore him. He'll not have Communion today. But he persists. "I suppose you're a bit confused right now." He grins.

"I've been assaulted, Willem, and I have no intention of turning the other cheek. I'm going to lay charges against you and sue you in civil court. I'll also write to the bishop and inform him of your sacrilegious rite."

"Yes, yes, of course," he replies. "I understand you suffered a bee sting and had an allergic reaction. The doctor said so."

He looks heavenward. "Before you ride off in the sunset, answer this, was it not an effective ceremony? We discovered the truth and the community came together. Even sister softened. I think it's a small miracle. Don't you?"

"It's no miracle, Willem. It's an infringement of human rights."

He laughs. "Who will you go to? The lawyer is one of us. The policeman is zealous in his vocation. Our bishop is in failing health.

He follows his monsignor's lead. Perhaps Rudy might assist you. He seemed to have a certain rapport with you."

"I will find a way, you snake. You pervert the cloth."

"Sticks and stones," he says. "I came to offer peace. As I said before, public confessions relieve the sins that affect us all, and we come together and heal. You can endorse these ideals. We in turn will let you carry on with your little secrets in the dark of the confessional."

"Get out of my church, Willem. It is defiled by your presence."

He doffs his hat and answers with a smile. "Does this mean you won't accept Peter's invitation to join the knights?"

Throughout the day, my muscles pain when I move. When I sit, they only ache. I think I'll try jogging but cannot reach my feet to tie on my runners. Strange, my eyeballs still ache. I decide to wait. Every two hours, I pry myself out of my recliner and retrieve a cold Coke from the fridge. Toward evening, I think I should cook a meal. Not tonight. Even ordering in is too much effort.

A knock on my door sends a spasm through my back. Before I can move, Greta is beside me. A pained expression gathers on her face, and a tear slips along her cheek. She holds my face in her hands. "I just heard, Thomas. I'm so upset. Will you be all right? I heard you had an allergic reaction. Lucky for you, the doctor was at the meeting."

I roll my eyes again and stop when they ache. "I'm afraid the doctor was the reaction. When I objected to the meeting, I got jabbed with a paralyzing drug. It couldn't have been an allergy. I've seen allergies on the street. I had no swelling, no wheezing, no rash."

I describe the meeting. Greta's pupils dilate, her expression pales, and hands begin to shake.

"Jesus," she says, "what are you going to do? What, other than pray, I mean."

I have no immediate answer. "I'll have to think of something. It's not fun anymore."

"Well, please do," she says. "I've grown to care for you and when you ache it bothers me."

For a while, we are silent. Then a grin appears on her face. "Lay down on the sofa, Thomas, I'll give you a back rub.

I've never had a back rub. She is merciless. Fingertips and knuckles make my muscles scream. Then she is gentle and soothes my aches. "There," she says, "feel better?"

After I put on my shirt, she brings me a glass of water and helps herself to a Coke. She looks at her watch. "Father's expecting me. I have to go." Then she moves toward me, kisses me and says, "Please be very careful. Sometimes you may need to bend."

Next night, darkness falls like an axe on a chopping block. I light the fireplace and turn on the lights. I am left with a residual ache, and my eyeballs no longer throb. Time and Greta's magic fingers healed my body.

On what microwave delicacy shall I feast tonight: Swanson's dinner, lasagna, chicken wings?

Meal planning is interrupted by repeated thuds at my backdoor. It is a foreign sound, quite unlike a normal tap. Espinoza uses his forehead to knock. I open the door, and he stumbles into my house. His face is muddied, tear stained, bruised. Beneath the mud, he is ashen. His shirt is lacerated from the stings of a whip. I lower him into my easy chair. He raises his hands to show me. Each finger is fractured and deformed to unnatural angles like twigs twisted on themselves. He tries to move his fingers. They move without strength or direction.

"We'd better get you to the doctor," I say.

His eyes widen, and he places his hands in front to indicate stop. He shakes and nearly faints.

"*No medico, por favor*. I was already at doctor."

"You need help."

"You fix, Padre. Please I beg you. I am strong."

I have no heroin or methadone to ease his pain. Before I begin, I hold many glasses of scotch his lips. My parish has supplied a full bar. Eventually, he speaks slurred Spanish and saliva drools from the corners of his mouth. I start with his thumb. It is broken between the joints and extends backward. I yank and slide the fragments into place.

Enrique moans and motions me to continue. Like an inverted salute, his index finger points backward. I wipe his forehead with a cool cloth and pour more scotch. With a quick snap, I realign his finger. By the last digit, we are both sweaty. I'm afraid the finger fragments will separate, so I place a tennis ball in his palm and tape over his fingers. I pray this will be enough splinting. He smiles and tries to kiss my hand.

"Please," I say, "this is only for popes and bishops."

Later, I pour more scotch into the drunken Espinoza and apply my recent expertise to the other hand. Practice is useful. My hands move more quickly. At times, he opens an eye and moans incoherently. Perhaps I should have been a surgeon. I shake the inebriated Espinoza to the state where his eyes are momentarily open.

"What now, Enrique? You can't be seen. The knight doctor will fix your hands again. No one must know you're here. I assume you are non grata, even with your own kind. I could hide you in the basement until your hands start to move. In the meantime, figure out how to get to Mexico."

I keep my houseguest hidden like an unsightly relative, a cellar-dwelling Quasimodo. I spoon food into his mouth. I wash him, wipe his anus after a movement, aim his penis into the toilet, and brush his teeth. It is not onerous. I serve my fellowman. I remove his clothes and place them in the washing machine. He will need fresh ones for his return to Mexico. Naked, I climb into the shower with him. I shampoo his hair and wash his body. It is my duty, and I discover neither of us is homosexual.

He lives in voluntary confinement. Often, when I visit, he's drenched in sweat from exercise.

Time is plentiful. After dark, we sit by the fire. He speaks broken English, and I more broken Spanish. We swap stories, he of material deprivation, and I of my former spiritually empty drugged life.

"Ah," he says, "las drogas. Muy mal."

After a silence, he begins to speak, hesitates, stops, and begins again, "We are paid, very good for working here—double. We travel from Mexico by boat and land. Each of us is given to wear a jacket with many pockets. When we get to here, we meet man who take jackets.

"My friend, Carlos, one day, get hole to jacket and powder spill. He knew powder and breathe powder. Body shook like earthquake, eyes roll under face. He breathing fast. Pink juice bubble from mouth. He fall down. Die.

"We save jacket. Boss say jacket more valuable than Mex.

"Some of us get jacket full of money and go back to Mexico every few weeks.

"Boss say if we tell, we die. I tell you, Padre. If not you here, I die."

I'm stunned. "Are you sure, Enrique? How can you get this far and not get caught?"

"Who cares if Mex is caught? We get rides and have protection."

What will I do? Run? To where? Shall I desert my flock? Where is the law? What of Greta? Questions in a blender. Where do I begin?

In two weeks, he is anxious to test his hands. They move. Stiff as they are, they move. Enrique is a dedicated physiotherapist, always in motion. I live in fear that my handiwork will be undone. Not so.

"I am ready," he says, "I must go. I walk at night and hide at day."

I've had instructions: backpack, boots, freeze-dried food, clothes-waterproof, gloves, lighter, etc.

One o'clock in the morning. Dew turns to gel before turning to frost. He kneels, "Thank you. I go now. Please, I confess. I a good man, work hard, pray. I have family. I true to *mi esposa*. Not fuck nobody."

"This is really not confession, Enrique. It is not a sin to be faithful and falsely accused. Go. God be with you on your journey."

He rises from his knees, embraces me, and gently closes the screen door as he leaves.

CHAPTER 32

At 2:00 AM, my telephone rings. "It's me, Bruce—your father. Your mother had a stroke. She's in hospital. She wants to see you."

Next morning, Greta knocks on my door. "Are you packed? You've got a plane to catch."

She hands me a return ticket to Bellingham.

"Of course I'm packed. What do you think I've been doing since 2:00 AM?"

I sit beside her in Peter's Explorer. She hands me an envelope. "Here you are," she says. "Since you want to be poor, I've given you my money and a credit card with a pin number. When you get back, I want the residual."

She seems tense. "You will come back, won't you?"

The Dash-7 is on the tarmac. It's props idle in the morning sun.

"Don't touch me, Father, and don't kiss me. It behooves you to be circumspect."

I am embarrassed to fly first-class and during the day. I can hear Greta in my mind—a little sin won't hurt you.

No one meets me at the Bellingham airport. I take a taxi and go directly to St. Joseph's Hospital. Mother is unable to speak but waves with her normal arm. I sit beside her. "I'm sorry this happened, Mom. I've been praying for you."

She squeezes my hand. I tell her of my pastoral life. I lie a lot and omit major segments—Greta, Peter, Willem, nuns, Mexicans, and drugs. I tell of my acceptance into the community and generosity of my parishioners. I beseech God to cure her. In time, I am at a loss for conversation and kiss her good-bye.

Bruce is waiting in the hallway.

"So you made it?" he says.

"Yes, I just got here."

"How was the flight?"

"Fine."

"You can stay at my house if you want."

I am suddenly furious. He calls it *my house. What happened to our house?*

"No thanks, Bruce. I'll find neutral territory."

I rent a car. *Why not?* I have a credit card. I need to talk to Al Maguire. I am still ashamed of how I treated him and need his counsel. Arrogance no longer suits me. If need be, I will grovel. I have doubts. Perhaps, I should leave him alone. He has a new life. *Why agitate old injuries?*

I drive north along the I-5 to Vancouver and find Al's name in the phone book. He is near his old church. On the way to his house, I pass my old haunts, and see people asleep in doorways and in alleyways. A young man in a torn shirt weaves along the sidewalk. "Welcome home, Tommy," I say to myself. "Ditch the car and tell them Jesus loves you."

I circle Al's house, a clean white building with green asphalt shingles. An old truck in the driveway has a sign—Al's Landscaping. Maybe I should phone ahead or write. I can't just barge in. Again, I drive around the block and nearly leave. *What's the worst my old friend can do?* I agitate myself and nearly back out a second time. Finally I knock on Al's door. He's balder now, a little fatter. "Hi, Al. I just happened to be in the neighborhood. Have you got any coffee?"

"Tom! My god! It's you."

He embraces me, the prodigal son. "Come in. Come in. Meet the family. Tell me everything."

"Thanks, Al. I just wanted to see you and apologize for the way I treated you."

"On fiddle," he says. "You were freshly minted. We can talk about that later. God, it's great to see you."

He drags me inside. "Cassandra, it's Tom."

She is nothing like my lascivious mind imagined. There is no haughty tilt to her head or tempting sway of her hips. She extends her hand. "I'm happy to meet you. Al often talks about you."

Two girls stop their game and run to their mother's side. "These are my girls, Alice and Zoe." Both girls step forward and shake my hand.

"Where's Tommy?" Al asks. He looks out the window. Tommy's in the sandbox.

Cassandra brings coffee. "Why don't you two go in Al's office? I'm sure you have a lot to talk about."

Al's office is cluttered, not organized like his old desk. This must be the new Al—a free spirit. He pulls a second chair into his office and leans back. "How are things with you, Tom? Is everything OK?"

I shake my head. "Nothing's OK. My life is a mess. I'm desperate and don't know where to turn."

"I tell him of Johnsburg, Willem, Peter, Espinoza, and O'Doul. Al shakes his head and says, "The bastards hung you out to dry."

Then I tell him of my dilemma—my love for Greta, and my love for the church.

"I wish I could help, Tom. You're at the crossroads. Whichever fork you choose, pain waits. If you think it helps, I'll tell you of my suffering."

"Maybe it won't be so bad, Al. I hope celibacy is just a blip in church history. Soon the rules will change and priests will marry."

"I hope you're right, Tom, but it may not happen in your lifetime. The problem is more fundamental. The church demands obedience to herself. Once you accept that she can ask any thing of you. She also demands faith. Everything she tells you is true."

"It's hard, Al. In my mind, I'm committed, but it doesn't sit right in my heart."

Al sighs. "Do you think it matters to God that his priests are celibate? For hundreds of years, they weren't. Did he send an angel to instruct the pope or was it something more earthly—like inheritance?"

I am uneasy. "You're on the verge of willful doubt, Al."

"Not on the verge, over the edge. Why did God give you a brain?"

Al squeezes his eyes shut. I think he has a migraine. "A priest does everything for the church. In return, she renders him penniless, demands obedience to unreasonable rules, and lastly, she castrates him. Then she promises heaven that no one has ever seen and life everlasting of which only the dead partake. I hate to break the news, Thomas, but the church is not God. Only God is god."

I fortify myself with the sign of the cross. "Jesus, Al. If you weren't defrocked already, you'd be excommunicated."

"I'm sure that's true. Would God bestow gifts upon us and then demand we not use them. I believe this applies to the brain as well as the pecker."

I'm upset. "It's blasphemy even if it is logical" .

Al nods. "You can submit to the church or be your own man. Doing both will shred you. You can't be free until your mind is free."

He rises and once again embraces me. "Good luck, Tom. Believe it or not, I can help. Keep in touch."

He shows me to the door.

CHAPTER 33

Every Saturday, between 5 and 6 PM, I wait in the confessional. During the quiet times when no sinner attends, I pray my rosary, reflect, and plan. I am deeply disturbed by Al's challenge to my faith. Yet I know that among the vast tomes of *Apologetics,* there is ample rebuttal for his assault. My mind wanders to the present. I am excited that Espinoza has left safely and pray that his safety continues. At other times, my prayers are for the wetbacks, and my truncated hopes to bring them the word of God.

From my left is a squeak as the penitent's door opens. Another squeak sounds as it closes. After a few seconds, I slide back the cover to the grill. My penitents remain anonymous. I have no wish to know the sinner's transgression when I am outside of the box.

Today, an unfamiliar voice confesses. It is muffled, somewhat garbled, as if speaking with a plugged nose and marbles in the mouth. At times, when a sinner is stressed, he consumes alcohol and disguises his breath with peppermints. This sinner has only a voice, no odors and no fidgety movements. Even age and gender fail to reach expression.

"Bless me, Father," says a voice that's flat. "I just wanted to talk to somebody to clear my mind. I'm not sure confession's the right word, and I don't know how to reconcile what I've done. What I need is someone to talk to. Someone who swears he won't repeat what I say, no matter what. You won't repeat what I tell you?"

"Let us begin with a proper confession. What you say then is sacrosanct, and I will not repeat it, even if I'm tortured and killed, I swear to God."

"That's reassuring, comforting. I need to be sure."

He clears his throat, rearranges the marbles in his mouth, and begins. "Bless me, Father, for I have sinned. My last confession was years ago. I just haven't felt like coming.

"You see the problem is that I'm quite fond of my sin. It's really only one sin, but I repeat it as often as I can. Actually, I'm not even sure it's a sin because it only yields enjoyment, and I've injured no one. Isn't that the definition of sin—hurting someone one?"

I clarify the question. "There are many sins—of thought, word, and deed. Some are against God only and therefore do not injure man."

I'm puzzled. *Is this person leading toward some intellectual or spiritual conflict?* A dilemma like those saints experienced.

"Perhaps," I say, "you could just begin and tell me whatever comes to mind."

"I guess it's just that I like kids. We have a lot of fun together. Sometimes we play, and I'm aroused. Sometimes we're intimate. But it's OK, Father. I wouldn't hurt them, and I always give them medicine so they don't remember."

"I think you play with me, and your confession is insincere. What have you done to save the children from your perversity?"

"Oh, lots of stuff: psychiatrists, aversion therapy, counseling, prostitutes. I even considered marriage. I had several Internet offers, but they were all disgusting. Compared to children, women are old, flabby, and malodorous. Nothing worked. There's a burning in my blood for which there is no cure."

He continues in that neutral tone. "My confession is sincere. Do you think I should kill myself?"

"What!"

"Kill myself. We know I'll never stop."

"No. It is not right to compound one sin with another. Pray, confess each week, meditate, and take in an extra Mass."

"Thanks, Father. Do I have absolution?"

"Yes, your sins are forgiven. Go in peace."

"That's great, Father. I feel better being pure. I can hardly wait. They're so nice to fuck."

I abandon my priestly comportment and shout at him.

"Your absolution is rescinded. You are insincere and toy with me. I hope you burn in hell!"

"Boy, are you ever touchy. It's a sickness you know, Father. I can't help it. I just want to be forgiven for what I've done, not for what I'm going to do."

From my confessional, I hear a laugh as he leaves my church.

I remain after confession. My church is my fortress. I seek comfort on the hardness of an oaken pew. Night encroaches, and still I am furious. I cannot resolve, or rationalize this self confessed pervert who lives amongst us. On my knees I beseech my Savior. I cannot summon words of understanding. I have become uncharitable, unforgiving. I pray for justice, punishment, and retribution.

Once in my home, I cannot sleep. Anger shreds my nerves. As dawn approaches, I am frazzled like a frayed electrical wire. Sleep is a fantasy that mocks me with its laughter and retreats at my approach. Violent screams ricochet inside my skull, ear piercing, thunderous, glass shattering like sonic booms. A raging migraine has subsided, another stalks, gathering force, then charging to attack.

Past fatigue, I squeeze my head and smother a scream. I swallow pills and vomit them out, spray my nose with analgesics. In desperation, I find suppositories—one, two, three. I am contaminated with the sins of others. And am myself unconfessed.

During the night, I pray on my knees, lie on the floor, arms outstretched like Christ on the cross. I try to capture his pain.

Twittering birds chirp in the predawn darkness. Every chirp recruits another as nature's miracle unfolds. Today, nature's miracle is an irritation. Another day is forced upon me. Is there no escape from this accelerating centrifuge that has become my mind?

I stumble into my gray jogging suit and well-worn runners. No conscious decision guides me. Soon I am aware of the Marsalaat. It's earthen dike, now freshly graveled and fortified stands ready for winter's wrath. The sun still rests low on the horizon, not quite willing to begin the day. A slight breeze, coolness, and solitude greet me. There are no eddies on the water. No visible currents. But the river moves slowly, imperceptibly. Quiet now, sleeping, gathering strength for next spring's rage. Then, she then transforms into a devil's churn of boiling muddy waters. It is inevitable. The present presages the future for my sinner. The future bodes shades of black.

A group of mallards swims near the shore, playing hide-and-seek among the bulrushes. Their staccato quacking is like laughter at a dirty duck joke. One tilts into the water, searching for food. His feathered bottom extends skyward, mooning passersby. Blue-green males display their beauty to the rising sun, while brown females are content to snorkel among the reeds. I come closer. They are not afraid. It is my first diversion. I whisper a thank you. A tear meanders along my cheek.

In the distance, oak leaves dance in the morning breeze, waiting their turn to parachute earthward. A chattering squirrel gathers acorns. He stops at my approach and sits on his haunches, paws held in front as if in prayer. I am humbled. In nature manifest is my god.

I am still on the dike and begin to jog. My head aches with each step. There is no doubt that my sinuses are at war. Each step jars a small explosion. I compromise with a stroll.

In the distance, two crows argue over breakfast, irritable like a divorcing couple. Their raucous voices rise, one stepping over the other.

I feel compelled to return to my church. It is my duty. I am obliged.

CHAPTER 34

Over the next few weeks, I often talk to Greta. "It's not right," I say. "They're not confessions. They're inquisitions." I complain about Peter, Rudy, and the truncated Mexican Mass. She remains calm. "Well, Thomas, I don't know what to do about it. But I'm willing to help if you come up with something."

"If I knew what to do about it, I wouldn't be a nuisance to anyone who will listen."

"Insight," she smiles, "can be very uncomfortable."

I am being a nuisance and am unable to discuss that which most perturbs me. After a few days, I visit Greta in her office. She has become a source of comfort in times of crisis.

Papers are stacked high on her desk. A telephone is a permanent attachment to her ear. She is an oasis in my life. Dark blue eyes, full red lips attract me. She is friendly, warm, animated. Her movements, fluid beneath a flowing dress, engender unpriestly desires. "Good morning," I say in a faked normal voice. "I know you're busy, but could I trouble you for a moment?"

"Never too busy for you," she smiles and lowers her eyes, "providing you don't take too long."

"Could I trouble you for Bishop O'Doul's address and phone number?"

She clicks a few buttons, and in a few seconds, I have the address, fax, phone number, and e-mail on a neat sheet of paper.

She stops for a moment and removes the phone from her head. "Well, since you're here, let's have tea. I need a break." She blows a lock of hair off her forehead, "Cream and sugar." she says."

I scratch my head. "I don't understand it. These people want a priest and when they have one, they don't avail themselves of his services. It's as if they were afraid."

"Yes," she says. It seems strange. They all think the same way. Have you heard the saying, 'money makes the world go round?' I prompt, but she won't divulge.

> *His Grace, Bishop O'Doul:*
>
> *I write for assistance in reconciling the Knights of Columbus to rational Catholicism. I was witness to public confessions. The Knight's chaplain, Willem DeRooy, led the ceremony. Actually, it was interrogation of a pregnant fourteen-year-old and an unjustly accused illegal Mexican. When I protested, I was injected with an agent that left me weak and temporarily paralyzed.*
>
> *These confessions are reminiscent of evil rites. I seek your assistance in expunging them from your diocese.*
>
> *Yours truly,*
> *Thomas Spanner, OSB*

Next week, at five in the evening, Greta locks her office and follows the covered walkway to my door. "I have a letter for you, Father, from the Holy See. Yes, I'd love to stay for a drink. Thank you for inviting me."

I open my mail.

> *Dearest Father Spanner,*
>
> *Blessings and spiritual gifts be upon you. We are not surprised that the road is rocky. We are aware the knights in your parish are zealous to a fault. However, we thank them for maintaining a spirituality, which in the past we were unable to provide. Yes, there are differences between the traditional church and them. Work with them, resolve. If necessary, unconvert them. Begin the process and let it evolve.*
>
> *If you are assaulted, please invoke the secular authorities, that's why they're here.*
>
> *The knights are a worthy arm of the church. Do not alienate them. Enlist their help.*

*Surely, a soldier of Christ can handle a group of women
elementary school teachers and the fund raising Knights of Columbus.
You have the power. Use it.*

Yours in Christ,
Fergus O'Doul, Bishop of Chicago.

I show the letter to Greta. She laughs. "Shall I summarize it for you?"

"No, I know what it says."

My mind rings like echoes in a hollow tub. "Jesus," I say, "Bishop O'Doul ignores the pleas of his priest. I can be assaulted and humiliated with no recourse. No effort is made to investigate my complaints. In addition to celibacy, I am now castrated. My charges of assault are ignored like those of a child who says, 'he hit me first.'"

Greta remains calm as a totem pole in an Indian village. She kicks off her shoes and swivels back in my easy chair.

"Well," she grins, "I'll have the specialty of the house."

"Tea? Yes, that will be lovely."

"That twelve-year-old scotch will do nicely, thank you."

"Wouldn't you rather have some sherry?"

"No, I'd like scotch."

"There is no scotch."

"There must be," she says and jumps out of the chair. "It's right here." Then she pulls out the empty bottle.

"Have you been drinking, Thomas? Come here. Let me smell your breath. No it's not like you. You exercise and get up early."

I opt for candor. *What have I to lose?*

"Would you believe it, Greta. I had a houseguest for two weeks, a Mexican wetback. He'd been whipped. His fingers were broken, twisted to grotesque angles. He was horrified of medical help. Seems he already had some. He was accused of raping a white girl.

"With God's help and a lot of scotch—for the Mexican—I was able to straighten his fingers. He left a while ago, before the snows."

She is silent, and then utters one word, "Sherry."

In a few moments, she extends her glass. "More sherry."

She sips slowly, stares into the fluted glass, trying to find the exact bottom. She frowns, puts down her glass, and rubs her temples. Then she says in a whisper, "Quid pro quo, Thomas. We all have our secrets. Some are harder to bear than others."

She is suddenly serious, far away. She sips her sherry and then say. "I was raised here and worked for the knights after school, mostly bookkeeping. Peter liked the way I worked and found a scholarship for me in Chicago. I studied: money, taxes, commerce, tax shelters. He let me work part time while I was studying and hired me for his Chicago office after I graduated.

"Life was wonderful. I married and lived in heavenly bliss for three months. My husband was the jealous type. At first, I was flattered. I was often late coming home. Soon he became suspicious—'who was I with?' At times he would twist my arms behind me. He started to hit me.

"He had a drinking and gambling problem. At times, he would come home beaten up and threatened for debts he couldn't repay. After I was unable to borrow any more, I lent myself money from the company without its knowledge. I got caught.

"The judge agreed to Peter's offer. I could serve my sentence in Johnsburgh and avoid jail. Then I would be on probation. Peter would give the parole board periodic reports. He still trusted me to look after the knight's money.

"Peter did show me a lot of intricate stuff. It's surprising what you can download or get on a disc. Offshore investments and money transfers are their own specialty. I did a lot of traveling, always with Peter. After all, he was responsible for the criminal.

"Well, Dad was failing. It was a good time to come home.

"So, Thomas, here I am, doing church taxes, land leasebacks, Mexican labor with rebates from the Mexican government, offshore investing, etc. It's like interning, and I have access to any financial mind that Peter knows."

"I'm lost," I say. "This is way out of my field."

"I know," she says. "But I'll tell you something that isn't. If they ever find out about you and the Mex, they'll get you for this. You're dead meat."

"Why, what have I done that's so bad?"

"You know about the drug trade. You'll never leave, and neither will I. Keep your mouth shut."

"Besides, what did I tell you before? The Johnsburgers believe they are part god. Insemination by a being close to the animal world destroys their sanctity. It's a heinous crime, Thomas. You negated the punishment and sided with the devil. It's the second criminal you've succored. Is there a three-strike rule?"

She rises from the chair and wipes the tears from her eyes. "Please, Thomas," she says and kisses my lips. "Please be careful. I've grown very fond of you."

CHAPTER 35

What does Greta know? *Everything I know and more. What can she do? One negative report from Peter will give her a job in the state laundry. Where shall I turn?* I ruminate and spend many sleepless nights. Winter encroaches on my life, and I am encircled in this prison that has no need for bars.

Greta has developed into a habit. She thinks my den is a roadside pub. "Ease up, Greta. This isn't a lounge. I'm not to be socialized by young ladies who have more experience than I do. Don't you have a life? Don't you know people? Isn't there some place you can go?"

"Actually, the only place is my house. And only Dad is there. There's no one else. I might as well be alone and when I'm alone, I'm very boring company."

"Well, if you want boring, just come to my sermons. You'll be happy to be alone."

"No, Tom. I like your company. I just get so lonely. Just talk to me, and tell me what drives you and what keeps you here."

With no real answer to give her, I compromise and make tea. She lingers a while, thanks me and leaves.

I continue to hear confessions on Saturdays. I alone hear valid confessions. I alone dispense the body of Christ. It is not arrogance. It is fact. In my confessional, children harvest forgiveness. In school, the guilty do penance. I maintain my policy of generosity and forgiveness. Even the sisters attend confession. They repeat after one another, "I am here to confess my sins. I will supplement the penance you give me to the appropriate level. I am not here to discuss politics."

All else remains the same. Public confessions continue. I rant and rave in my Sunday sermons. I pound my lectern. Stoic faces stare back at me. I have only words, and I am harmless enough.

Snow buries my parish. I prepare for Christmas and the holiday season. At the front of the church, the children and sisters have prepared a manger scene.

I am again reminded that Santa Claus is not formally acknowledged.

"We don't lie to our students and then retract the lie as they get older," Sister Mary James says tersely. "Besides, it's primarily a secular commercial concept."

I heard this last year. *Does she think I have an attention deficit disorder?*

Grizkovich left on holiday. "Going to visit my residual offspring," he says and grins widely as he boards the Dash-7. Greta is away for two weeks to visit in Chicago. "Time off for good behavior. Mandatory parole," she says wryly.

Snow continues until white is the only color of this world. Even Rudy and his snowmobile remain indoors. No ice fishers or snowshoers challenge the storm. Telephones are silent. TVs blanked out. From the garage, my standby generator purrs smugly. I am ensconced in my den and toss another log on the fire.

Like last year, I am alone for Christmas. I read, reflect, pray, and meditate. No one makes demands of my time or seeks solace in their time of need. *Am I strange that I don't yearn for company at this special time?* Before midnight, I prepare for Mass. I light two candles on the altar of my god, don my vestments, and begin the miracle that leads to life everlasting. My Savior loves me. That is all I need to know. I bow to his will. That is all I need to do.

I worry. Greta is on my mind too often. Now that she's gone for a while, I become aware how frequently I've gone out of my way to see her. And how I've come nearly addicted to her touch.

My eyes fix on the wooden cross above the altar. Jesus is nailed to that cross. His head has fallen to one side, and thorns in his head cause blood to obscure his vision. On his side a gaping wound marks his death.

This is why I am here, why I became a priest, and vowed my chastity. A small denial in the face of his sacrifice is all I require. I will speak to Greta.

Prayer and fasting are not enough to drive her from my thoughts. Even turning my mind away from her is futile. Two weeks pass quickly. On her return, my spirits lift. I am overjoyed.

Greta pervades my mind. She roams freely among the convolutions and valleys of my brain. *How would we love were I not collared to my church?* Even now my daydreams, unrestrained as those of night, blur the margins between the two. Dreams magnify my fervor. As their intensity mounts, my desires and frustrations rise. In that nether land, between sleep and wake, I dream that she lies beside me, soft, naked, warm in my embrace. Her breath is a soft tickle on my neck as her body nestles into mine. In my dreams, we are together. It is only a dream aided by imagination. I know it is only a dream. The covers of one side remain unruffled, that side that is cold, not warm. When I awake, there is no perfume; and the aura of her presence is no more.

With reluctance, I beg forgiveness. Yes, I am aware of prayer, of denial, of detachment, of my vows. But I have no desire to pray and lose this mortal blessing that possesses my heart and flirts with my soul. It's too late for thou shalt not, and much beyond yielding to temptation. Adam and Eve flash in my mind. *What need have I of their sin when I have my own?*

This morning's bright blue heaven is one of nature's gifts. No wind disturbs the layered snow. The dike is plowed, and I walk quickly, shielded from the glare behind my glasses. A few clouds propelled by the northern wind congeal to a blacker mass. In a sudden shift, the north wind builds on itself, menacing, gathering its sulking fury, and once more becomes master of its domain. I run along the dike to the shelter of my home.

Noon is dark as night, and Johnsburgh is imprisoned by the storm. I am in my kitchen, steeping another pot of tea. There is mail to read, sermons to prepare. Time passes slowly until 4:00 PM when I hear the click of Greta's heels as she marches along the covered walkway.

With a tap on the door and turn of the handle, she enters. A folder of papers is clutched in her arms. She thinks this is a diversion. Her arms enfold me while she lingers with her kiss.

I bribe her with gifts. "Oh, Thomas, sherry, Bristol Cream, Belgian chocolates. My favorites."

She licks her lips and makes a small smacking sound. Then sinks further into my chair, raises her feet on the foot piece, and closes her eyes. I rub lotion into the instep of her naked feet: light rubs over her toes, firm strokes on top of the arches. She purrs like a cat whose tummy fur is stroked against the grain.

Nothing in my life has warned about the eroticism of naked feet. She sips her sherry while I cast my mind to the mundane: lemons, pickles, onions. It is only a partial antidote to my arousal. She laughs as I reach into my pocket to adjust myself.

"OK, Tom, remember, we're just friends. Get out the Scrabble board. No made-up words, no cheating, and no Latin. Try to keep your mind on the game."

We play at the kitchen table (Scrabble on vinyl). Greta has lost her killer instinct and misspells even simple words. She seems agitated, her mind elsewhere. I assume the day has made its toll.

She folds the game and slides it from her, comes to me, and touches my face with short agitated strokes. She kneels beside me and touches the back of my hand with her fingertips. Her hand strokes mine, softly. "I can't take it anymore, Thomas."

Nervous fingers tangle her hair. "I can't take it, sneaking around, wanting to tell everyone of our love and not being able to. I get paranoid, wondering who knows what. The snickers behind my back depress me. I can't lie anymore, it's tearing at me."

She bites her lips in agitation, crosses her arms, and hugs her shoulders, shivers as if cold then folds her arms and sobs. "I love you, Thomas—there, I've said it; and it's tearing me apart."

I kneel beside her, touch her hand, her hair.

"What will we do, Thomas? There is nothing that can change the way I feel. You can't always be my love, be in my heart, while I remain at the edge of yours."

I become incoherent, inarticulate. "I am promised to God, vowed to him."

She cups my face in her hands and looks into my eyes. "So am I, Thomas, so am I. In all that I do, from all the sacraments bestowed upon me, I am a child of God. What kind of a god would endow his children with the power to love and then deny its fulfillment? Every one, but chosen priests, may love and have a mate. Can't you love me with your heart and leave your soul to God? Maybe get dispensation from the church, a chastity annulment. After all, it's a church rule not a celestial decree."

She strokes my hair, moves tears around my face with the tip of her fingers, and rotates a knuckle into her smudged eyes. She grasps my arms, indents the skin with her nails, and shakes me.

"What have you to lose? You are a priest forever. You are baptized. You can't be unbaptized. Poverty needs no effort to achieve. If you wish to obey, there's the army. You've already lost your chastity in your mind. How can you believe in priestly chastity when a married Protestant minister can become a Catholic priest and still remain married? Don't you think something's fishy?"

"Greta, I know all that. Don't you think I know? I'm half-crazy with wanting you? But it hurts with an endless pain, and I can't undo my calling no matter what the price."

Tears stream in rivers from her face to splash on the table. She screeches her fingernails on the vinyl. "At the beginning of time," she sobs, "God said, 'It is not good for man to be alone.' Do you think he's changed his mind? Choose, Thomas. Choose to hear your inner god. Allow my love into your heart. Love me in the light of day or forever let me go. I can't be a preacher's concubine or live as the reverend's whore."

There are no candles, no incense, and no perpetual flame to light our lives. Her body heaves with endless sobs. The present fills my heart with fear, and I tremble at the aftermath. I kneel beside her, a hapless fool, who finds no words of comfort among all those that he's learned. I cannot will my hand to touch her and ease the rawness of her pain.

IV-LOVER

CHAPTER 36

Greta's door remains closed. At times, I'm not sure she's even at work. I am possessed. Day and night, she haunts my mind. I barely fall asleep when I am startled awake. Sometimes I jump out of bed and hope she'll be at my side. My breviary cannot keep my attention. The words are meaningless when her image flows across my mind.

Black and yellow flashes blaze before my vision. A clang, like heavy metal, begins a drumming in my ears. Another migraine gathers and builds to a screaming peak. Nausea precedes retching, and I double over with pain. Greta punctuates my misery. Between aching thuds, I see her tears and couple them with mine.

Prayer precedes medicine, yet I have no relief. I use nose sprays, suppositories, and pills when I no longer vomit.

During the day, I run along the dike. Perhaps I'll meet her there. Beyond fatigue, I cannot sleep. I yearn to trade my collar for the solace of a fix. Just one hit, just one more time—to ease my battered soul.

I'm losing weight. I manage to recite a facsimile of the Mass. Then I tear off my collar and throw it on the floor. Empowered to enact miracles, I'm barred from normal life. *How much more can I withstand?* Possessed by Greta I cannot sleep. Nauseated, I dare not eat. I sniff medicinal narcotics and fear I'll readdict.

After dark I knock on her door. "Is that you, Thomas? You look awful. Are you sick?"

My verbal skills forsake me. Words stumble, I utter inanities. Finally, I blurt, "I can't stand it anymore. I can't live without you. You're always on my mind. I love you."

I fall on my knees. "Please, Greta, marry me. *Nothing else matters.*"

She smiles a sad and worried smile. "I love you too, Thomas, with all of my being and have no wish to be apart."

Greta accepts. I am filled to the brim.

"That's very brave of you, Thomas, to go against your church. Are you ready to be laicized? Can you go through life no longer part of the church? No parish? You'd be like a doctor who has lost his license. You better be sure, dead sure, because it's very hard to turn back."

"I know that, love. But a priest is a priest forever, and they can't take that away. At least I remain God's priest."

For a moment I think of Al Maguire. I shudder at his turn of mind. Now, I agree with him—*I love her, more than heaven or the threat of hell.*

At the next church committee meeting, I present my case. "Even though I am anointed, I am also human. I minister to you as another Christ. Unlike other religions, Catholicism prohibits marriage of its clergy.

"Greta and I will be married. I come not to ask your permission but simply to inform you. We accept the consequences of our actions and only ask that you formulate a consistent response. If you are unable to accept us, we will leave Johnsburgh."

They are nonplussed. "We know you and Greta love each other. We don't think being in love is a sin. Every animal in the world is paired. It's a natural state. We believe the church is evolving in a liberal direction. You're merely ahead of your time—or centuries behind. Either way, it is irrelevant to us."

Elsa Smith smiles, lunges toward me with arms outstretched, hugs me, and kisses my cheek. "Congratulations. I'm so happy for you."

"Don't you wish to discuss this?" I ask. "Have you no wish to clarify my position? Do you not wish to talk to Greta? Consult with my bishop? What do the sisters think?"

She smiles. "We have discussed and debated at great length. Our objections are theoretical and theological. We are unanimous and most of the sisters also see our point of view. In the normal course of tradition, you would be cast out. We think we are more enlightened."

I tell Greta the news. "It's great. The church committee is behind us. They want to keep us here, and they're not offended. Is it not wonderful? I can be a priest and keep my ministry. I'm not laicized, and we can live openly as a married couple. I'm so happy. God works in strange ways."

Greta looks at me quizzically, as if I too am strange.

"I love you, Greta, this is a great day for us."

She smiles and hugs me. "There's one little oversight, Thomas. What does your bishop say?"

"I wrote to him a few weeks ago and stated my intentions to marry you. I have no reply."

Greta shrugs. "Perhaps, he too is ahead of his time—or the mail is slow."

She embraces me, and I feel her softness, her comfort. "Congratulations," she says, "I'm so happy for us. Just think how miserable it might have been?"

I'm unsure how to ask so I blurt, "Greta, it's customary for those about to be married to receive instructions from the church. Have you considered taking a marriage course and rejuvenating your Catholic faith?"

Her eyes widen. "You've got to be kidding, Thomas. After all your complaints against the church, you ask me to become involved. Get real."

"I know, but there are a lot of good things in the church, and we could work from within."

"Sure, send a letter. The pope wouldn't listen to Luther, but he might listen to a green hick town priest who's hornier than his vows."

I assume she's not impressed.

"Tell you what," she says. "I'll look into it. If it looks good, I might try it. In the meantime, I have my own views. I believe there is a god in the logic and beauty of all living things. There is a spirit that dwells in our inner temple, an essence that is the gyroscope of our morals and ethics, the core of our being that longs for the elated expression of our life."

"That's wonderful, Greta, your talking about the soul."

"Oh, am I now? I am not. I'm talking about freedom, inner goodness, and love. I'm talking social justice and common sense. When the church has women priests, ask me about converting. Also, Thomas, I believe, as do your parishioners that I am part God. After all, God created man—and woman—in his image and breathed his life into them. His breath, a part of God became part of man. Henceforth life was sacred."

I pause. "Well, it's one view point, and I can't say that you're entirely wrong."

"Also, Thomas, I believe in the Trinity. Within this shell called my body is a trinity of heart and mind and soul. Here, logic of the mind and feelings of the heart mesh with mystery of the soul. It's something your church hasn't figured out."

I ask her to elaborate. "Figure it out," she says. "It will come to you."

Next Sunday, my sermon is the wedding at Canaan. I announce that Greta and I will exchange our vows immediately after Mass. I explain my views on celibacy, and I tell of my feelings for Greta. I explain that I too am human and love is a sacred emotion, a religious concept in which one person gives to another. God so loved the world that he gave his only begotten son . . .

When it comes to the part—if any one knows why we two should not be united in holy matrimony, let them now speak or forever hold their peace.

Sister Mary James stands and marches to the pulpit. She stares at my congregation. It seems she encounters each furtive stare on an individual basis. "It's all pie and ice cream, isn't it?" she says. "Father was young, he wasn't sure of the long-term impact when he made his vows. People promise to stay married for life and then divorce. Why should the priesthood be any different? It's uncomfortable for Father to remain celibate or at least to presume celibacy.

"In the meantime, cannon law still applies. The vows of poverty, chastity, and obedience have not been rescinded. I object to this union."

I reclaim the pulpit. "Sister is right. I break one vow and exchange it for another. No matter what I do, I am a priest forever. My sacraments remain valid. My love of God is unabated. I bring you the body of Christ and eternal forgiveness. I am subject to your will. I am also subject to mine. Greta and I will marry."

After Mass, Greta walks from the rear of the church. I have visions of my church emptying, but not so. My people stand and applaud.

No white wedding dress adorns her. She is alone, head high, jaw firm. I am apprehensive and hope her strength prevails. A dark purple dress flows from her. Modest to its ankle length, freely flowing. She has no veil, no flowers in her hair. She smiles and reaches out to touch me.

We hold each other's hands. With tears in her eyes, Greta says, "I pledge to you my friendship, my comfort when you're in pain. I am your salvation in a tumultuous sea. Alone, I long for you. Together, we are complete. As long as I live, I pledge myself to you."

What shall I say in answer? "I thank God for the gift of your love and pledge myself to you. No one shall come between us in this life or the next."

"Thomas, will you be my husband and love me with all your might and all your heart, as long as we both will live upon this earth?"

"I will. Greta, will you be my wife and cherish me for the rest of your life?"

"I will, Thomas, and more. I will love you with all my heart and mind and soul."

She kisses me, a long lingering kiss that halts my breath. Again, my people applaud.

Willem, in knightly robes, commands the lectern. "We can all be thankful," he says, "and pray for a peaceful time. We are at a new era. Father Spanner marries one of our own and therefore becomes one of us. We need have no doubts about his gender orientation, his alcohol consumption, or his desire to lead us in truth and sanctity. As you all know, the church's stance on celibacy is under attack and review. We are at the forefront of this revolution.

"Please welcome the new Father Spanner and his bride into our hearts."

CHAPTER 37

We live now, enveloped in our love. My people approve and are uplifted by our joy. Greta and I sleep in. We hold hands on the dike. At times, we stop for a kiss and stare at the river. Greta holds my hand, even when we're shopping. People smile, congratulate us, hug Greta, and pat me on the back.

I'm not used to shopping. The church ladies have always provided, and my cupboards were never empty. They are still willing to shop for us, but Greta refuses the offer. "It's a territorial thing," she says.

Greta drags me through the aisles.

"What do you like, Thomas? Come on. I can't make all the decisions."

She wrinkles her nose as I harvest pickled eggs and garlic sausage.

"On the other hand," she says, "some decisions need be unilateral."

At the check out the clerk smiles as I take out my wallet

"Sign here," he says. "We'll just put it on your tab."

There is no tab. I sign a piece of paper and know that I'll never get a bill.

I have assuaged my guilt, convinced my self that I am right. It was only a misguided medieval church that perpetrated celibacy. It is a church ruling, an ancient custom soon to be removed. It is not God's law. I believe all the arguments in my favor. Nothing is cast in stone.

My mind races even when I sleep. Greta's beside me and from time to time, startles me with her nocturnal noises. For short periods, I sleep then I waken, alert, ready to begin the day. I touch her, lightly and have no wish to waken her. My eyes are moist, and I thank my God for his gift to me.

I have fallen asleep when the telephone jars me to a painful alertness. An unfamiliar voice rasps in my ear. "We need you, Father. Meet us right away. The antichrist is born, and his wrath will soon be loosened upon the earth."

"What are you talking about? Play your crank calls with someone else. Phone dial a prayer. I'm busy sleeping and don't have time for nonsense. This is the third millennium, not the middle ages."

The voice becomes pleading. "Please come, Father. There may not be much time. I know this sounds strange, but you need to see for yourself before you judge. Hurry."

I am curious and angry. Not angry enough to stay home, but curious enough to go.

I stumble into my pants, put on my collar, and grab my kit. Peter's black Cadillac idles at the front of my house. It's not Peter at the wheel, rather one of the knights that I've seen but not spoken to.

I slide into the front seat. "Hi, I'm Tom Spanner."

An icy silence replies. We drive north, following the Marsalaat upstream to Grizkovich's house, then turn inland. I try to converse with the driver. "Where are we going? What's this about? Nice car. Is it yours?"

He gives no reply. No up yours or even a fuck you, only stony silence.

In the distance, lights surround a farmhouse. Every few feet small fires flicker in the dark. Tires crunch on crushed gravel. On either side of the door, a cross, painted in red, guards the entrance. For a moment I wonder *Is it blood?*

The driver grabs my arm and pushes me inside, then closes the door behind me. Sister Mary James cradles a child in her arms, a child, newly born, unbathed. The creamy cheese like vernix of the newborn still covers him. Sister removes the blanket from the scowling child. His hair is dark, complexion even darker. He opens his mouth and cries. Not the pitch of a normal newborn but a moist muffled growl from inside his chest. An oversized tongue sticks to the roof of his mouth. Two small teeth penetrate the lower gums.

Challenging and daring, sister stares into my eyes. Then she turns the babe's face toward me. She points to a deep purple mark on his cheek. A cross, inverted on itself, runs from eye to jaw bone.

"Is it any wonder," sister says, "that the antichrist should be born in our time, and in this place? Look at him. His features are those of the devil himself, and he speaks in a guttural tone."

"Just a minute, Sister. You're jumping to conclusions. I'm not a doctor and neither are you. Don't you think this child could have a genetic syndrome and be born with heart problems? Look how blue he is more than a blue baby, he's purple."

Her jaw sets and back stiffens.

"I am not here to argue with those who deny sin and break their wows. This child requires exorcism; if you do not exorcise this demon, Armageddon will be loosened upon this earth. Exorcise this child. Unfortunately, you are the only one who qualifies."

"Oh, please, Sister. Don't be so melodramatic. We are far from Hollywood. This child is ill. He needs a doctor and may require heart surgery. In the meantime, I'll be happy to baptize the child."

"Spare me your arrogance, Thomas. I suppose you're a doctor now too."

Then turning to others in the group she says, "The greatest danger to the exorcist is to become possessed of the demon himself. This is why the exorcist must feel free of sin and harbor no secret need for punishment. Otherwise, the devil can easily entrap him."

She pauses a full minute and stares at my collar.

"Is it any wonder that Father is reluctant? He is afraid. Are you free of sin, Thomas? Can you face the devil?"

Sister has obviously read the qualifications of an exorcist. Perhaps she watched a movie or found answers on the Internet. Nevertheless, fury overtakes me, and I smile. To sister, I give my sweetest response.

"I have sinned, and my sins are forgiven. Before my god, I stand anointed and follow his law."

I try not to bristle and misquote—let her who is without sin cast the first stone.

"Sister refers to the woman I love. A priest too may be blessed with this gift. My wife is my joy and God's gift to me."

Sister squeezes my arm until the muscles ache. "Exorcise this child," she whispers. Then I follow her gaze to the door. Two hooded knights flank Greta. She is still in her nightgown. Her head is high, and she stares at me.

Sister's eyes bulge in the flame. "Our priest is a weakling," she says. "Many times, Willem DeRooy would face the devil and cast him from us. This man hides from his duty."

I am not yet persuaded to cast out devils. *Shall I expound before I begin?* My mind reverts to those Sunday morning preachers who stick fingers in ears and release deafness devils from the mind— praise and hallelujah. Perhaps I could conjure a seizure in this child and have him spit while he rolls his eyes.

I address those before me.

"Dearly beloved, if this child is possessed, we need proof. Traditionally, speaking foreign languages and superhuman strength are the hallmarks. This child has no language. He is weak from the effort of breathing. I believe he's a poor excuse for a devil."

Sister begins to protest.

"Silence, Sister. I am speaking. Is this child the antichrist? An incidental birthmark on a sick child bodes poorly for one who would challenge Christ himself. This is not the antichrist."

I place my stole around my neck and dip my hand in holy water. I baptize the child. For some reason, I turn him on his side. The large tongue falls forward, his breathing eases, and color changes to normal.

There is a gasp from the people in the room then silence. I bless the gathering. "Go in peace."

One by one, they depart. Sister is not in prayer, but her head is bowed. I take Greta's hand and leave the cabin. We slide into the Cadillac. Greta shivers beside me. A few minutes later, we take a turn in the road and see the cabin engulfed in flames. Greta closes her eyes and covers her face with her hands.

My den is our sanctuary. Greta opens a bottle of scotch. I hear the clink of ice on glass as she pours. She wraps a blanket around her shoulders, closes her eyes, and leans back in the recliner. She inhales the fumes of her drink. I go to light the fire. "Not tonight, Thomas," she says, "I've seen enough fire for one day."

She shivers under her blanket and rocks in the chair. For a long while, she is silent.

"We have to get out of here, Thomas. What's next? Dead cats on the doorstep?"

I'm puzzled. I asserted church authority over sister and gained more credibility. "But, Greta, we won that round. Don't you think we prevailed?"

"Maybe you won, Thomas, but I didn't. I was kidnapped and held hostage. Maybe the church prevailed, but who do you think died in the fire?"

She stares at the floor. "I'm no martyr. What does it take for you to see the light? Let me make a list—false arrest, kidnapping, assault, child abuse, labor violations, drug running, money laundering. Do you think I want to stay here? I'm stuck. I'm still on parole, and Dad isn't mobile.

"I'm glad you think the Church prevailed, but you didn't win. I'm going to find a way out, Thomas."

Next afternoon, a hesitant hand knocks on our door. "Let's go fishing tomorrow," Grizkovich says, "Both of you. You need a break."

He is merciful. We sleep in until nine. "It's ice fishing," he says, "the fish can't tell night from day."

He drives in near silence to one of his favorite fishing holes. We stop when all four wheels begin to spin. On the frozen lake, about a hundred yards from shore, is a shack that looks like an outhouse. Mike reads my mind and grins. "It's not what you think it is."

He lights the propane heater and opens the ice hole. Breakfast is donuts and coffee. Later on he serves scotch for Greta and beer for himself. He sneers as he hands me a Coke. I inhale and pray that I don't become an alcoholic. Greta leans on my shoulder and falls asleep. A tug on her fishing line jars her awake. She reels in, like pulling a log out of the water, dead weight, and no fight. She whoops her excitement, kisses my cheek, and slaps Grizkovich on the back.

Mostly we sit, drink, and make benign comments. It's a conspiracy. I am ignored when I mention the parish. We talk hobbies, music, and fishing.

CHAPTER 38

On Sunday, I am invited for lunch at the Carlsons'. Greta declines the invitation. "Don't worry, she says. "I'll visit Dad. He's mostly bedridden but still refuses help. He takes forever just to feed himself and eats only pureed food. Sometimes it gets into his lungs. I'm afraid he'll get pneumonia."

I have been remiss. My personal life detracts from my mission. Alice Mary Carlson becomes increasingly pregnant. In the meantime, I fail to offer counsel and prayer. From the front door, I hear, "Get off your feet, Alice. Lie down. You're toxic. Lie down before you get a seizure."

Alice drops her magazine and shuffles toward me. Her eyes are puffed so that only slits remain. Her feet are swollen and skin glistens threatening to crack from the pressure.

"Hello, Alice, how are you getting along?"

"Oh hi, Father, I'm doing OK for a blimp. Can I have the baby today?"

"Well, if that's what's meant to be that's what will happen. You must be going to have the baby soon?"

"Guess so," she says.

"I suppose adoption has been considered?"

"Yeah," she says and shuffles away.

Her mother's voice rises from the kitchen "Did you hear that, Alice. Father Spanner wants to know if you've considered adoption."

Alice scratches her sides. "I dunno," she says, "maybe, I guess."

Mary Carlson looks for cracks in the ceiling. "See what I mean. Besides, it doesn't matter. There isn't exactly a line up to adopt a Mexican child."

I'm not sure why, but I kneel beside Alice and say, "God bless you, Alice. Everything must be very difficult right now. I pray for you, and I can help you feel better. Please don't be afraid to ask."

I look at Mrs. Carlson. "How are things going?"

"We're not sure," she says. "We're working on it. She's so clueless, so ambivalent. She's confused—why public confessions? Why Willem? Why Espinoza? Why . . ."

I ask, "Have you involved a psychiatrist?"

"In Johnsburgh?" she snorts. "There are none."

She rises from her chair and puts her arm around me. "Don't be so glum, Father. Things have a way of working out in the end."

We hold hands and form a circle. I try to express the prayer that resides in our hearts. "Let us pray . . ."

Now, I have an opportunity to help one of my troubled charges. Alice harbors guilt and shame. I explain, ask rhetorical questions. I show her she is blameless. I bless her and invite her back even if it's just to talk—about any thing at all.

Sunday after next, nature is on our side. Brilliant sunshine and clear blue sky welcome all. My people remove their sunglasses as they enter my church. I am in my vestments and welcome my parishioners. Today, another greeter stands beside me. Alice Mary cradles her child in her arms.

"Isn't she beautiful?" Alice says.

The child wears a pink bonnet. A few curls of red hair wave from the edges of the hat. Alice turns the child's face. A clear birthmark in the form of a purple S engraves her temple. "And look," Alice says, "there's this birthmark."

The back of my neck prickles. The child's birthmark is a miniature of Willem's. The curve of the S and deep purple could not be coincidental.

As usual, the knights enter from the sacristy and kneel in the front row. I am still welcoming the faithful when several muscular farmers drag Willem out of my church and strip his robes. Willem cowers naked in the churchyard. Before I can react, he is surrounded and beaten with belts that the farmers have removed from their waists. Welts form on his body, and he bleeds from cuts.

"Stop," I scream. "Stop." I try to break free but am restrained. Willem lies naked in the snow, and the beating continues. Snow turns red from his blood, and the beatings increase. In a fit of fury, I break loose and cover his body with mine.

A few residual blows sting my back, then nothing. After a while, a firm hand touches my shoulder. "Get up, Thomas. It's over."

Sister Mary James runs her hands over my back and legs. It seems she's satisfied that I'm uninjured. "Thanks, Thomas," she says. "We'll look after him for now. Even sinners deserve our comfort."

I thank her and try to find words to express my thoughts.

"Don't talk," she says. "Words are futile when the obvious stares you in the face. We'll talk later. We will decide about Willem."

First, I phone. Next, I knock. The answer is always the same. "Mr. DeRooy is recovering. He has no broken bones or damaged internal organs. His vision is intact. No, you may not visit."

Next Wednesday morning, I am still in my housecoat. A demanding knock shakes my kitchen door. Rudy turns the knob and enters. "Sorry to barge in. Get dressed. You've got to see this." He is unarmed and out of uniform. His dark green corduroy pants are held in place by a wide belt with a buckle in the shape of a steer horns.

Billy opens the door of the cruiser for me. "You can ride in front now, Father." He smiles at what he thinks is a joke. We drive to a small cottage, surrounded by trees and nearly invisible from the road. "Willem lives here," Rudy says. He kicks the door and is answered with a dull metal thud. "Cute, ain't it?" he says. "Wait till you see what's inside."

Incense mixed with the odor of burning candles penetrates my nostrils. Mozart's *Requiem* exults through the cabin. Strange, the funeral piece is joyous. Willem, in his knight chaplain uniform, lies dead on his sofa. On the table are three plastic containers: GHB, Rhohypnol, Ativan. Beside them is a stack of video recordings.

Rudy inserts one in the cassette player. "They're really all alike," he says. A naked Willem appears on the video screen. Beside him is a child, perhaps eight years old, as naked as Willem. Willem touches the child and then himself.

My thoughts collide and form no sound. Rudy looks at me only the way a policeman can. He sizes me up, debates in his own mind, shrugs, and passes an envelope with my name written on it.

Dear Thomas,

I have many regrets in my life. Most of all, I regret what I am. I regret that you and I were never friends. You are so constrained with your Catholic morals.

We are all incomplete, Thomas. Out of whack. One can have too much faith. I am harsh. Forgive me. I dared hope for love, even as I existed beyond the perimeters of your forgiveness and understanding. But I do love you, Thomas. I must confess to many joyous moments while I played on your naiveté. At least forgive me that.

Now that I'm dead, it's unfair for me to chastise. Yes, my reward is eternal punishment. I deceived the sisters and raped the children. Unimaginable torture in hell is insufficient retribution.

Thomas, you will never know the ecstasy, the transcendence of a humble monk in communion with God's innocents. I hurt no one and transmitted no diseases. My sweet children had no memories. Unknowing in their amnesiac dreams, they loved me. True, there was no agreement. But neither was there disagreement, and I loved these children as my own. Many would have chosen to honor me in mutual love, but our rigid traditions and laws of consent forbid. I reveled in the joy of lust and gratification. Could I have stopped? Sought help and counseling? Become like an AA member? "I am a pedophile. I haven't touched a naked child since . . ." I doubt it. How many of us leave jail only to reoffend? My love became clandestine, according to law. We love as we live, in hope that transcends fear.

I am as I am. It is not my choice. Women overpower me.
Men frighten me. Boys excite me. Little girls are sweet, precious,
innocent creatures, almost heavenly. In many ways, I am still
a child. I prefer the company of children. I am safe here. They do
not threaten or dominate. I laugh with them and teach them
to laugh.

Unfortunately, with therapy, I became attracted to older
children. Pregnancies were my undoing. Goodbye, Thomas. Pray
for me if you can. Live your life as best you can within the
confines of the religious box. Bless you. May your god love you
and cradle you always in his hand.

Your brother in Christ Jesus,
Willem

In conscience, I cannot bury Willem. He died by his own hand in mortal sin. Sin compounded on itself, unreconciled, unrepentant, and unforgiven. Willem is proud of his sins. He has no remorse. I kneel before the altar of my god and pray for Willem. *Where are my feelings?* In place of sympathy is a stone. No affection springs from my heart, only hatred and disgust.

I tell Sister Mary James of my decision. I tell her of Willem's suicide note. I show her Willem's letter. Then I remind her of Willem's birthmark on Alice Mary's child and the mark on the so-called antichrist. Most of all, I tell her of his unrepentence.

Sister Mary James sighs and clasps her hands. "Can you not find a spark of kindness in your heart? Willem did much for us. He explained the Bible to the children and helped many on the way to God. Can you not recount the good that he did and ask God to forgive his trespasses?

"How can you judge?" she says. "What were his thoughts as he became unconscious and slipped to eternity? Could he not repent at the eleventh hour? How do you know, Thomas, how do you know?"

"How does any one know," I reply. "As a man lives so shall he die." In my mind, a smiling Willem mocks me. I turn to sister. "I have seen nothing of repentance. He flaunts his evil. If you don't think so, view his movies."

She holds up her hand. "This is not your decision, Thomas. In the matter of suicide burial Cannon law states, 'If some doubt should arise, the local bishop is to be consulted, and his judgment is to be followed.'"

"Well, Sister, there is no doubt. Cannon law also clearly states, unless they have given some sign of repentance before their death, they are to be deprived of ecclesiastical funeral rites. I have seen no hint of repentance."

I get a phone call from Bishop O'Doul. "What are you trying to achieve?" he asks.

I explain that I am also aware of the Cannons. He replies in his thin voice. "I am also aware of Willem's monumental contribution to Catholicism and his faithful attention to his Bible books. These help to spread the faith. Also, in these times, I am grateful for his fiscal contribution. Willem and I have been colleagues for many years. Will you be the first priest to deny a funeral Mass for a Knight of Columbus?"

"But, Your Grace . . ."

"But nothing. Bury him, you dolt, and make it High Mass."

I obey reluctantly and with malice. The sisters attend, as is their duty. Willem's fellow knights and Peter also attend. A handful of parishioners attend. Videos play in my mind—images of images. I see images of Willem, grotesque and repulsive.

"People here present," I begin, "my bishop decreed that I bury Willem. I do so with much ambivalence. His sins are public and have damaged our community. Every one deserves prayer. God will decide if these prayers are accepted. Willem's good deeds are many. Let us pray for him. Also, let us pray for ourselves."

CHAPTER 39

Peter chairs the open meeting. During the day, the school gymnasium is less ominous. He wears a navy blue suit as do his fellow knights.

"We are a house divided," he begins. "Common goals are thwarted by divergent paths. Father Spanner's humanistic Catholicism clashes with our traditional discipline. The prosperity and safety of our community depends, in large part, on a peaceful labor force. Father Spanner wishes to minister to the Mexicans. In the past this has been disastrous. Can our community find a way to do this safely?

"While we constrain Father Spanner, he in turn coerces us and threatens to leave if his personal circumstances are not accommodated. We conspire with him and accommodate his wishes. To the objection of some, a married priest is our pastor. We adapt.

"Father Spanner thinks that the knight's generosity is a bribe. On the other hand, he preaches generosity and kindness. Can he not accept his own teaching?

"We need to address our justice system. It is, in effect, a jury system and has functioned efficiently. We have a town council and public confessions. We reconcile our differences.

"I hope, in time, we can educate Father Spanner and show the wisdom in our community. I hope he can educate us in the way of the church and we can live together in harmony.

"I, like many of you, am devastated by the death of Willem DeRooy. He judged himself and executed that judgment. Let us not bury the good he gave us."

I am invited to speak. I thank Peter for his summation and then say, "Firstly, we need to heal our hearts and souls. Also, we have long-standing issues that need to be addressed. There are flexibility problems. The sisters perceive they are right. The knights are right to protect the community. I am right because I speak for the church who speaks for God. Yet at the core, is a common belief. Let us pray and work from that belief."

Peter asks for dialogue, for discussion, for input. There is very little. The church committee is strangely quiet. "We need to resolve these issues," Peter says, "It's hard to do in an open forum. I propose, what business proposes—a task force. May I suggest Sister Mary James, Mary Stewart of the church committee, Father Spanner, and Ralph Dixon, our knight advocate. Surely, we can all get on the same page."

Greta insists that I wear nonclerical clothing when I'm at home. "You can wear your uniform at work," she says. "But this is our home, and I'm married to Thomas, not Father Thomas. Tea, Thomas? Let's just sit and stare. You can tell me everything tomorrow."

Greta lies beside me, restless in the night. At times, she clings to me. At times, she grasps my arms until they ache. I stroke her hair, kiss her forehead, and gently rock her in my arms.

When I return from morning Mass, aromas of fresh baked bread alert me. Greta feels better. She wears a floral apron. Her face is flushed a light pink, and he she hums a familiar tune—*try not to be angry, try not to be sad.*

"Good morning. Is this the new you?"

"No," she says. "It's the old me. Isn't this how I used to look?"

"I love you, sweetheart. When you feel better, I feel better."

She smiles and kisses my cheek. "Oh, you're so romantic."

I resume my priestly duties. Peter and I have reached an understanding. My car and stipend are re-instituted. The car is registered to CCC—Catholic Church Committee—and my stipend is drawn on the CCC account.

"It's more appropriate," Peter says. "Besides, now that you're married, you'll have expenses."

After dinner I tell Greta of the arrangement. She shakes her head and laughs. "Wow, Thomas. Nothing's changed except for third party involvement. He's a clever devil. But I'm happy you feel better."

We sip our tea and read. I've reached a compromise with Greta. She may use the rocker on alternate days—and when I'm away. Tonight, she sips her tea and smirks.

I answer a knock on the door. A smiling Sister Theresa clutches a bouquet of roses. She hands the flowers to me and curtsies. "A present," she says, "from the sisters."

Greta's curiosity has dislodged her from my chair. She hesitates for a moment, breathes in and reads the note—*To Thomas and Greta—Welcome—Best wishes from the sisters.* Silence, I am numb and have no thoughts. Greta is the first to regain the power of speech. "It's a major concession, Thomas. More eloquent than any sermon."

Perhaps the essence of democracy is mutual concession. Peter and the sisters have eased their stance. Even the knight advocate is agreeable. He says, "The knights will allow you free access to the Mexicans when they arrive. Provided you keep our concerns in mind."

Everyone gives a little and the people gain. I am elated we're making progress. Thanks to Peter, we dialogue.

Normality resumes. I say Mass, hear confessions, and am thankful for my priestly duties.

Greta spends more time with her Father. "He's failing," she says. "All he has left is his mind. I read to him. He loves it."

"Why don't I visit him with you? I can't cure his body but I might help his soul."

"Bad idea, Thomas. He's really quite against the church."

She continues her visits and becomes increasingly worried. One evening, she says, "Maybe you should come with me. He's dying."

Arthur Simpson sits propped in bed. His head nods, eyes droop. Even from the bedside I hear the rattle of his breathing. His skin is blue. Greta sits beside him and strokes his head. I kneel beside her and begin to pray. She yanks my ear and jerks me quickly to my feet. Then, she glowers at me.

Arthur's breathing quiets and becomes inaudible. His life fades away and he dies before our eyes. Once again I kneel and pray.

Greta slaps me on the back of my head. "Have you no respect? He wants no prayers. Do you need to impose your will over his?"

How shall I bury Arthur? The answer lies in his will.

> *Dearest Greta, my loving child.*
>
> *This is my last will and testament. All that I have, I bequeath to you. Big deal! To no avail, I've spent all my money on pills and doctors. All that remains is my thoughts. All I can give is my thoughts.*
>
> *Why did you marry that boy? He's without experience, brainwashed by the church. Perhaps you can convert him to reality. If not, dump him. He's of no use with that crap that circulates in his head.*
>
> *I am not an atheist. In fact, I am a devout theist. Now that I am rid of this encumbrance called my body, I am free.*
>
> *Do me one favor. Put my carcass in a wooden box. Bury it. Cry if you must. Do it without ceremony or prayer. Don't let your husband pray over me. It's an insult.*
>
> *Goodbye, my love. I wish for you a happy and satisfying life.*

It is difficult. Arthur Simpson is lowered into the ground. There is no incense. No holy water. No prayers. I hold Greta's hand and shut my mouth. I watch as a backhoe covers his coffin.

Greta is quiet now. She seems to have lost interest in our home and spends long hours at the office. I bring her coffee and make lunch. Some evenings, she sips her scotch while I prepare dinner. At times, she dabs at her tears. In the night, I hear her sobs.

Soon the Mexicans will arrive. Greta wants to organize food, housing, clothing. She delegates well. There is a constant stream of people to and from our house.

I also have my duties. One evening Greta is home before I return. The fireplace is alight. Candles decorate the den. Greta sits in my chair and sips her sherry. Her smile is brighter than the candles that adorn my church. She jumps up and wraps her arms around me, kisses me until I gasp for breath.

Well into her second sherry, she runs a finger along the bridge of my nose. "It's not aquiline," she says, "nor is it Roman." She plants a moist kiss on my cheek then nips an ear lobe until I feel the bite. I pinch her nose until her teeth unclench. She giggles, "Oh, Tommy, you're so yummy."

"You're cut off, Greta. From now on it's tea and juice and crackers."

"Sorry. I've just been working up my nerve. We need to talk. Have you given any thought to leaving Johnsburgh?"

A knot forms in my stomach. "I thought all that was behind us. Willem is laid to rest. The town accepts us. I minister to my people's spiritual needs, and they are more accepting of the true faith. The committee is making progress. What more could we want?"

Her voice, nearly a whisper, replies. "I'm glad that you're happy here and have been assimilated. I take it that the absence of a legal system and a thriving drug trade are not your concern. You are no longer informed of public confessions or exorcisms—they still occur."

I feel faint and the knot in my stomach tightens. "I thought all that was behind us, and we agreed to leave alone that which we could do nothing about."

She shakes her head. "That will never do, Thomas. It's too self-serving, too immoral, too easy, and too wrong. The sisters give you roses, and Peter puts a new label on his bribe. You wag your tail and acquiesce."

For a long while, she is silent, then fills her sherry glass. "You've become one of them, Thomas, and you don't even know it."

"I've been a good wife," she says, "I've kept my mouth shut because I'm still crazy about you. All those doubts and reservations I've kept to myself."

She dumps the remnants of her sherry into the flowerpot, moves away from me, and folds her hands on her lap. "Tell me again, Father, slowly. What's it all about?"

I explain, as I would to a child: God, Adam and Eve, original sin, Jesus Christ, crucifixion, forgiveness of sin, confession, communion, heaven and hell, limbo and purgatory. Satan.

She forms her lips into an O. Her eyes open widely. "Incredible. Is that what it's all about? Let me get this straight and don't stop me until I've finished. Once there was God. Complete in himself. Perfect. He decided to make a man a.k.a. Adam. Adam got lonesome so God took out a rib and made a woman for him—a.k.a. standing rib. Adam and Eve lived happily in the Garden of Eden. God devised a test of loyalty—don't eat the apples. Was it obedience or something to do with sex? He created Adam and knew every molecule of his being and since God could predict the future. He knew how the test would turn out. Adam and Eve had no choice. God got pissed and kicked them out of Eden to be miserable. It's not free will, Thomas. It's crap. Your god is a sadist."

She pours more sherry. Her voice remains level. There is no shouting, and there are no wild hand movements. Is this a research dissertation? My Greta is a heretic. I am paying the price for broken vows, and the Devil sniggers behind me.

"Before I believe what you're peddling, Thomas, it has to be logical. For me to be guilty of a two thousand year old homicide is not logical. I believe in God. Not the God your church has created. I don't believe the innocent need suffer to attain joy. The whole system stinks."

"Faith," she snorts, "It's the emperor's clothes. You see what isn't there, and what is there you don't see."

Greta remains controlled, cool as the ice of winter fishing. It's more than a difference of opinion. For a long while she stares into her sherry glass and gulps the remainder. "I'm sorry, Thomas. I wasn't brought up on this stuff, and I don't see it your way."

I am relegated to the sofa and waken early to seek solace at the altar of my God. I pray for Greta's soul and hope she will see the light. I don my penitent robes. *To which Saint shall I pray that has fallen from the path to Christ? What penance shall I self-impose?* Hidden in the sacristy, away from the altar, I begin my Mass. In fragments I pray—Our Father who art in heaven—*Miserere, mea culpa.*

Before me gleams the sanctified chalice. It shimmers even without sunlight. I am not worthy and dare not touch the vessel, nor turn its wine to blood. Power that saps my strength restrains me. Beside the chalice is a pure white host. Abhorrence, shudders my body. *How could I defile the bread of Christ?* Celibacy, my gift to God, lies in tatters on the floor. My soul reflects the fragments of that gift.

Words, like a ticker tape, traipse across my mind: obedience, faith, original sin, guilt, confession, crucifixion, heaven-hell, Satan, *mea culpa* . . .

I return to my home. Greta is dressed in jeans and a red-checkered shirt. Her hair is combed and makeup accentuates her beauty. She hums a lively tune while she peels carrots at the sink.

I am relieved and smile. "Hello, hello. What happened? The lovely Greta has returned. For a while, I thought you needed uppers."

"I've been thinking," she says, "and then I ran out of booze."

I am astounded. She decimates my way of life and then behaves as if all were normal, peaches and cream. "Greta, I'm still very upset and depressed at our conversation. Your beliefs confront all that my faith stands for."

"Oh, Thomas, It was just talk between the two of us. I'd never embarrass you in public or voice a contrary belief. But it won't hurt you to see another viewpoint. Even God's anointed can get too smug. Do you believe nothing of what I said? Have you no mind of your own. For a moment, put faith aside and use the logic of your mind."

She sighs and becomes suddenly serious. "But I don't care about that, love," she says, "I just want a normal life. I want babies to hug, their faces to wipe. I want to feel them suckle at my breast, teach them to walk, and see my joy reflected in their eyes. I don't care about heaven or hell. I just want to be normal. Is it too much to ask?"

CHAPTER 40

After lunch, I crave a cold Coors. Humidity to the edge of saturation and stifling inert air hang over Johnsburgh like a prelude to a temporal hell. From the distance, I hear the groan of the Maxim fertilizer truck as it lumbers fully laden across the bridge of the Marsalaat. Soon it will return, relieved of it's burden. Its multileafed springs easily absorbing a faster speed.

Two hours later, a small dust cloud rises from the bridge and a rumble of engine replaces the groan. The sun is at its apex now, centered at the height of the sky, equidistant from every horizon. Searing heat in thermal waves flows through the valley. For a moment, I stare, then cock my head to listen. First, a hum and point of light, then a cluster of lights, enlarge from the distance. *Are we at war?* The *whup, whup, whup* of helicopter blades assaults my ears. Bug-shaped choppers expand in size before the noonday sun. Each mechanical insect buzzes in search of prey. One blocks the road in front of the truck and hovers just above the ground. A loud speaker blares words I cannot discern, garbled by the distance.

A piercing noise hurts my ears. The helicopter flops on its side and gouges the road with its rotors. The truck reverses, but a tractor blocks its route. Hurried and animated, men tumble out of the truck. With hands clasped behind their heads, they fall face down on the dusty road. Agile men with blue uniforms and yellow letters on their jackets snap handcuffs on their captives.

Are we at war? Has Somalia arrived at our doorstep? Helicopters, why? What for?

Greta lunges against the door and halts abruptly. She remembers to turn the handle and nearly falls in her hurry. Another helicopter commands the schoolyard. Its rotors slices languidly as if resting in the heat. Greta claps her hands, skips, and whoops like a Red Indian. She hugs me, wraps her legs around my waist, tousles my hair, and gives me excessive kisses.

"Deliverance, Thomas. Freedom. Redemption. Escape. Judgment Day. Hallelujah."

She's demented from staring at the sun. Again, she runs in circles, hugs me then rummages in her closet. On her return, she carries two small handbags. "We're all packed, buddy, our chariot awaits."

I don't quite comprehend the movie. Helicopters, guns, and policeman invade my world. "What's going on, Greta?"

"It's a drug raid. Those choppers and uniforms are all DEA."

"So what has that to do with us? We're not involved. We don't gain financially from drugs."

She smiles again. "Where does the money for your stipend come from? Cranberries?"

"What's with the handbags? Is it some sort of evidence?"

She looks skyward. "Blessed are the innocent. That's our luggage. I've hoarded my salary and your stipend. There's clothing and toothbrushes. It's our ticket out of here."

"You're serious—about leaving?"

"What have we talked about? We can have a normal life. Didn't you hear anything?"

"But now that the law's involved, the place can be cleaned up, and we can live here."

"Oh my god. Are you crackers? This is our chance for a normal life, and you want to keep your head in a noose."

Two men in suits emerge from an air-conditioned red Buick. The shorter extends his hand to Greta. "Thanks, Greta," he says. I'm here to uphold our end of the bargain. You've held yours admirably."

"What's this all about?" I say to Greta. "Couldn't you have given me a clue?"

"Serious shit. I promised Smith here that I wouldn't say a word until it was all over. If I tell a secret then it's not a secret anymore. But you know that from confession."

She turns to Smith and hands him the satellite phone. "Thanks," she says, "I won't need this anymore."

"You're very welcome," he says, "and the department thanks you. We think we have a solid case against the knights. We've frozen the accounts whose numbers you sent us. We can't locate Mr. Krantz. Would you know where he's likely to be?"

"Peter is likely to be where you're least likely to look."

Greta, takes my hand. "Let's go, Thomas. Don't pack. We've got Master Charge."

The chopper's *swoosh-swoosh* noise and strobe lights flash through my window. I become a dead weight in Greta's hand. A giant hand restrains me and bars me from the door.

"I can't go, Greta. I just can't. Tears trickle down my face. Of all my vows, obedience to my calling remains. I have a duty to bring my people to their true god. I can't leave them for my selfish interest."

Greta slaps my face with all her might. "Snap out of it, Thomas. This is your only chance for a normal life." Then she turns to Smith. "Arrest him. Obstruction of justice, profiteering, aiding, and abetting, anything."

"I can't. I don't have a warrant or probable cause."

Tears, like the water of baptism well from her eyes. My face stings, more than any confirmation slap. Greta kneels and whispers to me, her voice hypnotic in its rhythm—liberty, redemption, deliverance—liberty, deliverance. One, two, three, you are free."

I wish it were so simple, like the words of confession—your sins are forgiven. I absolve you—one, two, three. You are free. I am still enslaved to my vows. Vows made of words. Words that indenture me more than brick and iron bars.

My stomach knots, and I'm near vomit. Between duty and desire lies a chasm that I cannot bridge. I shake my head and hear the splatter of tears on the floor. "How can I go, Greta? I've given my word?"

She cups my face in her hands and kisses away my tears. "You poor sap, Thomas. It all comes down to that. In the beginning was the Word and all else stems from the Word. Do you prefer the

Word to substance? I also gave you my word, and I'm with you in substance to back it up."

A weight, like a wooden cross falls from my shoulders. Greta reaches out her hand and pulls me across the chasm that still divides my mind.

Mike Grizkovich stands beside the Buick. He squeezes me in a bear hug. "Good-bye," he says. "I thought we'd never get rid of you."

EPILOGUE

My life is simple. I am with the woman I love. We revel in that love, discover, and grow. I have found a kindness that no one warned me of. Greta enriches my life—cookies, little touches, and hugs.

We live normal lives. Greta works for First Investors. I went back school and now have my psychology license. We are good friends with Al and Cassandra. Our child is a beautiful son. I hope to teach him all that I am and especially those things I am not. Greta's wishes for him are simpler. She says, "I hope he has the power to love, to think, and be honest."

Mostly, I am happy. At times, I become disconsolate, but not for long. I haven't sinned against God. I've only disobeyed my church, a church who demands faith and obedience. She demands faith without logic and obedience without question.

Yes, I miss the power of the priesthood, the power to grant life everlasting, power to forgive sins, and the power to create God from the bread in my hand.

I am no longer part of the cult. I can't fight faith with logic when logic is denied. Nor can I find the answers when questions are taboo

House-call fathers welcome me. Father Ron Larson is a man in his forties. He has a gray beard and a paunch.

He has a family, is happily married, and is still a priest—no parish but still a priest. I hear of his agony when he separated from the church. He tells me of his love for his wife and rails against celibacy.

"Please come back often and talk," he says. "You need to talk. We are a community, a subculture of priests. We support each other and are of like mind."

I wish him well. House-call fathers have found an answer. But it's not my answer. They still believe.

I pray and suffer to clarify my mind. Finally, I see that the emperor has no clothes. It's only words. What god would punish the innocent he created—for generations in perpetuity?

Of course it's true; faith believes anything, obedience does everything. *What can I expect from a church that demands obedience and usurps worship that rightly belongs to God? The church is detrimental to man's relationship with God. She has become her own god.*

END